DANGEROUSLY FIERCE

A BROKEN RIDERS NOVEL BOOK 3

DEBORAH BLAKE

D1522582

Dangerously Fierce (A Broken Riders Novel Book 3)

Deborah Blake

Interior design by Crystal Sarakas

PRAISE FOR THE BOOKS OF DEBORAH BLAKE

"Witchy and wild, this book has everything I'm looking for."
-Tanya Huff, author of the Peacekeeper series

"Paranormal romance at its best."
- Alex Bledsoe, author of the Eddie LaCrosse novels

"An addicting plot...I never had so much fun losing sleep!"
- Maria V. Snyder, *NYT* bestselling author of *Shadow Study*

"[Blake does] a fantastic job building layers in her world and developing interesting characters both old and new."
- RT Book Reviews

"An engaging world full of thoughtful, clever details, and a charmingly dangerous heroine...Tightly plotted, with great fidelity to the Baba Yaga stories from Russian folklore that inspired the book." - Dear Author

ACKNOWLEDGMENTS

I am deeply appreciative of Berkley/Penguin for publishing the Baba Yaga series and the first two books in the Broken Rider series. Sadly, publishing is a numbers game, and in this tough new world, the numbers just weren't good enough for them to justify giving me a contract for the third one. But there was no way I was going to deprive my readers of Alexei's story, so I decided to go ahead and write it anyway and self-publish, in the hopes that those who had loved these series would follow me on the next part of this journey.

Self-publishing is a whole different endeavor than traditional publishing, and although I still wrote the book the same as I would have otherwise, I would never have been able to get it into the readers' hands without a little bit of help from my friends. Okay, a lot of help. A LOT OF HELP.

Huge thanks to the amazing Sierra Newburn for formatting and brainstorming and general assistance above and beyond the call of duty. Without you, this book never would have seen the light of day. And kudos to cover artist Su from

Earthly Charms for doing such a great job matching the style of the previous covers. It wasn't easy even coming close to how Alexei was supposed to look (especially since we couldn't get Jason Momoa to pose, darn it), but she did remarkably well.

Big thanks and much gratitude to Karen Buys for the brilliant revision notes, which helped make the book much better, and to her and Judy Levine for proofreading and letting me know about the zillion tiny errors I'd made so I could fix them before anyone else saw them. You ladies rock.

More gratitude to my lovely agent Elaine Spencer, who was totally supportive of this project, despite the fact that it took me away from writing the next book for her to sell. The truly good agents care about their client's total careers, not just the next deal, and I am fortunate to have one of the best.

Thanks to Mindy Klasky for the self-publishing advice and general cheerleading, and to everyone else who knew I was working on this and said, "YES, go for it!" You know who you are.

Most of all, thanks to you, my readers, for taking this amazing journey with me from the first Baba Yaga novel through to this one. Believe me, we're only just getting started.

To the real Bethany, who is the most courageous and dangerously fierce woman I have ever met. You are my hero, and I hope you don't mind my borrowing your name for my heroine. Nobody could fight harder or do so more gracefully than you. (And your love story is more romantic than anything I could write. Jarrod is pretty damned fierce too.) FGBVs forever.

1

Alexei Knight swallowed the last of his beer, hid a grin in his beard, and aimed his pool cue at an innocent looking nine ball. The ball caromed across the felt to tap in three of its fellows before swishing into the corner pocket with an almost smug-sounding sigh. Across the table, his opponent let out a curse.

"Too bad," Alexei said, plucking the twenty dollar bill off the edge of the table. "Want to go again?" His slight Russian accent, stronger after an afternoon of drinking at a slow but steady rate, made the first word sound like "Vant." But his hands were still rock steady. When you were six feet, eight inches tall and weighed two hundred and seventy pounds, it took a lot of alcohol to made an impression, even if you didn't have the metabolism of a formerly immortal Rider.

While the man he'd beaten conferred with his companion, Alexei let his gaze swing idly around the room. He'd been in so many bars over the last year they were all starting to look alike. This one, *The Hook and Anchor*, was someplace in

Cape Cod, although he wasn't sure exactly where. He'd started out in California, methodically drinking and fighting his way across the country, hitting every state other than Alaska or Hawaii. (The thought of flying made him shudder, and there was no way he was leaving his beloved Harley behind.)

But eventually he'd run out of land, ending up here in this nautical themed bar, whose sign bore an anchor crossed with a pirate's hook. It wasn't too bad; clearly aimed more at the locals than the tourists, and slightly threadbare at the edges, which was just the way he liked them.

The floors were wooden planks, worn down by time and use, and the walls were hung with battered fishing gear—old harpoons, frayed netting, empty lobster traps, and the like. The lighting was dim and the music a low throb of jazz that would have seemed better suited to a more upscale establishment. But as long as the beer kept coming, he was happy to hang around for another few hours and use his considerable skills to separate his fellow drinkers from their money at the pool table. It wasn't as though he had any other place to be. Ever.

The two men came around the table, glowering, their ruddy faces alike enough to mark them as brothers. The one Alexei had just beaten clenched callused hands. "You're cheating," he said in a low voice. "You suckered us."

Alexei shrugged. "No. And yes," he said. "But nobody forced you to play. If you don't have the stomach for the game, run along and let somebody else have a chance."

The second brother growled and waved his pool cue threateningly in Alexei's direction, and a couple of other men who had been leaning against the wall and watching started to drift in their direction. "Give us back our money," the man demanded. "Or you'll be sorry."

Alexei grinned, large even teeth gleaming whitely in his brown beard. This was more like it. He'd been getting bored with pool anyway. "Not going to happen," he said, and as the others started closing in, he lifted his own stick in both hands, getting ready to break it over his knee to make it into a better weapon. But for some reason, the stick didn't move.

He blinked, looking down. A small, surprisingly strong hand hung on to the middle of the cue, pulling it downward and him along with it until his eyes were looking into the steely-eyed glare of a petite red-headed woman.

"NOT IN MY BAR," she said with the hint of a Scottish accent. "And not with my pool cue. Those things aren't cheap, you know." She plucked the stick out of his grasp and leaned it against the wall before turning her glare on the other men. "Tommy and Jonah, I think I've made my feelings clear on the subject of fighting in this bar. You've had enough. Go home."

"But he stole our money!" Tommy whined. Or maybe it was Jonah.

The woman snorted. "Nobody forced you to play pool, Tommy Carson. And nobody forced you to bet on it, and keep betting on it after it became clear that you were seriously outmatched. Go home and sleep it off, and take your brother with you. Get, now." She shooed them out the door, and everyone else scuttled off to sit at tables and try and look as though they hadn't been about to pile four-deep onto a perfect stranger.

She turned to Alexei, tilting her head up so she could look into his eyes. "You," she said. "Bar. Sit. Now." She pointed at an unoccupied stool towards the end, away from anyone else.

When Alexei didn't move right away, a little bemused by the small dynamo who had just ordered around a room full of men twice her size, she narrowed her eyes, crossed her arms over her chest, and added, "Unless you'd rather go after the Carson brothers than have another beer."

"Make it a vodka," Alexei said, trying to hide the laughter in his voice. "Since you've insisted on spoiling all my fun."

"Fine," she said, stalking off toward the bar. "You can pay for it out of your winnings."

She went to the other side and waited for him to sit before and pouring him a drink.

"I've been watching you," she said. "I'm Bethany McKenna. This is my place, or near enough."

"Alexei Knight," he said, holding out a massive hand. Alexei couldn't figure out how he missed noticing her. He must be worse off than he thought. There was something special about her. And considering the women he normally hung out with, that was really saying something. "You've been watching me?"

"I don't much appreciate you hustling my customers. I realize those two boys are none too sharp, but still, I figure you took about eighty-five dollars off them, and that's enough." She pushed a stray stand of red hair back into the clip that held the rest off her slender neck.

Alexei shrugged. "How am I supposed to get the money to pay for my beer, then?" he asked in a reasonable tone.

She pointed at an well-dressed man currently being rude to the lone waitress. "Feel free to entertain yourself with the tourists," she says. "Just don't hustle them. I don't need this bar getting any worse a reputation than it already has. Play an honest game. Anyone still dumb enough to bet you after the first one, well, I'll consider it a cheap education."

Alexei thought he might like this woman. He'd tell her so, but he had a feeling she'd just smash a bottle over his head. "Okay," he said instead. "Fair enough. You get a lot of tourists in here?"

The woman grinned. "At the end of March? Nope. Hardly any." She gave him an assessing glance. "You're not from around here, but you don't seem like the tourist type. What brings you to the Cape?"

He shrugged again. "I started out on the West Coast, and I've been drinking my way across the country. Near as I can tell, I've about run out of road."

Bethany took this in without any notable reaction. "Yup, I'd say that's probably true, although technically you've still got about half the Cape to go before you hit Provincetown." She shifted a couple of inches to the left so she could wash dirty glasses and still continue their conversation, her eyes constantly roaming over the bar to see if anyone needed her attention. "So what are you going to do now?"

"Not sure," Alexei said. "Turn around and do it all over again, maybe. Or get on a boat and go drink my way across Europe. Haven't done that in a while."

She put a clean glass upside down on a drying rack. "A boat? Not a plane?"

Alexei shuddered. "Not a chance. Flying is for birds and dragons. Not for people."

Bethany laughed. "I wouldn't have pegged you for a man who was afraid of flying."

"Not afraid," he said. "Just smart enough to know when

something is a bad idea. I don't have many rules. Do not trust a machine to carry you through the sky is one of them."

Another glass joined the first. "So, what are the other rules?" she asked, sounding half curious, half dubious. He understood that. He knew he didn't exactly give the impression of a man who followed many rules. And he didn't, although the few he thought were worth following, he'd stuck to without exception for more years than most could count.

"An empty beer bottle is an abomination," he said, looking pointedly at the one he'd carried over from the pool table, until she took the hint and replaced it with a full one. He took a swig and thought for a moment. "Never hurt an animal that isn't trying to hurt you. Picking on those weaker than you is wrong."

Bethany bit her lip, trying not to smile. It made the cleft in her strong chin stand out even more. "I'm guessing that doesn't leave many folks for you to pick on. That's a pretty short list. Anything else?"

Alexei took another drink and stared blankly into the mirror behind the bar, not really seeing his own reflection. "Never pick a fight you can't win, unless you're backed into a corner and don't have any choice."

She raised an eyebrow. "I wouldn't have thought you'd have ever lost a fight," she said, waving a wet hand to indicate his size, in case he'd somehow forgotten the way he dwarfed most other people.

"It only takes once," he said with a growl, and tossed down the shot of vodka, slamming the shot glass back down on the bar. "It only takes once."

BETHANY HAD the guy pegged as trouble from the moment he walked through the door. It wasn't just his size—although admittedly that was part of it. She'd seen men who weighed more, but that was usually mostly fat, and this guy was incredibly tall and broad, with muscles on his muscles. There wasn't an extra ounce on him that she could see, which was kind of amazing when you considered the way he was currently putting away the beer.

Some of it was how he was dressed; the black leather jacket dangling with chains, black jeans, and the black tee shirt that stretched tightly across his chest and abs as if it had been molded to him. Add in the long brown hair pulled back with a leather thong and the braided beard that made him look like something out of Lord of the Rings, and he stood out even in a bar full of tough sailors. But mostly there was something about the way he moved, the way he carried himself, that just shouted *dangerous* to every instinct she had. Dangerous in an attractive way, if that kind of man was your type (hers was more of a button-down shirt intellectual sort), but dangerous all the same.

When he gleefully prepared to wade into a fight with the Carson brothers, she figured he'd proven her right. She'd been tempted to toss him out of the place right then and there, and would have if he'd given her any sass at all. Instead, he'd let her take away the pool cue without an argument and sat quietly at the bar, even had something like a civilized conversation until she'd said something that had caused him to slide back into glowering silence.

She'd kept a subtle eye on him since, but other than devouring three of her extra-large burgers and a mountain of fries around dinner time, he hadn't done anything worth remarking on. Just sat there and drank slowly but steadily, without getting obviously drunk. Either he had an amazing tolerance, or all that mass burned up the alcohol as fast as he drank it. Or else he'd simply fall over as soon as he finally stood up. She'd seen that happen too.

By mid-evening, she'd almost stopped worrying about him when he suddenly appeared down at the other end of the bar, somehow moving so smoothly she hadn't even seen him get off of his stool. He stood next to a couple who'd come in a few minutes before; Bethany thought they looked vaguely familiar, so probably locals, but not regulars.

Please don't let him be hitting on some other guy's date, she thought, edging slowly in that direction. *That's all I need.*

But Alexei's expression was composed and his posture seemed purposely unaggressive as he said casually to the woman, "I don't think you want to drink that wine."

Bethany blinked. Admittedly, the house red wasn't exactly a prime vintage, but it wasn't *that* bad. She stopped where she was, waiting to see what happened.

"I beg your pardon?" the woman, a pretty blond in her mid-twenties said.

"I don't think you want to drink that wine," Alexei repeated in the same calm tone. "Your date put something in it."

"What?" The woman looked from Alexei to her companion. "Don't be ridiculous."

"Sorry," Alexei said. "I was looking in the mirror and I distinctly saw him drop something in your glass." He nodded at the man she was with, an attractive, slightly preppy sort with neatly trimmed hair and wire-rimmed glasses. "Nice job, by the way, distracting her by pointing at that fancy car as it went by. Smooth."

The preppy guy sputtered. "I did no such thing. You're drunk. Go bother someone else."

Bethany moved to stand in front of the couple, and looked Alexei in the eye. He gazed back unflinchingly, as if daring her to take his word for it.

"Well, isn't this just a wee bit awkward," Bethany said, purposely broadening her accent even more than it already had since she'd returned home to live with her dad. She gave the couple her brightest smile, flashing her dimples at the man for good measure. "But it's easily resolved, isn't it?" She turned to the man. "All you have to do is take a drink from her glass. If there's nothing wrong with it, I'm sure you wouldn't mind a small sip. Then this helpful gentleman can return to his seat and we can all go back to having a nice peaceful evening."

The man gave a small but noticeable flinch. "Uh, no. Sorry, but I don't like wine." He gestured at the beer mug sitting in front of him.

The blond stared at him. "Gary, what are you talking about? You had wine at the party we went to last week at Steve's house. You went on and on about how important it was to pair just the right cheese with it."

Alexei crossed his huge arms across his chest, making the muscles bulge, although he didn't say a word.

"Fine," Gary said, rolling his eyes. "You're all making a fuss about nothing." He reached over to pick up the wine, but somehow knocked it over instead, spilling red liquid over the scarred surface of the bar. "Oops. Sorry."

His date's face turned ashen. "Oh my god, Gary. You *did* put something in my drink. I can't believe it."

"It was an accident," Gary said. "I didn't spill it on purpose. And I certainly didn't try and drug you. Stop being such a baby." A petulant expression marred his previously attractive features.

"Do you know this guy?" Alexei asked. "Enough to trust him?"

Silent tears slid down the girl's face. "He's my best friend. I've known him for years." She shook her head. "I thought I could trust him with my life. Apparently I was wrong."

Bethany picked up the glass and gestured at the small puddle of wine on the counter. "Do you want me to call the cops? I'm guessing they could still get enough evidence from that mess and whatever is left in the bottom of this."

The blond shook her head. "No," she whispered, barely loud enough to be heard. "I just never want to see him again."

"You heard the lady, Gary," Bethany said. "Get the hell out of my bar." She thought for a second and whipped out her phone as he stood up, snapping a quick photo of his smug smile.

"Hey," he said. "What are you doing?" He reached out a hand to grab at the phone, but Bethany pulled it out of his reach.

"Here's the thing, Gary," she said. "Cape Cod is practically an island. It's not very big, and you'd be surprised how many people in my business know each other. I'm going to send this picture out to everyone I know who owns a bar, tavern, pub, or hotel, and ask them to send it out to everyone else they know. By the end of the evening, you won't be able to buy a drink from Provincetown to Boston. *Now* get the hell out of my bar."

Alexei stalked over to stand behind the smaller man, placing a firm hand on his shoulder. "If you don't mind, I think I'll escort this boy out the door. You know, just in case he has a tough time finding his way."

Bethany gave him a hard look. He stared blandly back.

"Uh huh," she said. "Try not to do any permanent damage. I already have enough of a mess to clean up in here." She started mopping up the spilled wine, ignoring Gary's shouted protestations as Alexei half walked-half carried him outside. The few other patrons in the place acted as if nothing were happening. Just another Friday night at the *Hook and Anchor*.

"Are you going to be okay?" Bethany asked the girl. "Is there someone I can call for you?"

The girl pulled out her phone with fingers that shook. "I've got a friend who lives near here. She'll come pick me up when I tell her what happened."

She wiped away tears with the napkin Bethany handed her. "I just can't believe he was going to do that to me. I mean, I knew Gary kind of had a crush on me, but we've been joking about it for years. I never thought he'd stoop to something like drugging me. If it hadn't been for that big guy spotting him…" she shuddered. "And to think, when I saw him, I thought *he* was the scary one."

There was a series of loud crashes and a bang from outside, then silence, followed by the sound of squealing tires as a car peeled out of the lot. A minute later, Alexei sauntered back into the bar and sat back down on his stool as if nothing had happened.

Bethany walked over and set a beer in front of him.

"What's this for?" Alexei asked, looking at the beer bottle. He still had part of one left.

"Consider it a reward," Bethany said. "You did good." She

nodded at his battered knuckles. "I hope you didn't do anything too drastic, although God knows the kid deserved it."

Alexei shrugged, a movement that reminded her of a video she'd once seen of a mountain during an earthquake. "He'll live." He thought for a moment. "But you might need a new garbage can."

Bethany raised an eyebrow. "You dumped him in a garbage can? Fitting, but my cans are metal. I don't see how that would hurt one."

"I might have kind of crushed the can after I pulled him out of it," Alexei admitted. "Then smashed the can through the rear window of his expensive sports car. Accidentally. Like he spilled that wine."

She tried not to stare. "You accidentally crushed a metal trash can with your bare hands?"

He gave her a flash of a grin, lighting up his face in an unexpectedly attractive way. "Naw, I crushed the can on purpose. It was tossing it through the window that was an accident. More or less." He peered dubiously at the bottle of beer. "You know, destroying personal property is very thirsty work. I might need a shot of vodka to go with this."

Bethany choked back a laugh. "You got it." She reached up to the top shelf for the good stuff. He'd earned it.

2

ALEXEI STAYED AT THE BAR UNTIL BETHANY CLOSED THE PLACE up around one AM. After all, he had no place else he had to be. And he liked bars; they were as close to home as he got these days, since he had walked—or driven—away from anything and anyone that might once have resembled such a thing. All the other customers had left by midnight except one exceedingly drunk older man whose resigned looking son picked him up about the same time Bethany turned off the neon signs in the window.

She clicked off everything but the main light and came to stand beside Alexei. "Sorry, big guy. 'You don't have to go home but you can't stay here.'" When he looked blank, she added, "The Gretchen Wilson song? Seriously, you hang out in bars across the country and you haven't heard that one?"

Alexei shook his head but he slid off the barstool and headed for the door. "Not that I recall. But I get the point."

The small redhead put one hand on his arm. "You need

me to call you a taxi? I mean, you've been here pretty much all day. You probably shouldn't be driving."

Alexei laughed, a deep sound that bounced off the walls of the empty bar. The sad truth was he couldn't really get drunk —not without putting a pretty substantial effort into it. Damned Rider constitution. What good did it do him, now that he was no long a Rider? But he didn't have any way to explain that, nor the fact that, if need be, his still-magical steed-turned-motorcycle could drive itself.

So instead he did his own version of the "prove to the cops you're sober" routine, walking a straight line with his eyes closed, touching each forefinger to his nose, and then, because he couldn't resist showing off to a pretty girl, doing a hand-stand that ended up with him supporting all of his weight on the palm of one hand, before springing to his feet and taking a bow.

"See? Sober as a judge."

Bethany snorted, but he could see the smile lurking at the corner of her full lips. "Actually, that drunk old man you just saw leaving? That's the local judge. But otherwise, a very impressive performance." She opened the door and waved him out before locking it behind them. "I guess I feel comfort-able letting you drive, although I still don't know how you managed to drink for over twelve hours and not get even a little buzzed."

"It's all in the pacing," he said.

"And being the size of a small mountain."

"Yep, that too."

Bethany glanced around the parking lot and spotted his Harley, a couple of spaces away from the battered dark green truck that was the only other vehicle remaining. She rolled her eyes. "Why I am not surprised?" she said. "I hope you don't have far to go. It's warm for the end of March, but still pretty brisk out for a motorcycle ride. Where are you staying?"

Alexei shrugged. "Don't know. I just rode into town this morning."

"Are you serious?" she put her hands on her hips. "You do realize that because it's the off-season, most of the smaller bed and breakfast places are closed, and the one hotel in town locks its doors at midnight."

"Doesn't matter," he said in a reasonable tone. "I don't have money for anyplace swanky anyway." He pulled a rumpled wad of mostly ones and fives out of his pocket. "Unless you think they'll rent me a room for what's left of my pool winnings."

A sigh gusted out into the night. "So it's my fault for not letting you go all pool shark on my customers? Don't you have a credit card like normal people?"

He also wasn't going to explain that it was hard to get a credit card when there was no actual record of your existence. At least not outside of old Russian fairy tales. "Don't believe in them," he said. He pointed at the bike. "I've got some gold coins in my saddlebags, but I doubt there's anyplace open that would take them. I'll just sleep on the beach. It wouldn't be the first time, and I've got my bedroll. I'll be fine. I like the sound of the water."

Bethany let out an inarticulate exasperated noise. "It's forty degrees out. Way too cold for sleeping on the beach." She shook her head. "Besides, I'm not going to just send you out into the night, not when you saved that poor girl from being drugged in my bar on my watch. I would never have forgiven myself." When he opened his mouth to protest, she just narrowed her eyes at him and he shut up. He'd spent too many years hanging around with Baba Yagas not to have learned when to let a strong woman have things her way.

"Come on," she said in a resigned tone. "I have a place you can stay. It's only a couple of miles away, so you can follow me on your bike. Try not to wake up everyone between here and there by revving your engine." She clearly wasn't a Harley fan.

Alexei swung one leg over the seat and leaned over to whisper to the motorcycle. When it started up, it was barely louder than a purr. He grinned smugly at Bethany. "I'll bet the exhaust on that rusty old beater you're driving makes a lot more noise than this." And it did.

BETHANY PULLED up in front of the long one-story house with its fading gray paint and peeling black shutters. As soon as the weather warmed up, she was going to have to add painter to the long list of other duties she was currently performing. Her father had never really cared about appearances. Only the wheelchair ramp was new and neat, an ironic contrast to the rest of the place.

She got out of the truck, closing the door hard because it didn't stay shut otherwise, and walked over to Alexei.

"Do you live here?" he asked, looking around at the scrubby plants that were all that grew in the sandy soil, and the path made out of crushed shells that branched off toward the house in one direction and a small mother-in-law apartment in the other.

Bethany nodded her head in the direction of the house.

"That's my dad's place. I'm staying with him for the moment. He had an accident about six months ago and I came home from Boston to take care of him and run the bar until he could get back on his feet." She winced at her poor choice of words. "Figuratively speaking. He broke his back, so he'll be in a wheelchair for the rest of his life."

"Tough luck," Alexei said, matter-of-factly.

She appreciated the lack of sentiment; she got tired of people feeling sorry for her father, or acting like she was some kind of saint. She was far from that. A saint would probably be a lot less resentful, for one thing.

"Shit happens," Bethany said, stifling a yawn. Her days started early and ended late. This one wasn't over yet, either. She pointed at the smaller unit and they walked up the path toward it. "My dad usually rents the apartment out during tourist season. It's not really set up for guests at the moment, but it should be habitable enough. Better than sleeping on the beach, anyway."

She hesitated at the front door with the key in the lock. "I should warn you, the place is already occupied."

Alexei raised an eyebrow, but followed her inside without comment. The eyebrow went up even further at the sight of the huge Great Dane sprawled over the entire length of a long flowered sofa. At their entrance, the dog lifted its head and let out a quiet woof. As she made an ungainly dismount and waddled over to greet them, it became clear that she was very pregnant.

"I hope you're not allergic to dogs," Bethany said. "I'm fostering Lulu here until after the puppies are born and ready to go out for adoption. The space was empty and I didn't have the heart to say no when the local rescue organization begged me to take her. She's too large for anyone else on their list. I assure you, she's really quite mellow."

Alexei knelt on the floor to bring himself down to the dog's level and rubbed her gently on the head, then scratching behind her ears until she whined in contentment. "I like dogs just fine," he said. "Big dogs especially. Some of my best friends are big dogs." He heaved himself back up again. "We'll get along, no problem."

Well, that was a relief, although seeing the gigantic man being so sweet to the equally giant dog gave Bethany an unexpected pang. The man really was damned attractive. She still thought he was trouble, but he clearly had a soft side underneath all that toughness. Still, not her problem. She'd let him sleep here tonight, and then in the morning, he'd be on his way. For now, she had other things to deal with before she could get the rest she so desperately needed.

"Swell," she said. "Then I'll leave you to it. The bedroom and bathroom are down that hallway. The bed won't be made up, but there are sheets and towels in the hallway closet." She was too tired to wait on him, and it wasn't as though he was a paying guest. He'd just have to fend for himself. "There's nothing much in the kitchen, I'm afraid, but I wasn't expecting anyone to be staying here until May. If then."

"No worries," Alexei said. "I'm used to roughing it. Shall I let the dog out before I go to bed?"

"That would be great," Bethany said. "The back door leads out to a small fenced yard. Just put her out there for a couple of minutes, then let her back in. There's food on the counter for her if her bowl is empty." She yawned.

"We're fine here," Alexei said. "Thank you for the place to stay. You should go to bed."

Bethany nodded and headed for the door. If only it was going to be that easy.

SHE LET herself into the house as quietly as possible, but Rosa must have been listening for her, because the stout Hispanic woman came barreling into the outdated kitchen as if she'd been shot out of a cannon, her coat and purse already slung over one arm. Her graying black hair was coming loose from its bun, its errant tendrils following the grooves time and stress had carved into an already homely face. Bethany had the sinking feeling those lines had gotten deeper since she'd seen Rosa earlier that day. And she was pretty sure she knew what put them there. Or rather, who.

"No more, Miz McKenna," Rosa said in her heavily accented English. "I no work with that man no more. He eez the devil. I quit."

Bethany took a breath in through her nose, trying not to panic. If Rosa quit, that would be the third home health aide to do so in two months. The agency had already warned Bethany that they were having trouble finding anyone willing to take the job. Without Rosa, she was sunk.

"Now Rosa," she said, trying to sound soothing, and not as though she was begging. "I know my father is difficult, but he *is* in a lot of pain, and he's not used to being dependent on other people. He's just having a hard adjustment. He really doesn't mean to take it out on you."

Dark brows beetled together as Rosa shook her head. "He in a lot of pain because he no willing to do his physical therapy. He no willing to do nothing. Today he throw his dinner at the wall when I bring it him. I no work here no more." She shook her head even more vehemently, as if to reinforce her point.

"Rosa, please," Bethany said. "I'm so sorry. I'll pay extra if you'll stay." Although heaven knew where she would get it. They were barely managing as it was. "Please."

"I sorry," Rosa said, putting on her coat. "You a nice girl. But that man, he is *loco. Un hobre muy malo.* I no work with him no more." She stalked out the door without a backward glance, slamming it decisively behind her.

Bethany sighed, leaning against the table for a moment while she worked up the energy to go further into the house. Truth be told, she didn't blame the older woman at all. Rosa was right. Calum McKenna was a mean man. He'd always been that way, and falling off a roof and breaking his back hadn't improved his temperament one iota. Her mother had loved him despite all his flaws, passionately and completely, but for the life of her, Bethany didn't know why.

Finally she made herself walk from the kitchen through the shabby but neat living room and down the hallway to her father's bedroom, one door past the bedroom she'd moved back into six months before, thinking it would be for a month or maybe two at the most. Now it was beginning to feel as though she'd be there forever. Ironic, considering that she'd spent most of her teens counting the days until she could get away. Sometimes the universe was a bitch.

She braced herself, then put her head up high before walking into the room. It didn't do to show weakness around Calum McKenna; he'd jump on it like a lion on the weakest member of the pride.

"Hi Dad," she said in as cheerful a tone as she could

manage. "I hear you had a rough day." Her heart sank as she took in the mess still clinging to the wall near the doorway; the remains of the stew she has so painstakingly prepared that morning now looking like a piece of demented modern art in 3D meat and carrots. "You know, if you don't like the dinner, you can always just say 'no thank you' like a normal human being. And why are you still awake? It's almost two in the morning."

Calum glowered at her from his bed, his craggy face sullen in the dim light on the bedside table. "I know what time it is, lass. Dinnae treat me like my brain is broken just because my back is. I'm not a child to be told when to go to sleep."

Bethany slanted her eyes pointedly at the wall. "Well, if you don't want to be treated like a child, perhaps it would be best if you didn't act like one." She went into his adjoining bathroom and got a wet cloth, kneeling down to start cleaning up the disgusting mass. "And by the way, Rosa just quit. I suppose you're pleased with yourself."

There was silence from the bed for a minute. Her father wasn't stupid, just bad-tempered and frustrated. Finally he said, "I never liked that woman anyway. She was too bossy. You'll just have to get someone else."

"We're running out of 'someone else's' Dad," Bethany said softly. "Home health aides don't exactly grow on trees. And if you want me to keep the bar going, that means someone has to be here to take care of you while I'm gone. You won't let me get someone to live in, which means an aide on the nights I work late at the *Hook and Anchor*. You can't have it both ways. If you're determined to have me run the bar, you're going to have to be nicer to the people who come in to take care of you."

"I don't *want* to be taken care of," Calum shouted. "I don't like having strangers in my house! And I don't like being told what to do by a snip of a girl who thinks she's too good to be running an honest business."

Bethany had heard this litany more times than she could count, and she was too tired to argue. "Well, Dad, there's a lot I don't like about this situation either. And as neither of us is likely to get what we want tonight, I'm going to go to bed." She stood up slowly, one hand wrapped around the soiled towel, and the other pressed against the small of her back. "I'll see you in the morning. Try and get some rest."

"I'll rest when I'm dead," her father muttered, turning off the light and easing himself back down on his pillows with a grunt of pain. "And if we're both lucky, that will be soon."

In the hallway, Bethany leaned against the wall and closed her eyes for a minute. She was never quite sure if her father really meant what he said about wanting to die or not. She wasn't sure he knew either. But if he didn't start eating, sleeping, and doing his exercises, she was afraid they were going to find out. And as difficult as the old man was, she really wasn't ready for that.

3

ALEXEI WOKE TO THE FAINT GLIMMER OF SUNSHINE COMING through flowered curtains and the warm weight of a body next to his. For a moment, he was caught between the strangely erotic dreams he'd been having about a woman with flame-colored hair and the reality of a new day. Then he realized that the female sharing his unaccustomed bed had four legs, a bulging belly, and doggy breath, and the pieces fell back into place.

"Idiot beast," he muttered, trying to move her out of the way without falling off a bed that was already too small for a man his size. "I thought you were supposed to sleep on the couch."

Lulu lifted her head and licked his neck, then made her ungainly way down to the floor, looking pitifully at the doorway. "Out," she whined. "Now."

"Da, da, I'm coming," Alexei said. He was never a morning person at the best of times, as his brothers had so often teasingly noted. Now he was hearing a dog talk. He needed coffee.

He tied his bedroll together and dropped it and his saddle-bags next to the front door; he hadn't bothered with the sheets his hostess had so kindly pointed out to him—way too much trouble for one night, and he wasn't planning on staying any longer than that. Then he made his way to the back door and let the dog outside to do her business before scooping a generous helping of food into her bowl on the floor.

Unfortunately, a quick exploration of the kitchen didn't turn up anything that resembled people food, and he wasn't going to be fit to ride until he had at least one cup of coffee. Preferably a whole pot. Lulu had resumed her position on the couch, apparently worn out by the strenuous work of peeing and eating, so he left her lying there and walked up the narrow path to the main house. Hopefully Bethany was up and around, and he could beg a mug full of coffee before hitting the road.

The path led to a kitchen, empty at the moment, but the lights were on and the door was unlocked, and no one answered when he knocked, so he let himself in. He opened his mouth to call out when he heard the sound of a voice coming from the next room. It didn't sound happy, so he halted in the doorway.

Bethany stood with her back toward him, already dressed for the day in jeans and a flannel shirt whose green and orange checks clashed endearingly with her hair. One hand held a phone up to her ear, the other was clenched into a fist down at her side.

"Are you sure?" she was saying to the person on the other end. "I realize he's—" The fist clenched tighter, the knuckles turning white. "Yes, I know you only have limited staff, but I can't—" A sigh. "Okay. I understand. Well, do the best you can. I appreciate it." She tossed the phone down on the sofa and let loose with an impressive stream of rude words before turning around and realizing that Alexei was standing there.

"Crap," she said. "Sorry."

Alexei shrugged. "I came into your home uninvited. You owe me no apologies. Besides, I am not exactly a sensitive flower."

Bethany snorted. "There's an understatement. Did you need something? Is Lulu okay?"

"Lulu is fine. She hogged the bed all night, and has already gone outside and had breakfast," Alexei did his best to look pitiful. "I was hoping I would be rewarded for my services with a cup of coffee."

"Sure," she said. "It's on the counter in the kitchen. There are mugs right there. Help yourself."

Alexei began to go back into the other room, then hesitated. "There is a problem?" Not that it was any of his business, but her obvious distress was hard to ignore.

"Multiple," Bethany said with a grimace. "But at the moment, the crucial one is that my father chased off another home health aide last night, and the head of the agency just told me that the soonest he could get me more help is next week. And he's not making any promises for then."

"Your father is difficult to work with?"

"My father is a pain in the ass," she said flatly. "But he also can't be left alone all day. I get him up and dressed and fed in the mornings, and I have someone who opens the bar for me so I don't have to go in until about two in the afternoon, but I can't afford to pay anyone to run the place full time, whereas the aides are covered by insurance. So my father needs someone here until I get back, in theory to help him with his physical therapy exercises, although he won't do them, and to give him his dinner, which he won't eat. Plus, of course, there are fun things like getting him into the bathroom."

As if on cue, a voice bellowed from down the hallway, "Dammit, girl, I need to take a piss! Where the hell are you?"

"I see where you got your accent from," Alexei said, hearing a much stronger version of Bethany's light Scottish burr. "Not to mention some of your vocabulary."

Bethany rolled her eyes and pointed him toward the kitchen, then hurried in the direction of the bellow. Not quite sure why he did it, Alexei ignored the caffeine he so desperately needed and followed her.

The man sitting up in the bed glowering at the doorway didn't look much like Bethany, other than his fading red hair and the cleft in his squared-off jaw. Bushy eyebrows shadowed bloodshot hazel eyes, and his pajama top strained over a barrel chest and once-muscular arms. Bethany had moved a wheelchair next to the bed and was working to shift her father's legs, with him cursing at her to go faster.

Alexei shook his head. "Let me," he said, pushing Bethany out of the way with a nearly gentle nudge. He scooped the older man up in his arms and carried him effortlessly into the bathroom, then waited until he was done and carried him back to prop him on the edge of the bed. Bethany was strong enough, but what was an effort for her was nothing to him. "Clothes," he said, holding out one hand. Bethany raised one eyebrow, but wordlessly handed him a pair of gray sweats, a blue tee shirt, and a zip-up hooded sweatshirt.

"Who the hell is this?" Calum asked, as he let himself be

helped into the pants. The rest he managed on his own well enough. The change from pajamas to shirt revealed a thatch of gray hair on his chest and a colorful tattoo on each arm. "The agency is hiring giants now?"

Bethany sighed. "Alexei isn't from the agency, Dad. They won't be able to send us anyone new for at least a few days. I met him at the bar yesterday and he didn't have a place to stay, so he slept in the guesthouse last night."

Calum snorted. "Oh great, another stray. As if that huge dog wasn't bad enough. I hope you're not expecting me to feed this one too."

Alexei ignored the man's rudeness, which didn't faze him in the least. He once taken care of a Baba Yaga in the last stages of her life, and she'd been even grumpier than Bethany's father, not to mention being able to turn him into a toad if she was having a really bad day.

Most Baba Yagas chose to live out the end of their long lives in the comfort of the Otherworld, where they would have servants and luxury provided by a grateful queen if they so desired, but old Berta hadn't wanted to leave the deep woods of Russia where she'd spent her entire existence, and Alexei had quietly started spending more and more time with her, until in the last year he was there all the time except when he needed to be off helping her replacement. Taking care of a crippled old Human was no big deal, comparatively speaking.

"Breakfast," he said cheerfully. "Good idea. I believe some-body promised me a cup of coffee." He placed Calum into his chair and wheeled him in the direction of the kitchen with Bethany trailed behind looking somewhat bemused.

Once in the kitchen, however, she put mugs down in front of both men and started filling the kitchen with the welcome aroma of frying bacon and eggs. Alexei poured a generous dollop of cream into his coffee, then dug into the huge heap of food Bethany set down in front of him. In contrast, Calum's single egg on a piece of toast seemed like meager fare. The older man pushed the plate away with a grimace.

"Not going to eat that?" Alexei asked. "Shame. Your daughter is a good cook." He grinned up at Bethany as she put another pile of buttered toast near his elbow.

"Not hungry," Calum grunted.

Alexei lifted an eyebrow. "Huh. I thought Bethany said you were Scottish."

"Of course I'm Scottish, ye big oaf. Do ye not hear the way I speak?"

"Well, sure," Alexei said. "But I'd always heard that the Scots are hearty eaters. *Almost* as much as Russians, who can eat more than three people from any other country. But here you sit, not even able to nibble on a piece of egg. Seems like I've heard it wrong." He folded two pieces of bacon in half and stuffed them in his mouth, as if to emphasize his statement.

"Any Scotsman worth his salt could eat a Russian out of house and home," Calum muttered, picking up his fork. "Put some of that cream in my coffee, will you? I'm sick of drinking it black." He scowled up at Bethany. "Are you saving all that bacon for this stranger you dragged home, or is there a piece left for your poor father?"

Bethany walked over and put some on his plate, mouthing the words "thank you" at Alexei as she went back to the stove to get her own food. He winked at her when Calum wasn't looking, and enjoyed the slight blush that colored her cheeks pink in response. He'd had worse mornings, and worse sights to look at over the breakfast table, that much was sure.

———————

AFTER BREAKFAST, Bethany loaded the dishwasher while Alexei wheeled her father back into the living room. She couldn't believe the man had actually gotten Calum to eat a real meal. Without a five-round knock-down drag-out fight, either, which was the only way she ever got him to do it.

When she was done, she paused in the doorway to listen to the conversation, eavesdropping shamelessly once she realized what she was hearing.

"Now then," Alexei was saying, "what's this I heard about these exercises you're supposed to be doing?"

"I'm stuck in this damned chair," Calum said with a growl. "It's not as though I'm ever going to be hauling in another load of fish or carrying a keg of ale. Those exercises are a stupid waste of time and I don't see the point."

"Well, maybe the point is to get yourself strong enough to be able to get in and out of bed and onto the toilet without the help of that pint-sized daughter of yours," Alexei said in a mild tone. "Nothing wrong with your arms and shoulders is there?"

"What the hell business is it of yours, anyway?"

"Oh, none at all, none at all," Alexei said. "I couldn't care less. It's just, well, that Scotsman thing again. I'd always heard about how tough your people are supposed to be, and I'm kind of disappointed to find out it isn't true."

"The hell it isn't," Calum roared. "A Scot is more man

than some damned Russian any day of the week, and twice on Sunday."

"Is that so?"

In the kitchen doorway, Bethany had to put a hand over her mouth to keep from laughing.

"That it is."

There was a moment of silence, then Alexei said thoughtfully, "Care to have a wager on it? I'll bet you can't finish your exercises before I can do three hundred pushups."

"Away and boil your head," Calum said, his thick accent making it sound like "Awa' an bile yer heid." "You can never do three hundred pushups. Yer just having me on."

"I've got twenty dollars that says I can," Alexei said. "Unless you think you can't lift that little weight a few times."

Bethany risked a small peek into the room and saw her father struggling to lift the small dumbbells through the various motions he'd been given. On the floor nearby, Alexei had stripped off his shirt and was doing pushups, seemingly without effort, the muscles in his arms and back rippling in a way that did disturbing things to her insides. A dragon tattoo in black and red looked as though it was going to slither down his shoulder. She ducked back inside the kitchen before either of them could see her, a crazy idea beginning to form.

AFTER HE'D WORN the old man out and left him sitting in front of the television, Alexei went into the kitchen to get one more cup of coffee before he hit the road. The three hundred pushups hadn't even left him out of breath, but he had to admit it had almost been fun to get Calum to do what he was supposed to. No matter what people thought, there was more to Alexei Knight than just brawn. Maybe his brothers' brains and charm had finally worn off on him a bit. Or maybe not.

Bethany was waiting for him, sitting at the kitchen table with two mugs and a determined expression. Alexei had only known her for a day, but he already knew that face meant trouble. Maybe he didn't need the coffee after all. He'd just won twenty bucks off her father—he'd get some at a diner somewhere. He started edging toward the door.

"Sit," Bethany said firmly, reminding him for a moment of Barbara in one of her moods. He sat, looking at her warily.

"If this is about the money," he started to say.

She shook her head. "Don't be ridiculous. I would have paid that much just to see you con him into eating." She raised an eyebrow. "Not to mention the floor show."

Alexei pulled the larger mug toward him, secretly tickled by the idea that she'd been watching him. "What then?"

"I have a proposition for you," Bethany said, chin lifting as if to ward off an argument she was sure was coming.

It was his turn to raise an eyebrow. "Fabulous. I haven't had one of those in weeks."

"Not *that* kind of proposition, you oaf." But she said it with a smile. "This is business. You said you hadn't made up your mind where you were going next. I'd like you to consider staying here and taking care of my father for the next week, until I can get another aide."

She went on, talking fast as though afraid to let him get the word "no" out before she had finished. "I can't afford to pay you much, but you could sleep in the guest house for free, and I'd feed you three meals a day. And I have a neighbor who is willing to come over for a few hours in the evenings to sit with

Dad until I get home, so you could still get your drinking in, seeing as how that's so important to you. What do you say? It would only be for a week, probably."

Alexei gazed at her across the table. It wasn't as though taking care of one crippled old man—and a talkative pregnant dog—would be that tough. Or that he had anyplace else to be. Spending another few days with Bethany wouldn't be any hardship either, although he wasn't about to tell her that. She amused him, and not much had done that in quite a while.

"You barely know me," he said, not wanting to give in too easily. "Are you sure you want to trust your father's care to a stranger?"

She shrugged. "A stranger who can get him to eat and do his exercises? You bet. I trust him to strangers all the time; they just come from an agency instead of a bar. Besides, there's nothing here worth stealing, and you're not likely to murder him while he's watching *Jeopardy*. So, what do you say?"

Alexei pretended to ponder the offer for another minute. "I get to drink for free? Beer *and* vodka? And I can play pool?"

Bethany rolled her eyes. "Fine, beer and vodka. But not the good stuff. Not at the rate you swill it. And as long as you're honest about it, you can play all the pool you want. But no ripping people off and no fighting."

"Bah," Alexei said, but held out one huge hand anyway. He was tempted to spit on it, just to see how desperate she was to have his help, but decided he'd just wait and torture her in other ways. This was going to be fun. At least, as much fun as you could have with a stinky dog, a cranky old man, and a bar owner with silly rules. "Deal."

A small, callused hand reached across the table to clasp his. "Why do I have a feeling I'm going to regret this?" Bethany said, a smile twitching at the corner of her mouth. "For what I'm going to give you in food and booze, I could probably have sent him on a cruise for a week instead."

"Yes," Alexei said with a grin. "But then you wouldn't have the pleasure of my company. And that would be just tragic."

4

Len Morgan was out on his fishing boat much too early in the morning, as usual. Fishing was definitely the wrong occupation for a man who hated to get up early. But hell, he hated fish, too. And the truth was, he was a lousy fisherman. Unlike his two older brothers, who seemed to love the life they were all raised to, Len despised the hard work, the smell of fish, and the constant ache in his back and shoulders. Given the choice, he'd much rather be a pirate. But since there wasn't really such a thing anymore—and if there was, it would probably be hard work too, if he was realistic about it—he settled for supplementing his meager legitimate earnings with some judicious smuggling on the side. Now that was easy labor with a good return.

Just today, he'd earned five thousand bucks. And all he'd had to do was meet up with a Russian trawler out in international waters and pick up an innocuous-looking duffle bag filled with heroin. Said duffle bag now resided underneath a load of cod, waiting to be handed off to a guy once he got back to shore. It had taken him a few years and a bunch of successful trips like this one to work his way up to being trusted enough to do the big hauls—that plain gray bag contained two million dollars worth, so he'd been told by a mean-looking dude with a scarred face, a gravelly voice, and a nose that had been broken more than once. "Don't lose it," the man had joked. As if Len would be crazy enough to lose two million dollars of the Russian mob's money. He was lazy, not insane.

A crackle from his radio roused him from his musings. Then the message he heard woke him up the rest of the way, slamming his heart into overdrive and sending his pulse racing. *Shit.*

Crackle. "This is the Coast Guard. Please bring your vessel to a halt and prepare to be boarded. I repeat, this is the Coast Guard."

Shit, shit, shit. Len looked frantically over his shoulder and saw a small boat approaching rapidly from behind him. *Should he try to outrun them? No, their boat was much faster than his. Besides, maybe they were just looking for lost tourists or something. No, no, they'd just radio and ask if that was it. Shit. He was screwed.*

He slowed the fishing boat to a stop as directed, then ran to the hold while the Coast Guard ship was still easing up alongside. He couldn't risk them finding the heroin, he thought in a panic, sweat dripping down the back of his wool sweater. He'd never make it in jail. Frantically, he rooted around under the pile of slimy fish until he finally found the handle of the duffle bag. It pulled loose with a plop and he raced to the aft side and dropped it overboard. It sank below the waves without a sound. *There. Safe.*

Len sauntered around the end of the boat to meet the two

Coast Guard men on the port side, hoping that the perspiration on his face would be taken for spray.

"Morning, gentlemen," he said with a smile. "What can I do for you?"

"Sorry to bother you," the larger man said. "We had a tip about a ship about this size bringing in illegal aliens. But we got a call just now telling us it has been found near Provincetown. Thank you for your cooperation."

He and his companion headed back toward their boat. The smaller man tipped his cap. "You have a nice day, now."

A nice day? A nice day? Len watched them go with stunned disbelief. He'd just dumped two million dollars worth of the Russian mafia's heroin overboard for no reason. Unless he could figure out a way come up with the money to replace it, he was never going to have a nice day again. Of course, that might be a challenge, since if he'd had that kind of money, he wouldn't have been smuggling for the mob in the first place!

NOTHING. Nothing. Len tossed the contents of another box over his shoulder and continued rooting around in the attic of what had been the family home, now occupied only by him and the occasional disappointed rat. (Len didn't keep much food in the house, mostly preferring to subsist on diner meals and beer.)

He knew it was up here somewhere. Along with the rest of the crap that he and his brothers had accumulated over the years. In theory, his brothers had taken their stuff with them when they'd moved out to get married, but so far Len had found a stack of his older brother Cal's yearbooks and high school trophies—useless—and a box of his younger brother Phil's old Playboys. Marginally less useless. Still, Len wasn't any closer to finding the object he sought.

Not that it was likely to do him that much good; it certainly wasn't worth any two million dollars, or he would have dug it out and sold it already. But in his desperation, it was the only thing he could think of that might have any value. Or that maybe he could convince someone else it had value, even if it didn't. Len didn't much care which.

Another box went flying, creating an even bigger mess than the one he'd found up here when he'd pulled down the folding stairs that led to the small room at the top of the house. The sides of the space sloped down on either side, so he had to do part of his search bent over like an old lady. His back hurt and his calves ached from crouching, and his nose was stuffy and dripping from all the dust. Bah.

Len wiped his sleeve across his face and pushed open the lid of an old steamer trunk. The thing promptly snapped shut again, almost taking his fingers with it. His cursing scared the dust motes away as he propped it open with an old umbrella that was missing half its ribs, then leaned forward to root through the chest. He'd hidden it so long ago, he had no idea where he'd put it and only the vaguest idea of what it looked like, beyond being ugly and kind of odd.

His grandfather had called it a talisman, whatever that meant. Family legend said that the old man was descended from a pirate, and the gnarly taciturn seaman swore he'd inherited the strange piece from his own father, who had stolen it from some more famous pirate. Len's grandfather said he'd used the talisman to help the Nazis sink boats during World War Two, but Len had always dismissed that as the rambling bragging of a crazy old man. Just like he'd dismissed the talk of a lost treasure ship off the coast of Cape Cod, which was how his grandfather had supposedly wound up there, chasing after mythical gold. The man was a drunk in his later years, so no one took him very seriously.

But right at this moment, Len was desperate enough to try anything, even a wild family legend.

The talisman had actually been left to Cal as the eldest grandson, their father having been lost to the sea many years before their grandfather finally made his own journey to the briny depths. But it looked like it might have been valuable, so Len had taken it when they'd cleaned out his grandfather's house. As far as Len knew, Cal never missed it. Len had tried to hock it off island, but no one had been interested in it except as an oddity, and its dull yellow metal turned out to be brass and not gold.

He finally found it under a faded framed photograph of his parents' wedding, his brother Cal already making an appearance in the slight bulge of his mother's second-hand dress. A dusty black leather pouch, only slightly gnawed around the edges. It didn't look like much, but Len clutched it close and took it back down to the first floor, heaving the stairs back into place and leaving the mess behind for another day.

At the grimy kitchen table, he finally loosened the leather thong that held the pouch closed and spilled the talisman out into his hand. It wasn't any more impressive than when he'd first seen it, and if anything, even odder than he'd remembered. Still, there was something about it that set his blood humming in his veins.

Slightly larger than his palm, the gold-colored metal was still shiny, although the brass should have tarnished over the years. A large stone was set in the center, with detailed metal tentacles writhing all around it, suckers and all. The medallion hung off a thick metal chain. Truth be told, the thing was ugly and not a little creepy, but it must have had some value, or the men of his family wouldn't have kept it all this time. Not a sentimental one in the bunch, Len included.

The couple of pawnbrokers he'd taken it to had poked at the stone in the center and shrugged. Some kind of rock, they'd said, but nothing they could identify. And if they couldn't identify it, they couldn't put a price on it. Len had shrugged back, tucked the talisman into its bag, and gone home. Even then, he hadn't really wanted to sell it, and was almost relieved to discover there wasn't any point. Now, well, now he was just desperate enough to see if there was anything to the family legends.

ONCE HIS BOAT was far enough out to sea that the only witnesses were a couple of gulls swinging in aimless circles above the mast, Len took the talisman back out of its bag, feeling more than a little foolish. The problem—besides the fact that the family legends were probably all nonsense—was that none of the stories gave any details on how to use the thing. Tales about pirates and gold, those they had plenty of. Fantastical stories of monsters that sank ships on command, fishing out the treasure they carried like pearls from an oyster? Those too, although Len had stopped finding them entertaining when he hit about ten. It would have been a lot more useful, he thought bitterly, if the damned thing had come with written instructions.

Rather sheepishly, he tried saying a few so-called magical words out loud: abracadabra, alakazam, open sesame. Even he knew that last one wasn't going to work. He tried to think like an ancient pirate, but what he knew about ancient pirates was pretty much limited to talking parrots and telling people to walk the plank, and he didn't see how either of those would be helpful. Finally, he just cursed at it, which seemed as pirate-like as anything else, but it just sat there, a useless hunk of ugly metal and rock.

He was pretty sure the damn thing was laughing at him.

Finally, he bashed it against the side of the ship in a fit of temper. The talisman didn't even get a dent, but the edge of one brass tentacle slice into the hand holding it, making him yell out loud as blood beaded up on his palm and dripped onto the stone.

An odd vibration seemed to make the talisman ripple and the greenish-brown gem developed a crack down its center. Then the crack opened like two round eyelids, and a swirling golden eye with a green tempest at its center stared up at him, unblinking.

"What the hell!" Len yelped and dropped the talisman onto the deck, where it rocked back and forth with the motion of the boat, still staring upward. The eye seemed to follow his movements, the whirling green pupil shifting slightly from side to side.

"I'll be damned," he whispered, crouching down to look at it more closely. "What the hell kind of thing are you?" There was no answer, just an uncanny glow. "Can you get me some treasure?" he asked. "Gold? Jewels?" *A two million dollar bag of heroin?*

The eye blinked at him once, and the wood planks under

his feet shuddered. Off the starboard side, the water began to churn and bit by bit, a monster emerged from the sea. A bulbous head with two eerily shining eyes, and tentacles longer than Len's boat thrashing the sea into a froth.

"Holy crap," he breathed. "What the *hell* are you?"

One dripping tentacle hovered over the bow and Len just about peed himself, but all it did was uncurl its suckered tip and drop a small object on the deck with a muffled thud. Then it vanished back under the waves as silently as it had arrived. When Len looked at the talisman again, it was simply an ugly, inert piece of family history.

He placed it almost reverently back into its bag and tucked the leather pouch carefully inside his shirt. Then he examined the gift the monster had brought him. It wasn't much; just an old coin. But Len knew it was the beginning of something much, much bigger. He just needed to figure out what to do next.

Hayreddin stirred in his cave, startled from his decades-long nap by a restless tremor that made his massive body shift atop its bed of golden coins, precious gems, antique vases, and other treasure. In his natural dragon form, he took up most of the space in the underground cavern, his shimmering black scales and yellow belly—almost the same color as the metal he hoarded—gleaming dully in the dim light. A ray of sun snuck in through a crack in the rocks above, illuminating the bounty that stretched from wall to wall, bits and pieces slithering down to the floor as Hayreddin stretched and yawned, trying to pinpoint exactly what had awoken him.

He looked about rather hopefully for a would-be thief, but this was the Otherworld, and few of its denizens cared for Human treasure, and none were foolish enough to brave a dragon in his den. Too bad. He would have relished a little excitement. Since the high queen had decreed that all paranormal creatures retreat to the Otherworld permanently, life had been rather quiet. Boring, even.

And the queen had made it clear that killing any of her other subjects, no matter how stupid or useless, was a fate punishable by whatever whim struck her fancy at the time. Too bad. Hayreddin liked killing things. Most dragons weren't as bloodthirsty as Human legend painted them. Some, like him, were. But the queen's whims were nothing to be trifled with.

He missed his days of adventure on the other side of the doorway, where he would take on the guise of a Human and lead bands of pirates in search of treasure and glory. Mostly treasure, of course, but he'd rather enjoyed being feared and admired, too. Through the years he'd had many names and faces, and had gathered much wealth which he'd brought back to his cave in the Otherworld. Gold and jewels had no intrinsic value here, of course, where you could find entire paths paved with rubies and trees whose bark was made of precious metals, but he was a dragon, and for dragons, it was more about the having than the value in the items themselves.

The having and the getting. Being a pirate king had been fun. There had been a lot more freedom on the other side and no one to tell him what to do. Or who he could and couldn't kill.

Hayreddin sighed, causing a cascade of tarnished silver goblets. When the queen's edict was issued, he had assembled one last huge haul, but the ship it was on had sunk in a storm before he could get it to land and through the doorway he was using back to the Otherworld. The Queen allowed occasional short, authorized visits to the Human lands, as long as you kept a low profile, but on his few visits there, he'd never been able to track down his lost treasure.

It had become something of an obsession—not an unusual hazard for a dragon who didn't have enough purpose in his long, long life—but he still felt as though his hoard would never be complete without that final piece. It was annoying, like a broken scale that itched at the back of one's neck, just where it couldn't be reached by claws or teeth.

The small tremor happened again, more of a mental twitch than a physical one, and he realized why he'd awoken thinking of his adventures in the Human lands. During that last storm, he'd lost a magical talisman, created for him by a particularly talented witch with a taste for the delicacy called haggis which could only be procured on the other side. Hayreddin had used the talisman to summon a kraken to attack other ships and empty their holds as they tumbled to the bottom of the sea. He'd thought it was lost forever, but now someone, somehow, had activated it. It called to him through the impossible distance, like an old friend singing his name in the night.

And if it had been found, it would be his again. Nothing and no one would stop him from finally reclaiming his lost treasure. Hayreddin would be a pirate one more time, and the oceans would run red with blood. It was going to be *so* much fun.

5

ALEXEI STARED INTO THE BOTTOM OF HIS BEER MUG AND sighed. Not over the beer—it was good enough, some local brew as dark and bitter as his spirits. But drinking wasn't the same anymore. Nothing was the same. He'd never liked sitting still for long, but now there was no next mission, no next adventure. He had no idea *what* he was going to do next, and Alexei had never been very good at doing nothing. He took another swig of the very good beer. Even that didn't seem to help anymore. Dammit, he was turning as broody as his brother Gregori. That wouldn't do. It wouldn't do at all. One deep thinker was all any family could stand.

And that person had never been him.

Gregori was the thinker, Mikhail was the charmer, and Alexei was the fighter. Which was all very well and good when there was something to fight. Besides boredom.

It wasn't as though he minded sitting in a bar drinking. He *liked* sitting in bars. But he'd usually had his brothers for company, and it had been a lot more fun traveling and drinking and brawling with them than it had turned out to be when he was on his own. Damn it.

But that had all changed when they'd been captured by Brenna, a deranged former Baba Yaga, who had tortured him and the others in an insane attempt to gain immortality, which had ended up draining them of theirs instead. That had seriously sucked. Yes, Bella's dragon-cat Koshka had eventually burnt the witch to a crisp—that was kind of satisfying, admittedly—but the damage had already been done.

Alexei gazed sightlessly at the dark liquid in front of him. He was the eldest. The strongest. He should have kept his brothers safe. But he'd failed, and they'd all paid the price. Nothing he could do would ever make up for that. He hadn't even been able to face them, after. Everyone said that no one blamed him, but he blamed himself.

So as soon as the worst of his wounds had healed, he'd left the Otherworld without a word to anyone. Just started moving and kept moving, drinking and fighting his way from the coast of California all the way across the country. As long as he was moving and drinking and fighting, he wasn't thinking. And that was a good thing, because thinking only depressed the crap out of him, and seriously, what was the point of that?

It wasn't as though he'd been completely out of touch. He'd kept track of his brothers' progress through the network of paranormal creatures still on this side of the doorway; the sprites tied to their earth-bound trees, the selkies and merpeople who had no ocean to retreat to on the other side. And he'd sent occasional postcards to the Baba Yagas, Barbara and Beka and Bella, so they wouldn't worry. He wasn't a complete jerk.

True, he'd skipped Mikhail's wedding, but he'd sent a

present. At least, he was pretty sure he had. And frankly, not showing up was probably a bigger gift. He was happy to hear that his brothers had managed to build new lives for themselves, but to be honest, he just didn't see the point. If he couldn't be the man he was meant to be, then he was going to embrace his lack of purpose with gusto, just like he'd always done everything else.

Speaking of which, his mug was empty. "Barkeep, I'll take another," he said, banging it down on the counter. With gusto, of course.

"If you break that mug, you'll get glass splinters and no more beer," Bethany said, rolling her eyes at him. "And if you spend one more night watching old cowboy movies on the television, I'm disconnecting the cable in the guest house. They're clearly a bad influence on you."

"Ha!" Alexei said. "As if I need a bad influence."

"You've got a point there," Bethany said in a wry tone, but since he'd just finished watching her father for eight *very* long hours, he looked at her pitifully until she poured him another one anyway.

A thin, weather-beaten man wearing a damp waterproof jacket and an exhausted expression slid onto the stool next to his and nodded at a couple of his compatriots who held down the seats further down the bar.

"Lousy fishing today," he said to no one in particular. "Bethany love, who does a man have to kill to get a beer around here?"

Bethany put a bottle down in front of him. "Tough day, Joe?" she asked. "The weather seemed okay. A little rain doesn't usually bother you."

"Weather's fine for this time of year," he said, draining

half the beer in one long swallow like a man who had been dying of thirst. "Fish just don't seem to be around a lot of the regular spots the last few days. Don't know why."

"Robbie did okay yesterday," the guy sitting on the stool next to him said. "He was in here bragging about it last night."

Joe shook his head and gave a half-hearted laugh. "He's not bragging today. They had to tow his boat into the dock. What's left of it. He's telling anyone who will listen this crazy story about some kind of giant squid attacking *The Marlin* when he was on his way back in. He swears the thing was so big, it nearly tipped the boat on its side and then ripped a hole in the deck to get at the fish in the hold."

The guy next to him guffawed. "Come on, pull the other one. A giant squid?"

The thin man shrugged. "That's what he's saying. Some of the guys think he was drinking and had some kind of freak accident, just made up the story so his wife wouldn't kill him. But I saw his face. *Something* spooked the hell out of him, that's for sure."

Another guy further down chewed thoughtfully on a tooth-pick. "Wouldn't look forward to putting 'giant squid attack' on all that damned insurance paperwork, that's for sure. He'll be lucky to get a penny."

"Oh, I dunno," a third man said from a table nearby. "I remember my grandfather talking about a monster that was seen further down the coast in his time."

Alexei perked up a little at the word monster. This was more like it. Nothing boring about monsters.

"What did your grandfather say it looked like?" he asked, swiveling around on his bar stool to face the man who had spoken.

"Well, I was only a kid at the time, and my mother used to shush him when he brought it up—I think she was worried he'd scare us little ones—but seems to me he could have been describing a giant squid. Said it had lots of legs and huge suckers, and maybe some kind of a beak, and it was so strong, it tossed a big ship around like it was a children's toy in the bathtub."

"That's the stupidest thing I ever heard," the guy next to Joe said with a scowl. "There's no such thing as monsters or giant squids. It's impossible."

Alexei shook his head. "Ha. The impossible is just the possible you haven't met yet." He'd met a *lot* of impossible things in his time with the Baba Yagas.

The guy snorted. "Want to bet?"

Excellent. Finally, some fun. "How about fifty bucks?" Alexei said.

"How about a hundred?" the guy countered, obviously thinking Alexei was kidding.

"Done," Alexei said, sticking out his hand for the man to shake. "I bring you back some proof there's a monster and you owe me a hundred dollars."

"Sure," the man agreed. "And when you can't get any proof, you owe me a hundred. I hope you're good for it."

"What the hell are you doing?" Bethany hissed, leaning closer over the bar.

"I'm going looking for a monster," Alexei said cheerfully, downing the rest of his beer. "Want to come?"

IN THE END Bethany went with him, more to keep an eye on

him than out of any belief that he was going to find anything. She didn't even want to think about where he was going to come up with a hundred dollars to pay off Duke, who wasn't exactly known for his forgiving nature. She was starting to second-guess her maybe-not-so-brilliant-after-all plan to have Alexei take care of her father. The man was clearly three pretzels short of a snack bag.

Although she had to admit, at least he'd gotten Calum up and dressed and fed with a minimum of fuss and a relatively small amount of cursing the last few days, and then walked Lulu without being asked, although it was a little odd the way he kept up a one-sided conversation with the dog. So the next day, as soon as the lunch rush was over, she'd called in her relief bartender for a couple of hours and asked Mrs. Masters from next door to come over for a bit while Bethany drove Alexei down to the wharf.

Calum complained bitterly about being forced to watch the neighbor's soap operas, but Bethany figured without a minder, there was no telling what kind of trouble Alexei might get into. Even with one, she wasn't feeling all that complacent. She had a feeling he could get into trouble in an empty room with all the doors and windows locked and one arm tied behind his back.

Maybe both arms.

She pulled the truck up to the wharf and put on the parking brake, overwhelmed for a moment by a flashback to the days she and her mom used to drive over to meet her father at the end of a long day's fishing. When they'd first moved here from Scotland, he'd taken whatever jobs he could get, going clamming or lobstering when he couldn't get a job on a fishing boat. Eventually he'd saved up enough money for his own boat, which should have made things easier, except it was right around then that her mom had started getting sick.

Nothing was ever easy after that. Still, right up until the point where she couldn't get out of bed, Bethany's mom had insisted that if she was going to keep their only vehicle during the day, she'd go pick up her husband when it was time for him to come home. Margaret McKenna might have been the only person in the world as stubborn as the man she'd married.

She had also been the only one in the world that Calum listened to, and sometimes actually behaved for. Bethany shook off the feeling that she might be starting to be that person for Alexei. That was just nuts. He meant nothing to her, and she sure as hell meant nothing to him. She'd be crazy to think otherwise, and while she had her flaws, Bethany was anything but crazy.

"You okay?" Alexei asked, sounding more curious than concerned. "You're gripping that steering wheel like you're trying to choke it."

Bethany relaxed her white-knuckled fingers and took a deep breath. She never got tired of the briny scent of the ocean, flavored with the slight tang of fish. She'd missed it, when she'd been going to law school in Boston. She hadn't missed Calum's temper and bad moods, or their constant disagreements while they were stuck together in that small house after her mother died, but she'd sometimes gone to the harbor just to breath in air that smelled like home.

"I'm fine," she said. "Just childhood memories rearing their ugly heads. You know what it's like."

He raised one shaggy eyebrow. She'd never noticed before, but they were slightly pointed in the middle, which added to his general devilish air. "I do not, actually," he said, his Russian accent stronger than usual. "My childhood was…unconventional."

Ha. And why didn't that surprise her? "Raised by wolves?" she asked, getting out of the truck and slamming the door hard so it would close.

"A few," he said. "Also some very nice bears."

She glanced at his huge body, long brown hair, and braided beard. Somehow, that wouldn't surprise her at all. "Right," she said. "*The Marlin* is usually docked down this way. If the damage isn't too bad, they might be trying to do the repairs in her berth, instead of putting her into dry dock. Cheaper and faster." Fishermen couldn't afford to miss too many days on the water. Most of them were barely making a profit as it was.

Various men greeted them as they made their way down the pier.

"You seem to know a lot of people," Alexei said after one particularly exuberant "hallo!" "Do they all come to your bar?"

"Plenty of them," Bethany said. "But you have to remember that I grew up on these docks. Fishermen are a pretty close-knit community. There are some newcomers, of course, but half these guys brought me cookies when I was a kid, or showed me how to bait a line. When my dad sold his boat to buy the bar after my mom died, most of them showed up out of loyalty and kept him in business. A few of them even helped me with my algebra homework."

Not well, of course. But she'd kept her grades up, even through the grief of losing her mother at fifteen, because even then she knew that getting into a good college on a scholarship was her ticket out of town and away from her father.

She came to a stop in front of a familiar spot.

"Wow," she said. "I guess Joe wasn't exaggerating after all."

The boat in front of them was listing slightly to one side, its usually neat red and white paint marred by scratches and gouges. A sizeable hole gaped in the splintered wood plank deck, although fortunately the damage seemed to be restricted to the area above the waterline.

"That doesn't look like a drunken accident to me," Alexei said, his grin suspiciously bright. "And I ought to know."

"I'll bet," she muttered. "Hey, Robbie, you here?"

A grizzled head wearing a warm navy blue cap and a wispy beard popped out of the ship's cabin. "Bethany, darlin', what are you doing here? Did your father send you here to gloat? He always was jealous of my *Marlin*." A crooked smile belied his harsh words, but it didn't touch the shadows behind his eyes.

"Just checking in on you," she said. "This giant person is Alexei. He's helping me look after my dad for a few days. Permission to come aboard?"

"Not sure why you'd want to," Robbie said glumly. "But sure, come on up."

Once on deck, the damage looked, if anything, worse. "Holy crap, Robbie. This is terrible." Bethany gave the older man a hug. "I'm surprised you're not already trying to repair it."

"Have to wait for the man from the insurance company, don't I?" Robbie said, tugging fretfully at the edge of his worn wool pea coat. "Can't so much as hammer a nail into a board until they take fifty zillion pictures, measure everything, make me repeat my story another seventeen times, tell me they don't believe me, and then hopefully, cut me a check anyway." He slumped against the side of the boat, his entire body a study in discouragement.

"About that story," she said hesitantly. "Joe was in the bar and he was telling everyone you said, well—"

"He said there was a monster," Alexei chimed in, as though that was the kind of thing people said every day. "Was it a big monster or a little monster? What color was it? Did it have tentacles?"

Bethany thought he sounded more excited than a kid on Christmas morning, as though a monster—not that there was such a thing—was the best kind of present anyone could get. Looking at the huge hole, she suspected Robbie didn't share his sentiments.

"Sorry," she said. "Alexei isn't exactly sensitive about other people's feelings."

"*Hey*," the big man said. "I'm taking care of a gigantic ugly pregnant dog and a cranky crippled old man. I'm completely sensitive."

Robbie coughed, clearly covering up a laugh. At least Alexei hadn't offended him. That was something. Bethany shrugged, offering him a wry smile.

"There actually was a monster," Robbie said, taking a pipe out of his jacket pocket and lighting it up. The smell of apple tobacco filled the air. "Not that anyone is going to believe me."

She looked at the gaping wound in the deck again. *Something* had made it, that was for sure. And short of someone dropping a huge safe from a ten story building, the way they used to do in the old movies her dad liked to watch, she sure as shit couldn't figure out what.

"What happened?" she asked. "Did y
ship?"

The old sailor snorted. "Weren't nothi
there but us, honey. We were coming back
pretty good haul when all of a sudden the l
shake, like it had run aground on somethii

deep water, and there weren't nothing to hit. I ran to the aft side and saw this long rubbery thing flopping around on the deck; I thought maybe one of the men was pulling some kind of practical joke until the damned thing wrapped itself around a spar and tore it right off the boat.

"Whatever it was, it was big. Really big. I only saw two of them tentacles, but what I saw was bigger than a grown man, and they weren't but part of the way out of the water." He shuddered. "I don't ever want to see the rest of whatever they were attached to. One of the men who was on the other side of the ship said he saw what looked like a giant beak sticking up. Looked like an enormous squid to me, but I ain't never seen no squid that could grow to that size. The thing tore open the deck over the hold like it was opening up a can of tuna, and rooted around inside like it was searching for something. Took a few fish, but I don't reckon that was what it was after, since it left most of 'em behind."

He chewed furiously on the stem of his pipe. "Damned cod are still in there, rotting in the hold instead of making me good money selling them at market. Insurance guy was supposed to be here an hour ago, but it won't matter none. Too late now." He spat on the deck, then gave Bethany an apologetic look.

"I'm sorry, Robbie," she said in a quiet voice. "This all sucks."

, I don't know," Alexei said cheerfully. "Sea monsters pretty rare these days. Maybe you can get on one of those reality shows Calum watches."

Bethany smacked his arm. It was like hitting a brick wall. With a rubber mallet. "Ow. No more TV for you, I mean it. Now unless you can think of a more helpful idea, I suggest we get out of Robbie's hair. I have a bar to run, in case you've forgotten. And you have a crabby old man to deal with."

"Um," Alexei said. Which might or might not have been agreement. "Did you say the fish are still in your hold?" he asked Robbie.

"Yep," the sailor said, sighing. "The ice is starting to melt down there, so you'll be able to smell 'em soon enough." He turned and gazed down the length of the dock, as if doing so could conjure up the elusive insurance inspector.

"Mind if I go have a look?" Alexei asked, already heading in that direction.

"Help yourself," Robbie hollered after him. "But if you hurt yourself down there, you're on your own." He blinked at Bethany. "He's kind of an odd duck, isn't he? Where did you find him?"

"In the bar," she answered.

"That explains a lot."

"You have no idea," she said.

A few minutes later, a whooping noise echoed up from the hold and Alexei hauled himself over the crushed edge, holding on with one hand and tossing a couple of large cod with the other. The fish hit the deck with a wet, meaty thwap, almost hitting Bethany in the legs.

"Oops, sorry," Alexei said, clambering the rest of the way

up and ambling over to where Bethany was staring down at the cod at her feet.

"Any particular reason you're throwing fish at me?" she asked in a milder tone than she actually felt.

"Look," Alexei said, picking up the biggest one and turning it over so she and Robbie could see the other side. One huge finger prodded at a strange mark on the fish's skin.

"What the hell is *that*?" Bethany asked. She put out a much smaller fingertip and touched it gingerly.

"That's a damned sucker mark," Robbie said, his voice a study in mixed awe and alarm. "But I ain't never seen one that size in all my years on the water. It must be fifty times bigger than any sucker on even the biggest squid I've ever come across. Holy crap. It really was a giant squid." He held up the fish gleefully. "I can't wait to show this to that damned insurance guy. You shoulda heard him laughin' at me on the phone."

Alexei quirked an eyebrow and gave Bethany a look she couldn't quite decipher, but which she figured boded nothing good for her peace of mind. "Can I keep this other one?" Alexei asked Robbie. It too bore the mark of an unusually large sucker. It was also starting to give off a distinct odor of not-quite-fresh fish.

Bethany scowled at Alexei. "You are not carrying that thing in my truck."

"Got to," he said. "I have to see a man about a bet."

Oh, hell. This was not going to end well.

WHEN HIS SHIFT with Colum was over for the day, Alexei took

the cod out of the fridge where he'd stuck it at Bethany's insistence (wrapped in two layers of plastic bags) and drove his motorcycle over to *The Hook and Anchor*. Luckily, the man he was looking for was already there, sitting at a table with a couple of his cronies.

"Ha!" Alexei said, slamming the fish down between their beers. "Take a look at that."

Bethany looked up with alarm as Duke shoved his chair back, out of reach of the beer that slopped over the edge of his mug.

"What the devil is wrong with you?" Duke bellowed. "You owe me another beer."

"Ha," Alexei said again, at a slightly lower volume. "You owe *me* a hundred bucks. You wanted proof of monsters, there you go."

Duke rolled his eyes. "I don't see how that cod is proof of anything other than the well known fact that dead fish smell. Jeez. Get that thing off my table, will ya?"

"Sure," Alexei said with a grin. "As soon as you give me my hundred dollars. Look at that sucker mark and tell me that didn't come from a kraken."

"A kraken?" Duke guffawed, and his two friends joined in. "There's no such thing as a kraken, you jackass. Maybe Robbie ran into a giant squid—they're rare, but they do exist —but krakens are no more real that mermaids and fairies."

"Some of my favorite people are mermaids and fairies," Alexei said in a low rumble that would have signaled trouble to anyone who knew him better. "And even an idiot like you should be able to tell the difference between the sucker mark from a giant squid and one from a kraken that could eat it for dinner and still have room left over for a whale or two. A bet's a bet."

"Who are you calling an idiot?" Duke said in a threatening voice. He stood up so fast he knocked his chair over, and his friends rose to join him. "Because as far as I can see, the only idiot in this room is the one that thinks I'm stupid enough to pay him a hundred bucks for a dead fish." He knelt down to pick the chair up, then swung it at Alexei's head with all his might.

All right then! Finally, a decent fight. True, it was only three against one, so it wouldn't last long, but at least for a minute, Alexei felt like himself again, instead of lost and untethered the way he had for months. "Son of a goat!" he yelled in Russian, turning over the table as he ducked away from the chair as it whistled through the air right over his head. "Is that the best you can do?"

Another chair connected with his shoulder, but he barely felt it as he picked up the man wielding it and tossed him across the room. More men joined into the fight as their drinks got knocked over, or more probably, just for the fun of it. Alexei roared, his blood pounding in his head and his muscles bunching as he held a sailor over his head with one hand.

A piercing whistle rang out and everything stopped as all heads swiveled toward the bar. Bethany stood on top of it like a red-haired avenging angel, a baseball bat gripped in both small hands.

"Put him down, Alexei," she said through clenched teeth. "And the rest of you, you know the rules here—no fighting, and no breaking the furniture. What would Calum think of you lot, destroying the bar he worked so hard to build? Shame on you."

All around him, men sheepishly straightened tables and chairs, sitting down and trying to act like they hadn't all been trying to kill him a minute ago. Alexei carefully lowered the guy he'd been holding until the man's feet were securely on the ground.

"But Bethany," Alexei said.

"Do. Not. But. Bethany. Me." She swung the bat in his direction. "I warned you. Didn't I? No fighting I said. No breaking things. But no, you just had to do it." She glanced around the room, her jaw set rigid with anger. "The place is a wreck. You've seen the way we live. Do you really think I have the money to replace all this stuff?"

The bat swung around until it was aimed at Duke. "Speaking of money, you owe Alexei a hundred bucks. He may be an ass, but he was right about the monster. I saw Robbie's boat, and no normal squid did that. Pay him, and get out. You started this fight, so you're banned for a month."

Duke narrowed his eyes at her, looking for a moment as if he might argue, then reached into his wallet, pulled out five twenties, put them on top of the now three-legged table, and stalked out of the bar without another word.

"See, it wasn't my fault," Alexei said. "He started it. You said so yourself."

Bethany hopped down off the bar and stood in front of him, five feet three of steaming fury. "You provoked him. And don't think I don't know you could have stopped him without creating this disaster area. I think you just like destroying things. I grew up with a man just like you, remember. And for now, I suggest you go back to the house and figure out a way to explain to him that you helped tear his bar to pieces. Maybe it will finally motivate him to get his ass back in here, so I can get on with what I laughingly refer to as my life."

She waved the bat toward the door, and Alexei opened his mouth, closed it again, and left. He suddenly missed his brothers so much it made his chest hurt. Even fighting wasn't fun anymore. Nothing was the same, and he had no idea what the hell to do about it.

6

BETHANY SWEPT SHARDS OF BROKEN GLASS AND SPLINTERED wood into the pile she'd already amassed in the corner, muttering obscenities under her breath. The few customers left in the bar were clustered across the room in a section left reasonably untouched by the fight; wisely, they were all drinking quietly and keeping their heads down. Nobody wanted to mess with Bethany when she was in this mood.

While some of her curses were aimed at Alexei, she saved most of the choice words for herself. She was an *idiot*. It wasn't as though she didn't know better, with Calum as a role model. She'd grown up with a man who dealt with his frustrations by drinking and brawling, and yet she'd still somehow let herself feel even the tiniest sliver of attraction to a man who'd made no secret of the fact that he was exactly the same. Okay, maybe more than a tiny sliver.

The truth was, she'd been halfway to falling for him, even though he was completely different from the calm, controlled type she normally went for—boring, predictable, and completely safe, everything that Alexei wasn't.

Just because he'd been gentle with a pregnant dog and surprisingly good with her father, that was no reason to believe he was anything other than the wild man he'd seemed to be on that first day he'd walked into *The Hook and Anchor*. She was a thrice-damned empty-headed shit-for-brains fool, that's what she was. It was a wonder they'd ever let her into Harvard Law School, much less almost allowed her to graduate. She was a moronic nincompoop.

And she had four broken tables and nine smashed chairs to prove it. She'd bang her head against the bar a couple of times, but with her luck, she'd just crack that too.

First thing in the morning, she was going to call the agency and *beg* for another aide. Then she was going to kick Alexei Knight out of her guest house and out of her life. Absolutely, positively, resolutely. That was the plan, and she was sticking to it.

Alexei sent the neighbor lady home early, got Calum comfortably ensconced in front of the television in his pajamas watching one of his favorite crime dramas, and then went outside to sit on the back steps with Lulu. He left the door open a crack so he could hear if Calum yelled for him, even though he was pretty sure that the old man's bellow was audible three houses away.

"I really screwed things up this time, Lulu," Alexei said, giving her an illicit treat. Bethany said the dog was supposed to be on a very specific diet until the puppies were born—which ought to be any day now—but Alexei figured that all pregnant women deserved a little treat now and then.

The Great Dane mouthed the biscuit daintily then lowered herself to the ground with a sigh, large paws resting on Alexei's similarly oversized motorcycle boots. He rubbed her ears absently, still brooding.

He didn't know what he was more upset about; that he'd wrecked the bar, or that he really hadn't had fun doing it. In a way, both issues were equally upsetting.

The truth of the matter was, in all the years that he and his brothers had spent brawling and fighting, he'd never really considered the damage they'd left behind. Never really thought about Human lives at all, except in the context of whatever job the Baba Yagas had them doing. They'd always been on the move and he'd never had time to get attached to any one place or any one Human. Not that he was attached now. Not really. No, not at all. He barely knew Bethany. And she was a Human, for heaven's sake. But still. At least this time he was able to see the after effects of what he'd done, and he didn't much like it. Didn't much like himself right this very minute, and it wasn't his nature to think about things that way.

He felt terrible about wrecking Bethany's place when she'd been nothing but good to him. But that was only part of the problem. Because if drinking and fighting didn't make him happy anymore, he had no idea what to do with the rest of his life.

Alexei groaned, resting his head in his hands. This was why he'd never wanted to think about things too much. It made his skull pound, and put a funny hollow feeling in the pit of his stomach.

"What did you do now?" a deep growly voice asked. A

rough tongue swiped across his cheek.

Alexei sighed. He hadn't made up his mind if he believed the dog was actually talking to him, or if it was just a symptom of his new mortality, a sign that he was, as the Humans said, "losing it." Of course, considering that after they were changed by Brenna's evil magic, his brother Mikhail became a shapeshifter and Gregori developed powerful psychic abilities inherited from his shamaness mother, Alexei supposed anything was possible.

"I made a mess at the bar and Bethany is mad at me," he explained to Lulu. "Hell, I don't blame her. I'm mad at myself."

Another lick followed by a huge, stinky dog-breath yawn. "When I make a mess, I just look sad and she forgives me. You look sad. Girl forgive you too?"

"I don't think it's going to be that simple, Lulu." Alexei fished another treat out of his pocket.

The smart thing to do would be to just move on. This was only ever supposed to be temporary anyway. Bethany would find someone else to deal with the cantankerous old man— although maybe not someone who could get him to eat right or do his exercises. Still, that wasn't Alexei's problem. He was just passing through on the way to someplace better. Someplace without a feisty flame-haired dynamo who could stand toe to toe with him. He'd find someone else to watch across the room when she wasn't looking, just to catch a glimpse of that dimpled smile. And as for Lulu…he didn't care if he never saw her puppies born.

Okay, that one was definitely a lie.

"I don't suppose you could have your babies tonight, before I go?" he said to the Great Dane.

Lulu gave him a sad-eyed look. "Man go?" She whined, resting her head heavily on top of her paws. "No. No go."

"I wish I knew if you were really talking to me," Alexei said. He could call one of the Baba Yagas and ask for their opinion, but he wasn't ready to face them yet. Not when he'd let them down so badly. Because of him, they had to fight all their battles alone now, with no Riders at their sides.

No, he couldn't call any of them, not tough and cranky Barbara, who would probably tell him he was crazy and it served him right. Or sweet Beka, who would say something New Age about the universe speaking to him through nature's creatures, or Bella, whose red hair and fiery temper just made him think of Bethany.

That only left two people he could ask. The two he had let down the most. The two he couldn't imagine ever being able to look in the eye again, but didn't know how to live without.

"I miss my brothers," he admitted to Lulu. The hollow feeling in his stomach moved up into his chest, settling there like a stone. A boulder, more like.

She whined again. "Call?" she said. "Talk?"

Alexei fingered the cell phone in the inside pocket of his leather jacket. The Riders had never used such things, and Barbara hated them. But when the evil former Baba Yaga Brenna had stolen the Riders' immortality, rendering them Riders no more, it had also broken the bond that had allowed the Baba Yagas to communicate with the brothers through the symbols permanently attached to their bodies. His dragon tattoo was nothing more than decorative now.

While they were still all healing in the Otherworld, Beka had created a mix of technology and magic; as the youngest and newest of the Babas, this was something that came much more naturally to her than to the others. Messengers had delivered the cell phones to each of the broken Riders, with all of their numbers and those of the Baba Yagas already programmed in, and the information that the spell that powered them meant they would work anywhere and never need to be recharged.

Alexei had never even turned his on. He had nothing to say to anyone. Nothing except "I'm sorry I failed you," and that seemed inadequate under the circumstances.

Now he took it out and stared at it. He'd meant to throw it away a million times. Had even tossed it into the ocean once, back when he was on the west coast. But the waves had brought it back to his feet, and the magic apparently meant it was waterproof as well, which made sense since Beka was a surfer and spent so much time at the shore.

But maybe it was time to finally put it to use. And under the circumstances, there was only one clear choice for who to call. After patting Lulu on the head one more time for moral support, he powered it up and then touched the icon that said "Gregori."

THE CALM, melodic voice on the other end said, "Hello, Alexei," and didn't sound surprised at all, despite the fact that they'd had no contact in almost a year. Alexei wasn't sure it if that was just Gregori being Gregori—he almost always sounded serene, even in the middle of a sword fight with ten-foot-tall fire-belching ogres—or if his brother's new psychic abilities had predicted this phone call. In the end, it didn't much matter.

For a minute, Alexei couldn't think of what to say. So many words tumbled over each other in his mind, spilling into his mouth and choking him until he couldn't talk at all. He hadn't realized until this very minute how hard it had been to spend so long without contacting the brothers he'd spent centuries with, since they were all children of varying ages playing in the realms of the gods.

"Alexei?" Gregori repeated. "Are you there?"

"More or less," Alexei mumbled. "Hello, Gregori."

His brother's low chuckle crossed the many miles between them. "How are you, you big lout? And where are you? We were beginning to think you'd disappeared off the ends of the earth."

"Close enough," Alexei said. He could hear the ocean from where he sat, although he'd have to walk down the road to actually put his feet in it. "And I'm…okay, mostly. You?"

"I am well. Still adjusting to all the changes in my life, but well enough, for all of that. Content. Happy, even." His brother paused for a moment. They'd never been an emotional bunch, or talked much about their feelings. "Are you happy, Alexei?"

Alexei snorted, making Lulu jump and give him a disgruntled look. "How would I know? I don't even know who I am anymore."

"Ah. That explains the call, I expect. Has something happened?" Another pause. "Have you discovered what your new gift is?"

"Pfft." Alexei scowled into the night sky. "Gift. Is that what we're calling our brother turning into a big green creature and you suddenly being able to predict the future? Gifts? I'd rather have a bottle of vodka and a nice box of chocolates."

"Wouldn't we all?" Gregori said lightly. But Alexei had heard through the paranormal grapevine of how hard his brother had had to fight to come to terms with his new talent. It had almost killed him, if the reports were right.

"I suppose so." Alexei took a deep breath. "Um, do you think hearing a dog talk could be my *gift*? Or is that just crazy?"

He could practically see the raised eyebrow through the phone.

"A dog? Or all of them?"

Alexei glanced at Lulu, who simply yawned back at him, uninterested in the fact that his life was unraveling. "Only one so far. A very pregnant Great Dane."

"I see," Gregori said. "And what does she say?"

"Well, she told me to call you."

Gregori laughed quietly. "Then she is either the voice of your subconscious, or a very smart dog."

"Isn't there some way to find out which one it is?" Alexei asked, only a touch plaintively.

"Have you tried talking to any other animals?" his brother asked. "That might tell you something."

"Bad enough I'm having conversations with one," Alexei grumbled. "Besides, I'm at the end of the world. Not many animals here, although I suppose there are other dogs and cats and such." He thought for a moment, then said more cheerfully, "And maybe a kraken. I wonder if I could talk to a kraken."

"A kraken?" Gregori repeated. "Have you—no, of course you haven't."

There was a moment of silence when they both thought about the days when it would have been automatic to contact one of the Baba Yagas if they ran into something odd and paranormal. Those days were over now, blown away like so much dust in the wind.

"Not my business," Alexei growled. "Besides, I haven't seen it. Just heard a story and saw a giant sucker mark on a dead fish. Might be nothing."

"Uh huh." Gregori sighed. "Leave it to you to stumble across trouble even at the ends of the world, wherever that is."

"Cape Cod," Alexei said, not sure why he was so reluctant to tell his brother where he was. After all, it wasn't as though he was staying. "But I'm leaving soon."

Another pause while his brother—always the smartest of them all—processed what he'd heard, and hadn't heard. "You don't sound all that happy about it," Gregori said finally. "Are you finally getting tired of traveling from place to place? Nothing wrong with that, if you are. Mikhail and I are both finding it surprisingly pleasant to finally set down roots. Endlessly moving isn't quite as attractive as it used to be when we had forever to do it in. And the Baba Yagas to do it for."

Alexei sighed. "Maybe. A little bit. There's this woman. Well, and the dog, and the woman's father, and a bar…" His voice trailed off when he thought about the bar. *Damn it.*

"This woman, you like her?" Gregori sounded torn between amusement and concern. "She's a Human?"

"Bah," Alexei said. "I wouldn't say I like her. She drives me nuts. I'm helping to take care of her father, who also drives me nuts. The dog is nice. I like the dog." Lulu reached up and licked his face. "Aw, cut it out, Lulu. That's disgusting."

"Is Lulu the woman?" Gregori asked. "In which case, should you be on the phone right now? It sounds like you're busy."

Alexei rolled his eyes. "Lulu is the dog, and she just gave me a stinky dog kiss. Bethany is the woman, and she runs her father's bar for him, since he broke his back. I'm um, kind of helping out with him. Just for now, because she'd giving me a place to stay for free. Besides, he's a stubborn old man, and you know how I like a challenge."

This time the silence on the other end of the phone went on a little longer.

"Let me get this straight," his brother said finally. "You found yourself a woman who runs a bar. That sounds pretty perfect for you. And you're taking care of her disabled father, which sounds slightly out of character, but I've seen you do odder things. So what's the problem?"

"How do you know there is one?" More silence, flavored this time with the air of a knowing older brother. "Fine, fine, you win. There might be a small problem. I might have kind of trashed the bar tonight."

"Alexei!"

"Hey, we used to wreck bars all the time. And the other guy started it." Alexei kicked a pebble with the toe of his boot. "But Bethany is furious with me, and I don't blame her. She told me the first night I got here not to get into any fights in her place, and I just kind of forgot. You know, for a second, it felt like old times." *Except that you weren't there.* But he couldn't say that.

"So what are you going to do?" Gregori asked, more gently than Alexei felt like he deserved.

He shrugged, even though his brother couldn't see it. "Leave, I guess. She's probably going to kick me out as soon as she gets home anyway."

"I thought you were helping with her father. Doesn't she need you?"

"She needs me not to wreck her damned bar, that's what she needs," Alexei said, wishing he could kick himself instead of the stupid pebble.

"Do you want to stay?" Gregori asked. "Because it kind of sounds to me like you do."

Alexei mumbled something that might have been an assent.

"Then maybe you should offer to fix the things you broke," his brother suggested. "You screwed up, then stay and fix it. You always were good with your hands. Apologize to the woman, make it better, and don't do it again. Maybe do something symbolic to show how sorry you are."

Huh. Gregori always managed to make things sound so simple and reasonable. That used to aggravate the crap out of Alexei, but this time he was kind of grateful. Assuming, of course, that he could find some tools, and that Bethany would listen to him long enough to let him make the offer. He thought it was more likely that she'd throw things at him until he was bleeding and lying on the ground. Well, he was tough. He could take it.

"Yeah, okay. I'll give that a try, I guess. Thanks."

"What are older brothers for?" Gregori said lightly. "And keep me posted on the talking dog thing, will you? It doesn't sound as perilous as what Mikhail and I went through, but you want to be careful nonetheless."

"Huh." Alexei glanced down at Lulu, lying at his feet and panting, her swollen belly making her look ungainly and uncomfortable. "Somehow I don't think I'm in any danger from a pregnant Great Dane, but I'll try and stay alert."

Gregori chuckled. "You do that. And Alexei?"

"Yes?"

"It was nice to talk to you. Try not to make it so long the next time, please."

"Maybe," Alexei said. "And Gregori, I, um, I'm sorry."

"Sorry for what?" his brother asked, sounding genuinely baffled. "For not calling? We've all had to deal with this change in our own way."

"No, not for that. For not protecting you and Mikhail from Brenna, when we were all trapped in the cave. I let you both down, and I'm sorry." Alexei rubbed one hand over his eyes, which prickled strangely. Must be some strange side effect from the sea air.

"You did not let us down," Gregori said. "Why would you think that?"

"I'm the strongest," Alexei said simply. "I should have been able to break us out. I should have been able to beat one small aged witch. But I didn't. I wasn't strong enough. And so you and Mikhail had to endure unending torture. It was my fault."

"Oh, Alexei. Is this why you have been avoiding us all?" Gregori's voice sounded immeasurably sad. "You were tortured just as much. I still remember when you held on to those magically reinforced bars to distract Brenna, even though your fingers burned and your skin melted. If strength alone could have gotten us out, you would certainly have done it, my large brother. Don't you think that Mikhail blamed himself for being tricked by Brenna and get us all caught in the first place? Or that I felt as though I should have been able to outsmart her?"

Alexei had never considered that his brothers might feel as guilty, as responsible as he did. "But, it wasn't your fault. Not either of you. The witch was just too powerful. And too evil."

"Exactly," Gregori said. "Too much for even your immense strength to overcome. Please do not blame yourself. We all survived—and now we are both less and yet somehow more than what we once were. It is what it is. The only thing left is to figure out what you want to be now that you cannot be who you were."

"What if I have no idea what that is?" Alexei asked.

"Perhaps it might be good to start with the woman who drives you nuts. At the very least, it sounds like it should be entertaining."

Alexei was fairly certain that was laughter he heard in his brother's voice.

"I'll think about it," he said.

"Perhaps you might also think about contacting Mikhail and the Baba Yagas," Gregori said. "They all miss you too."

Alexei sighed. "Not yet, Gregori. I'm just not ready."

"Very well," his brother said. "Then I hope you will call me again. If nothing else, I am curious to hear whether or not you can talk to animals now."

"He can," Lulu barked.

"Not helping," Alexei muttered. "We'll see," he said to Gregori. "But thanks for the advice." He ended the call and sat there for a minute, then heaved himself up and went into the house to ask Calum if he happened to have any woodworking tools lying around. You know, just in case Bethany didn't kick him out the minute she came home.

Plus, he needed a pair of scissors. He was going to do something symbolic. It remained to be seen if Bethany would understand just how deeply symbolic it was.

7

IN THE END, SHE LET HIM STAY. THE APOLOGY HELPED, BUT IN truth, Bethany didn't have much choice. The agency said the earliest they could sent someone new would be the beginning of the following week—if they could find anyone willing to work with Calum at all. She tried convincing the manager that Calum was being a lot better, but in her heart, she knew that was mostly because of Alexei's combination of sneakiness and sheer brute force, and not an indication that Calum was likely to be more cooperative with anyone else.

Besides—when she'd gotten home, he'd gone and cut his beard. He didn't say a word, just left the braided end sitting on the table, like a note from Samson to Delilah, and shown up at breakfast the next day with it shorter and more neatly trimmed. A little less wild man, a little more civilized. Not subtle, but then neither was Alexei.

So she gritted her teeth and told him he could stay for another week. But he was banned from the bar, and at the first sign of trouble, he was out. Alexei didn't argue. Didn't even balk at her cool tone and the distance she kept. Just took her father's woodworking tools, left over from the days he did repairs on his boat, and set to work fixing the worst of the wrecked furniture that she had hauled home in her truck.

The tables, when she got them back, were a revelation. She'd seen him working on them in the evenings when she'd gotten home from the bar, his huge form bent over in the dim light of a hanging lantern in the back yard, wood shavings littering the ground at his feet like late snow. But when she took them back to *The Hook and Anchor* and really looked at them, she was taken by surprise. Stunned, even.

The broken pine legs had been replaced with sturdy pieces of oak, adorned by fanciful carvings. Mermaids danced up one set of legs, frolicking amidst the seaweed and chests spilling over with treasure. On another table, dolphins swam in pursuit of schools of fish, the details so clear that the regulars chortled and pointed, recognizing the different types they caught so often. A third table featured fierce pirates, battling with each other or sailing the sea through shark-infested waters. The tops of each table had been stripped of their worn varnish and refinished, so they glowed in the soft lights of the bar. Here and there small scenes were etched into the surface —shallow enough so they wouldn't interfere with the function, but matching the more intricate carvings down below. The damn things weren't just repaired. They were works of art.

The customers were fascinated and word of mouth brought in the curious to see them, all of them staying to drink a beer or two. Bethany made enough from the extra business the first few days to more than make up for whatever she'd lost in cheap broken glassware.

At the end of the week, she came home from work,

slammed the door, and glared at Alexei, who was putting together a picture puzzle with her father in the kitchen.

"Fine," she said. "Come back to the damned bar. You might as well fix the rest of the chairs there; I'm tired of hauling them back and forth. But no drinking. And if you so much as chip a coffee mug, I'm going to kill you and bury you in the back yard, even if I have to hire three guys to carry you there for me. Got it?"

The two men stared at her.

Alexei nodded slowly. "Got it," he said. "It was okay, what I did with the tables? Not too fancy? I can do them again if you don't like them." His accent was stronger than usual, which Bethany had found usually indicated some strong emotion. This time, it probably just meant he was tired or something. Not much to get emotional about when you were talking about furniture.

"They are…nice. People like them. They're a conversation piece," Bethany said. "You're very talented."

Alexei blushed, something she would have guessed was impossible. "Bah," he said, ducking his head. "Just an old hobby. Something I used to do to pass the time by the camp-fire. I started out carving little wooden toys for…for some little girls I knew. I've just had a long time to practice, that is all."

"Well, whatever. They're okay. People like being able to keep finding new little details whenever they look at them. I keep getting requests."

"Like what?" Calum asked. "Naked ladies?"

Bethany rolled her eyes. The mermaids had been bad enough. "No, more like favorite sea birds, or whales. One guy even asked for dragons. Who knew our customers had such vivid imaginations?"

Calum snorted. "There's a lot of time to daydream on a boat, in between the hours of backbreaking work and the long trips in and out of port." He got a distant look in his eyes, and he rubbed his stubbly chin, his whole body drooping a little.

"Time for bed," Alexei said, his sharp eyes picking up on the signs. He looked at Bethany. "You're sure it is okay I come back? I promise this time I'll remember. And I'll carve you some dragons. I like dragons."

"Fine," Bethany said. The truth was, she'd kind of missed having him hanging around the place. It had been oddly quiet, and there always seemed to be a giant, Alexei-shaped hole at one end of the bar. "Just until the agency finds a new aide to send."

Calum made a rude gesture and wheeled his chair toward the bedroom.

"Good night to you too, dad," Bethany said with a sigh, and went to go walk the dog.

———

It was Monday and Alexei was back at the bar and something was wrong.

Bethany couldn't quite put her finger on it. He was behaving. Which, let's face it, maybe was part of what felt off, but it was more than that. He'd come in at ten in the evening, gotten a cup of coffee without a protest, and sat in the corner using some hand tools to mend a chair that had seen better days even before it had been whacked across someone's shoulders.

This was the third night since she'd allowed him back in, and he'd mended a few more pieces of furniture, along with a few other things around the place that her father had let go.

Occasionally he'd joined in on a game of darts or pool, but his heart hadn't seemed in it. In fact, if she had to pinpoint what was wrong, she would have said that something inside him seemed as broken as the chairs, but she didn't know what, or how to fix it.

She'd had to remind herself that Alexei Knight wasn't her problem. It wasn't her job to fix him, or anyone else, except maybe her father, who she was pretty sure was beyond help. Alexei was just passing through and would be gone in a week or two. It was a waste of her extremely limited time and energy to worry about him.

Needless to say, that didn't stop her. She wasn't even sure why she bothered to talk to herself if she wasn't going to listen.

So she was almost relieved when later that night, his interest was caught by a conversation between her and two men sitting at the bar.

"So what is it you do, exactly?" Bethany asked the tall, quiet one wearing glasses and carrying a bag bulging with files, a small laptop, and a stuffed parrot, of all things.

"I'm an oceanographer," he explained. "I work out of Woods Hole. I'm supposed to be researching changing ocean currents, but we've had so many reports lately of disappearing fish and sea mammals, I was assigned to look into it."

"Sea mammals," the fisherman sitting next to him said in a disparaging tone. "He means whales and dolphins. I don't know why you science geeks can't just say what you mean." He drank down a huge gulp of his beer. "Every damn thing in the ocean is disappearing. Might as well say so."

The oceanographer shook his head, but drank down his own beer faster than usual.

"You mean because of global warming and such?"

Bethany asked. There was always an ongoing debate among the locals as to whether or not climate change was to blame for the worsening fishing.

"Well, that too," the oceanographer said. "But in this particular case, there seems to have been a dramatic change in the last week or two. We can't find anything to explain it. The water temps have stayed more or less steady, there are no unexplained shifts in the current patterns, salinity is unchanged. But the fishermen who called us are right. The fish aren't where they should be, and there aren't nearly as many whales or dolphins as there normally are. Frankly, we're baffled."

Bethany noticed Alexei listening intently to the conversation, so when she brought his a refill for his coffee, she asked, "Do you think what they're talking about has anything to do with your hypothetical kraken?"

Interest sparked in his eyes for the first time since the night of the bar fight. "I wouldn't be surprised. After all, think about how big a kraken is. It has to eat something, right? Probably a lot of somethings."

Bethany shuddered, envisioning a great monster lurking under the ocean's surface, just waiting to grab a passing dolphin. Or maybe one of the fishermen who went out every morning, no matter what the weather, trying to keep their families fed.

"Should we tell the scientist from Woods Hole?" she asked. The research institute was widely respected locally, even by people who usually had little patience with what the other man had called "science geeks."

"Or warn the fishermen?" Although what they'd warn them about, she wasn't quite sure. She'd seen the sucker marks on the cod Alexei had found, and against her will she believed there was *something* large and dangerous in the waters off the Cape. She doubted it was a kraken, or anything else mythological. Still, even a real life giant squid could clearly take out a sizeable boat.

Of course, there was probably no need to spread the word among the locals. The fisherman's grapevine had probably already done that. Nonetheless, the ships still set out every morning. They had to make a living, no matter what.

The light went out in Alexei's eyes again. "There is nothing to do," he said, sounding unusually bleak. "It's not my job anymore."

What the hell was he talking about? "What do you mean, not your job anymore? Did you used to work with oceanographers or something? How was tracking sea monsters possibly your job?"

But he just grunted at her and gouged a large chunk of wood out of the chair leg he was working on, sending it flying through the air to land in someone's mug. Bethany sighed and gave up for now, reminding herself yet again that the big man was Not Her Problem as she went to get the poor guy staring into his beer a new mug.

She had watched her mother practically twist herself into a pretzel for years, trying to please a man who was determined to be discontented. Hell, Bethany had done it herself for the first couple of years after her mom lost her battle with the cancer. Bethany was still a teen, trying to fulfill a deathbed promise that it would have taken a saint crossed with a fairy godmother to achieve. It had taken her a long time to realize that you can't make someone happy if they are set on being miserable; all you can do was make yourself miserable too.

Then she'd spent another few years dating men who were so undemanding, they were practically catatonic. That hadn't been much better, although it was less exhausting. But at least it was better than beating your head against a brick wall over and over again.

Bethany liked Alexei—hell, if circumstances were different, maybe more than liked him. But there was no way she was going to turn into her mother. If the man wanted to sit in the corner and brood, she had better things to do than try and talk him out of it. All those drinks weren't going to pour themselves.

———

LEN HAD BEEN OUT to sea every day for a week, trying to get the damned talisman to work for him again and failing miserably. He'd done everything he could think of to recreate the moment it had called up the monster, but nothing had worked. If it weren't for the solitary gold coin, hidden securely under his mattress, he would probably have decided he'd imagined the entire thing.

Just his luck. He had finally caught the break he deserved, only to have it let him down. Figured. Wasn't that always the way?

He staggered home from the dive bar he frequented, pretty sure he'd been running his mouth off when he shouldn't have been, but equally certain that none of those cretins had believed a word he said anyway, when he suddenly became aware that he was being followed. Or at least, that there was a set of loud footsteps echoing his own. If someone was following him, they weren't being subtle about it. Len wasn't sure if that was a good sign or not.

He stopped under the street light closest to his house, leaning against it slightly for support, and turned around. "Come on out, whoever you are," he said. "I don't know what you want, but I got nothin' worth stealin', if that's what you're thinking."

A man stepped out of the shadows and took a confident step in Len's direction. "No worries, my boy. I don't mean you any harm. In fact, I think we might have some business together that will benefit us both."

Ah, someone who needed a smuggler. That would explain why the guy followed him, instead of approaching him in public.

Len peered blearily into the darkness. The man was a stranger; an odd-looking fellow with a faintly menacing air. He was large—burly, tall, and wide—with a third of his head shaved and the rest with straight graying hair combed over so it dropped to the edge of his chin, along with a slightly wild beard, hooked nose, and cold gray-silver eyes. Gold hoops hung from each ear and tattoos peeked out from the top of his navy pea coat and on the skin of his wrists. As he took another step forward and lifted a pipe to his mouth and lit it, Len spotted one on each finger, which read Black on one hand and Beard on the other. Smoke drifted toward him on the night wind, smelling like cold iron and bitter ashes.

Ha, Len said to himself. Another guy who grew up wanting to be a pirate. Len thought maybe the fellow had taken the look a bit too far, but he wasn't about to say so out loud. Not if the guy was a paying customer.

"What can I do for you?" Len asked cautiously. The guy

looked pretty wild, but that didn't mean he wasn't some kind of undercover cop.

"It is more a matter of what I can do for you," the man said smoothly, taking another step forward. For a second, Len thought he saw a huge shadow of something with a long spiky tail stretching out into the night, but another step brought the bearded man into the shining circle of illumination from the street light and the illusion disappeared.

Still, the hair stood up on the back of Len's neck. "I don't think so," he said, shaking his head. "It's late and I'm tired, and whatever it is you're selling, I'm not in the mood to buy. So buzz off."

"Buzz off?" the man repeated, sounding puzzled.

Len swayed, holding on to the lamp post. What was this guy, stupid? "You know. Buzz off. Fly away."

The man laughed, a great big guffaw that came up from his belly and shook his whole body, such a natural sound that for some reason it put Len more at ease.

"Fly away," the stranger said. "How amusing. You know what would be even more amusing? If I made you wealthy beyond your wildest dreams."

"Oh, I don't know," Len said. "I've got some pretty wild dreams. And why should I believe you?" He didn't really think the guy was some kind of cop—he just didn't have that feel to him. But *something* was off about him. Mind you, that could be said for most of the people Len knew who sailed on the wrong side of the law.

"Perhaps because you have something that used to belong to me," the man said. "An amulet, in the shape of tentacles wrapped around a central stone of mysterious origin. Sound familiar?"

Len took a step backward, his heart stuttering. "What do you mean it used to belong to you? The thing has been in my family since before my grandfather's time. There's no way it's yours." He clutched the front of his sweater, where the talisman hung on its chain, tucked underneath his worn flannel shirt.

"Ah, I misspoke," the man said. "Of course it could not have been mine. Time is so fluid. I meant it had been in my family for years. Then, alas, it was lost, I thought forever. But I sensed, rather, I heard, that it had come into your possession." His craggy face twisted with frustration, like an immigrant struggling to speak in a foreign language. "I can help you learn to master its magic."

"Magic!" Len snorted. "There is no such thing as magic."

"Then how do you explain the monster you called up from the depths with its aid?" The man grinned, showing sharp white teeth that glinted in the glare of the streetlight. "I know how the amulet works. I know how to summon the kraken to sink the ships of your enemies, to bring long lost treasure back to the surface. So much wealth, waiting on the bottom of the sea for the man brave enough to claim it. Are you that man?"

Long lost treasure. Wealth waiting on the bottom of the sea. Enough to satisfy the Russian mafia for the loss of their product, and still have something left over. The guy might be a little creepy, but he clearly knew about the talisman, so maybe he really did know how to make it work. Len remembered the shine of the gold coin, and longed to see it sitting in a pile of many like it. And let's face it, there might be something a little off about this guy, but Len was a lot more scared of the Russian mob than he was of some big guy with a strange haircut. "Hell yeah, I'm that man," he said. "Len

Morgan, descendent of pirates," he said, holding out his hand. "And you are?"

"Hayreddin, also of the pirate kin. You can call me Red," the man said, sticking out the hand not holding the pipe. Smoke drifted through his beard and up to wreath around his head. "Together, we shall make the seas run the color of my name, and reap a bounty of gold and precious jewels."

"Gold and jewels," Len said. "Excellent." *And when we're done, maybe you'll meet with a terrible accident and fall overboard, so I can take your half and not worry about you running off with my talisman.*

"EXCELLENT," said Hayreddin. *Stupid Human. And maybe when I've reclaimed* my *treasure, I'll eat you, and spit your bones into the sea.* He didn't quite dare break the Queen's rules against Para-normal folk influencing the Human world, but if he found a Human who already wanted to do what Red needed, well, that didn't exactly break the rules. The Fae folk were big on techni-calities. He could almost feel his treasure back in his grasp. Finally, it would be his again.

The queen might punish one who actively used a magical tool in the Human realms…but nothing said he could not get a Human to use it for him. Not one damned thing.

8

EVENTUALLY, ALEXEI RAN OUT OF THINGS TO FIX AROUND THE bar. So he fixed some things at the house, and when he ran out of those, he fixed some things around the guest house. Finally, even Lulu got tired of his banging and leaving wood shavings everywhere.

"Go do something," she barked at him one morning, licking her belly restlessly. It was so large, she could no longer get up on the couch easily, and it was making her grumpy. "Go chase a squirrel or a car or something. Mate with the woman. Do something. You make me crazy."

Alexei could feel his ears turn red. "I am not going to mate with the woman. Bethany. She doesn't even like me." He put down the pipe wrench he'd been holding and stared out the window in the direction of the house. "And I don't like her," he added, belatedly.

"Liar," Lulu said in a fond tone, or what Alexei interpreted as one. He wasn't really sure how he knew. Assuming he hadn't lost his mind. He still hadn't had any other animals talk to him.

"Fine," he said. "I like her. She stands up to me. I find that endearing. But still, no mating. I'm leaving soon."

"Humans always make things more big trouble than they are," Lulu said, turning around three times before settling into a lumpy heap on the rug. "But have it your way. Go do something else, then. Or nap. Napping is good. Napping, mating, eating. But not the noisy around the house things. Do something outside."

Great, even the dog didn't want him around. Alexei sighed. He had to admit, she had a point. He was getting tired of his own brooding. And he was Russian, so that really said something. So he wasn't a Rider anymore. That didn't mean he couldn't at least go take a look around. Right? Maybe there was some simple, non-Paranormal answer to the monster sighting and the disappearing sea creatures. And if there was something more to it, maybe it would at least give him something to fight.

Even Bethany couldn't object to him fighting a monster.

He walked over to the house, helping himself to a cup of coffee as he walked through the kitchen. It was Sunday, so the bar was closed. He'd come over first thing to get Calum up and dressed, then left the old sailor and Bethany alone. From the glares that met him as he walked into the living room, perhaps that hadn't been such a smart move.

"Tell this stubborn woman that I don't have to do any more exercises today," Calum said. A scowl made his scruffy face even more homely than usual. "I already did them."

"That was yesterday. Yesterday's exercises don't count. You know the doctor said you have to do them every day."

Bethany's scowl matched her father's, although Alexei thought it looked a lot cuter on her. Even he wasn't stupid enough to say so out loud, though.

"Do you still own a boat, Calum?" he asked instead.

Both faces turned their scowls in his direction.

"What's it to you?" Calum asked, at the same time Bethany said, "How is that helpful?"

Alexei rolled his eyes. "So that's a yes or a no?"

"Yes, I have a boat," Calum said. "Smaller than the one I sold to buy the bar, but I used to still go out fishing sometimes. Just for fun." He banged the side of his wheelchair with his closed fist. "Might as well sell this one too, since I'll never go out on it again."

"Never say never," Alexei said. "How about you do your exercises, and promise to do them every day this week without being such a cantankerous old bastard about it, and I take you out on the boat later?"

"What? Are you insane?" Bethany put her hands on her hips.

"Jury's still out on that one," Alexei admitted. "But I don't see any reason why your father can't go out on the water for a bit, if he misses it. I can handle a boat." That was one of the benefits of a long, long life—eventually, you get good at just about everything you have any interest in. "Come with us, if you don't trust me to handle both him and the boat. We can leave the chair on the dock and I'll just carry him around on board."

Since Alexei had been carrying Calum in and out of the bathroom, bed, and numerous other places with ease, Bethany could hardly argue with him.

"Well…"

"Are you serious?" Calum's face brightened for the first time since Alexei had met him. "You'd take me out on the ocean for the day?"

"For a few hours, maybe, dad. Not the whole day." But Alexei could tell Bethany saw the longing in her father's eyes.

She bit her lip. "You'll do your exercises? And listen to me and Alexei out on the boat, even though you'll want to do everything yourself because you know better?"

Calum laughed, displaying rarely used smile lines running through the deep grooves worn by pain and unhappiness. "To get back to the sea, I'd let you dress me in pink and call me a pig, darlin'."

Bethany's lips quirked up in answer to her father's rare good humor. "Well, I don't think that will be necessary, dad. But don't think I'm not tempted."

THEY SPENT a pleasant few hours out on the boat, which was as old and worn as its owner, but in much better shape. Calum, once he was comfortably ensconced in a seat on the aft side, a blanket tucked around his legs and a thermos of coffee at his elbow, contently ordered Alexei and Bethany around as if they were his crew. Bethany took it surprisingly well, probably used to it from a childhood spent on her father's boats.

Alexei followed orders cheerfully, just happy to be out in the fresh air again, doing something more active than carving a table leg or mending a crooked cabinet. The pregnant dog had been right, damn it. He wasn't made for sitting around.

The wind in his face made him nostalgic for his days riding his motorcycle across the country. He'd loved the feeling of freedom he'd gotten, even back in the old, old days in Russia when it had been an enchanted horse, covering the miles much faster than any normal equine could. It had transformed itself to keep up with modern times, much as the Baba Yagas and their huts did, but to Alexei, it was still his faithful steed. Maybe it was time to saddle up again and ride, even if he didn't know where he was going or what he'd do when he got there.

A musical giggle rang out across the boat as Bethany teased her father about something Alexei couldn't make out from where he stood. The sound seemed to call forth an answering chime in his chest and he laughed for no particular reason other than happiness in the moment.

Bethany glanced in his direction and grinned, her red hair blowing wild in the breeze and her eyes alight with pleasure instead of their usual shadows of worry and responsibility.

Maybe the motorcycle would have to wait for just a little longer.

Not because of her, of course. Although there had been a moment earlier when a random wave had rocked the boat and knocked them together. He'd put his arm around her to steady them, and it had felt oddly...right. That would be foolish, since there was no chance of a future between a broken Rider with a hidden past and nothing to offer anyone and a feisty Human who lived her entire life out in the open with her heart on her sleeve. But he couldn't just abandon her and her father until they got another aide from the agency. Besides, there was a mystery to solve.

Mind you, he hadn't spotted anything interesting or helpful all day, but maybe now that Calum had watched Alexei handle the boat, he'd let Alexei take it out again on his own. It would be better with two people, one to steer and one to keep watch, but Bethany would be busy with the bar the rest of the week, so he'd just have to manage.

With that in mind, Alexei was extra careful steering back into harbor, keeping all his attention on the task at hand so that he docked the boat back in her berth with nary a bump or bobble. Which is probably why he didn't see what was waiting for him on shore.

"Alexei! Alexei!" an excited cry greeted him as he carried Calum off the boat and deposited him gently onto his waiting wheelchair.

"Who's that?" asked Bethany, an odd look on her face.

Alexei glanced up and saw a gorgeous blonde racing down the dock in his direction, her long hair streaming out behind her. At first he thought he must be mistaken, since the only woman he knew who looked like that should be all the way across the country, on the California coast. But then he saw the gigantic black Newfoundland bounding along in her wake. There was only one pair in the world like that.

"Beka!" he shouted, forgetting for a moment that he was hiding out from all his friends in shame and sorrow, and simply reacting to the joy of seeing her. "What are you doing here?"

"I might ask you the same thing, you great big idiot," the blonde said, throwing her arms around him. "No one has heard from you since you left. We've all been worried sick."

Obviously Gregori hadn't told the others Alexei had called. Of course, Gregori always was the honorable one. If he said he wouldn't tell, his lips were sealed. "Hey, I sent postcards," Alexei protested, hugging her back. "Some of them even had pretty pictures on them."

"Most of them smelled like beer," said the Newfoundland, wrinkling his nose. Of course, to anyone else it would have sounded just like barking, since the dog was really a Chudo Yudo—a Baba Yaga's dragon companion—in disguise, and could make himself understood, or not, to whomever he chose.

"Nice to see you too, Chewie." Alexei bent down and scratched the dragon-dog behind the ears. He didn't have to bend far, since Chewie came up to his waist. "What on earth are you two doing on this coast?"

"I got a Call from the local Paranormal community. The merpeople and selkies have an issue, and while Barbara usually handles problems on this side of the country, since it is ocean related, it made more sense for me to come." She reached up and hugged him again, her normally sunny disposition even more shining than usual. "Oh, wait until Barbara and Bella find out you're here! They're going to be so happy I found you."

Alexei sighed. So much for hiding out. "I don't suppose your issue has anything to do with a sea monster," he said. "I was actually just out looking for one."

Beka's blue eyes widened. "That's great. You're already on it. It will be just like old times."

Hardly. "I'm not a Rider anymore," he reminded her gently. "I'm not anything. Just your average mortal."

"Pfft. You'll never be an average anything. Have you looked in the mirror lately?" Beka squeezed his arm, not so much missing what he meant as telling him she intended to ignore it.

"But we'd better talk about this later, when your friends aren't here." She nodded her head in the direction of Bethany, who was slowly wheeling Calum down the rough surface of the dock. "She's pretty. Is she your girlfriend?"

Alexei seriously considered throwing himself into the sea. "NO," he said, maybe a little more forcefully than necessary. "She's my employer. That's it." All he needed was a perky Baba Yaga matchmaker. He'd rather deal with a sea monster.

BETHANY ARRIVED in time to overhear the last part of their conversation. She was distracted from the bits she didn't understand by the unexpected pain of Alexei's adamant denial of a personal relationship. Not that she wanted one—with that giant, bearded brawler? No thanks—but still, he didn't have to sound so repulsed by the idea.

It was bad enough that seeing a beautiful woman throwing herself at Alexei had made Bethany unaccountably jealous. It was ridiculous. She didn't own him. Hell, she barely knew him. And didn't like him more days than not. Still, it stung a little. Just because…well, it just did.

She plastered a welcoming smile on her face anyway, although she might have been gritting her teeth a little. "Hello," she said. 'I'm Bethany McKenna and this is my father Calum. I had no idea Alexei knew anyone out here besides us."

"And all the guys at the bar," Alexei added.

The blonde rolled her eyes. "Well them, of course. Nice to see some things haven't changed." She held a slim hand out to Bethany, who was taken aback to find unexpected calluses in familiar places.

"You work on a fishing boat?" Bethany blurted. The woman looked like a model or an actress or a California surfer girl, not like someone who would do physical labor for a living.

But the girl just laughed. "Is it that obvious? My husband has a fishing boat he runs out of the Monterey Bay area. I help him when I can, although it's partially just an excuse to spend time with him." She blushed becomingly. "My name is Beka, and I'm an old friend of Alexei's. This is my companion Chewie." She patted the dog on the head and the mammoth Newfie barked as if saying hello.

"I had no idea Alexei was in the area when I came out here, but it certainly is a pleasant surprise. It has been too long." She mock-scowled at him, although the expression just looked cute on her open all-American face.

The gorgeous girl was married, and clearly madly in love with her husband. Who was a fisherman. Bethany suddenly liked her a lot better. Also, the fact that she referred to her dog as her companion was just adorable.

"Your dog is amazing," Bethany said. "Is he a Newfoundland?"

'Most days," Beka said. "So how did you meet Alexei?"

"I run my father's bar, *The Hook and Anchor*. He showed up there one night and I haven't been able to get rid of him since." Bethany grinned to show she was kidding.

"Shocking," Beka said dryly. "Alexei at a bar. How unusual."

"Well, to be fair, he isn't just hanging around," Bethany added. "He ended up helping out with my dad after Calum chased off the last home health aide. He's staying in our guest house."

Beka raised one eyebrow. "Huh. That *is* unusual. Alexei being helpful. Go figure."

"It's just temporary," Alexei growled. "I'm mostly staying for the dog."

"And he's not all that helpful," Calum said with a wink. "Just bossy and annoying."

"There's a dog?" Beka sounded slightly bemused. "At the bar?"

"In the guesthouse," Alexei said. "But to be fair, she was there before I was. A very pregnant Great Dane named Lulu. I think she and Chewie would get along quite well. They both talk a lot of nonsense."

"Goodness," Beka said. "I can't wait to call Barbara and Bella. This just gets better and better."

Alexei rolled his eyes. "Barbara and Bella are also old friends. Kind of like Beka's sisters," he explained to Bethany. "Family. There will be teasing."

"I look forward to seeing that," Bethany said. "But in the meanwhile, I think we should get my father back home. It has been fun, but this is his first excursion out, so we probably shouldn't push it."

"I'm fine, girl. Don't fuss," Calum said. But she noticed he didn't protest any further, and his drooping posture gave away his fatigue.

"It was lovely to meet you," Beka said, giving Alexei a meaningful look. "Do give me your address so I can stop by and visit. I'll tell you what, Alexei; give me your address and I'll come by later and we can catch up. I just need to talk to the harbormaster about renting a boat."

"Ah," Alexei said. "You mean for the thing."

"Yes, the thing," Beka nodded.

Bethany had no idea what either of them was talking about. "What thing? Fishing? I know almost everyone here who owns a boat, so maybe I can help you find one, if I have a better idea of what you need it for, and for how long."

Alexei narrowed his eyes, glancing from her to Calum and back again. "Actually," he said slowly, "I was going to talk to your dad about maybe borrowing *The Flora MacDonald* now and again. What do you think, Calum? Would you trust me with her? Beka is an able sailor, and has logged plenty of hours on her husband's boat. Together, we're more than capable, I promise."

"And what would you need a boat for?" Calum asked. "You're tired of breaking up my bar and you thought maybe you'd try your luck on a moving target instead?" He waved one hand through the air when Alexei protested. "Ach, I'm just having at you. Sure, the boat is just sitting here doing nothing. Worse comes to worse, you sink it and I collect the insurance. Buy one of them fancy electric wheelchairs with it."

He nodded at Beka. "No need to look any further for a boat, miss. If this giant oaf says you're okay, I expect you are. Come to dinner later and we'll talk about what the two of you have planned. But for now, I think I'll go home and have a bit of a rest. I'm not used to all this fresh air after being locked in my house for so long." He glared at Bethany. "Well? Are you just going to stand there, or are you going to drive me home?"

Bethany shrugged. "Sorry," she said. "He's a rude bastard, but at least he's loaning you his boat." She was amazed by that, and puzzled by why Alexei wanted one in the first place, but for now, she needed to get her obviously exhausted father home. She'd deal with the rest later. Plus, of course, figure out what the hell she was going to make for dinner. Who knew what blonde goddesses from California ate. Twigs and leaves, maybe, with some tofu on the side. Not likely in their house. It was going to be a long day.

9

ALEXEI HELPED CALUM GET INTO BED FOR A MUCH-NEEDED NAP (with only a token protest, so the old man must have really been tired) and borrowed the truck from Bethany, who was acting odd. Women. You could live thousands of years and never understand them. Alexei had given up trying long ago. Of course, he'd spent most of his time with Baba Yagas, who weren't exactly normal women, so that probably hadn't helped.

Bethany had asked him if Beka ate twigs and leaves for some reason, to which he'd responded with a baffled, "Not that I know of. I think she just eats, you know, food." Then he grabbed the truck keys and ran away before she could get any weirder.

As he's expected, Beka was waiting for him at the docks, sitting patiently in front of Calum's boat with Chewie stretched out in a patch of sun at her feet. Dragons enjoyed lying in the sun almost as much as cats did.

"I like her," Beka said as Alexei walked up to her. "She's tiny, but she's tough.

"The boat?" Alexei said, not sure that's how he would have described it.

Beka rolled her eyes. "Your friend Bethany. I'm glad you've finally met someone nice."

Alexei scowled at her. "Bethany is not 'nice.' She's a pain in my ass. Never lets me get away with anything. I'm just hanging out for a little while because I get free drinks and a place to stay. It's not a big deal."

"Uh, huh. How long have you been here?"

He shrugged. "Dunno. Couple of weeks. Maybe three."

Chewie made a coughing noise that might have been dragon-dog laughter.

"And you're living at her house, taking care of her crippled father, and her pregnant Great Dane?" Beka grinned at him. "Sounds like kind of a big deal to me."

Alexei growled at her. "I'm living in the *guesthouse*. I'm just helping with her father for the free drinks and because the old bastard scared off his last minder, and it's not her Great Dane. Bethany is just fostering Lulu until she has her puppies and they're old enough to be weaned. It's a temporary situation, just like me hanging around here. Do not make something out of nothing."

"I saw you when you got off the boat earlier. You were smiling. That's a big deal." Beka patted him on the arm. "I'm just glad she makes you happy, that's all."

"I'm always happy," Alexei protested.

"Sure," Beka said. "So happy you've been avoiding all your friends and your own brothers, who you love more than life itself, and drinking your way across the country." She sighed.

"I get it, Alexei, I do. Mikhail and Gregori both had a hell of a time getting over what happened too. It's okay not to be okay. But maybe it is also okay to let yourself find a new path, the way they did. They both found a purpose and someone to share their lives with. There's no reason you can't too."

Alexei crossed his arms over his chest. "I don't *want* a new path, Beka. I want my old path back. I'm never going to find a purpose as satisfying as being a Rider. It was what I was born to do, and there's no second choice. It's who I *am*. At least it was, until that damn Brenna stole it from me. From us. I'm glad Mikhail and Gregori have made their peace with it, but I'm not them."

"So what?" Beka asked, a blonde eyebrow quirked up. "You're going to spend the rest of your life drinking and fighting and never staying in one place for more than a few days at a time? That's your plan?"

Alexei felt tears of frustration pricking at the back of his eyes. It was ironic—the evil witch had tortured him and his brothers for days, and he had never gotten emotional about it. Never cried, or begged for mercy, or gave in to the gnawing beasts of hopelessness. But since he'd recovered, it seemed as though he fought those things constantly. Nightmares haunted him. It was…hard. And being here had only made it worse.

"That was my plan," he said flatly. "But lately I don't seem to enjoy drinking and fighting either. Now I got no plan. No plan at all." He shook off his melancholy with an effort. "So why don't you tell me yours? I assume that you've got one, or you wouldn't have needed a boat."

Beka looked as though she was going to continue to argue with him, but Chewie butted her in the leg and said, "Leave it, Beka. He's a big boy. He'll figure it out. We have a job to do."

"Spoken like a true Chudo-Yudo," Beka said. "How would we Baba Yagas manage without you?"

Chewie gave one of his barking laughs. "What makes you think you would?"

She bent down and kissed him on the top of the head, her fair hair a stark contrast against his curly black coat. "Well, I hope I never have to find out." Straightening up, she was suddenly all business, the pretty surfer girl replaced by the powerful witch with a mission to accomplish.

"Okay, yes, I have a plan. Or at least the start of one. We got word that the local ocean dwellers—Selkies and Merpeople, primarily—were having a problem with some kind of mysterious sea monster that suddenly appeared out of nowhere. So I figured the first thing I would do was search out some of the Paranormal folks, so they can tell me exactly what's happening."

"Hmm." Alexei nodded, and gestured her toward *The Flora MacDonald*. They might as well get underway while they talked, since he had to get back for dinner. "I might know a little something about that. A few of the fishermen who come into the bar have been complaining about the fish vanishing, and one guy swore his boat was attacked by a giant squid."

"A giant squid?" Beka shuddered. "Ugh. That's not good."

"It's worse than not good," Alexei said, steering them carefully out into the open sea. "I saw some fish from his hold, and the sucker marks were as big as a dinner plate. I think we're dealing with a kraken."

"A kraken!" Beka turned pale under her California tan. "There hasn't been a kraken sighting in over a hundred years. Where the hell would it have come from, and why show up here now?"

"I guess that's what we're going to have to find out," Alexei said, a trifle grimly.

"Ha! You said 'we.'" Beka jabbed him in the chest with one pointy finger. "I knew you were going to help me."

He set his jaw. "I'm just here to drive the boat. I told you; I'm not a Rider anymore. This isn't my job."

Beka grinned at him, her blue eyes sparkling like the water that surrounded them. "Maybe not, but it sounds like you need a new hobby. Kraken hunting sounds like an excellent place to start. You know, unless you want to take up needlepoint."

Alexei just growled at her. Women. They were all going to make him crazy.

BEKA HAD him sail to the small island of Monomoy. Once inhabited but now abandoned, it was home to about three thousand seals, and apparently, a number of the local Selkies. Not that most people knew about that second part, of course.

During the summer, visitors to the Cape took tours of the island, but at this time of year, they had the place to themselves. Alexei steered *The Flora MacDonald* into a quiet cove and he and Beka rowed the dinghy into shore and settled themselves onto a couple of rocks to wait. It didn't take long.

Two men and a woman walked out of the wind-battered trees, dressed in only jeans and tee shirts despite the cool weather. All three had straight dark hair, intense black eyes, and strong, lithe physiques. A few steps behind them were an older couple, both of them with long greenish-blonde hair, green eyes, and an odd, slightly limping walk. The Selkies and the Mer had arrived.

They all came to a stop before Alexei and Beka, and when Beka rose to meet them, they bowed in unison. Alexei and Beka bowed back. The Paranormal folk tended to have Old World manners, much more formal than the modern era they now found themselves living in. Of course, they rarely mixed with Humans, so that wasn't so surprising.

"Baba Yaga," the male Mer said, clearly the senior member of the greeting party. "I am Niall, and this is my mate Niamh. Our companions are Connor, Sean, and Anna, of the Selkie people. We are grateful you came."

"Of course," Beka inclined her head gracefully. "I am honored to come when my Selkie and Mer brothers and sisters Call me. As I'm sure you know, I have many friends in the communities of the water people back home."

"Indeed," Connor said. "It was they who suggested we ask for your help." He shifted his dark eyes, as deep as the caverns of the ocean, in Alexei's direction. "Is this not…that is, we had heard…"

"Yes I am," Alexei said, gritting his teeth. This was why he'd stayed away from anyone Paranormal for the last year, and why he hadn't wanted to get sucked into this particular task. He couldn't stand the pitying way people looked at him. At least Humans just gave him strange looks because he was so large and intimidating, not for any personal reason. "And yes, it is true. I am no longer a Rider. I'm just along—" he couldn't say because "because Beka twisted my arm." "I'm just here to help out an old friend, because I happened to be in the area."

The Selkies and Merpeople bowed again. "We count ourselves fortunate that it is so," Niall said smoothly. He glanced from Beka to Alexei and back again. "I suspect this challenge will require all the strength and magic we can muster."

"There seems to be a monster infesting our waters," Niamh said, twisting her hands together. "None of our people have seen it as yet, but we are hearing strange rumors from the fishermen who sail these seas, and our scouts have reported many fewer dolphins and whales than would normally be around in this season. Even the fish are disappearing, and if they don't return, we face a hungry spring and summer."

"I think you're facing much worse than that," Alexei said in a grim tone. "It is possible that your monster is a kraken."

The Paranormals looked more resigned than shocked, as if this possibility had already occurred to them.

"You don't seem very surprised," Beka said, clearly having expected a bigger reaction.

Anna shrugged. "There are tales from our parents' time that tell of such a creature infesting our waters during the age of the last pirates. The early seventeen hundreds, that would have been, as Humans measure such things."

"What do the tales say?" Beka asked. "Perhaps they have nothing to do with our current situation, but it can't hurt to know."

Niall shrugged. "Supposedly there was a particularly fierce pirate who had a magical talisman that could call a kraken to do his bidding. Mind you, in the tales, all pirates were fierce. And it seems unlikely that a Human pirate could ever have controlled such a creature. But those are the tales. According to my father, both the kraken and the pirate disappeared over three hundred years ago and were never heard from again. As I said, a story told to children."

"Hmm," Alexei said. "Three hundred years ago would

have been about the time that the high queen decreed that all
Paranormals return to the Otherworld to live, excepting those
like the Selkies and the Mer who could not leave their oceans,
or the tree sprites who could not abandon their trees. Did the
tales you heard ever suggest that this pirate was anything other
than Human?"

Niall and his companions all looked shocked.

"No, that is impossible," Niall stuttered. "How could that
be? It was a story, nothing more. Surely we would have known
if it was so."

Beka narrowed her eyes, looking pensive. "Still, that was
the last time this kraken was heard of, right? That would be an
interesting coincidence."

Anna shook her head. "But that doesn't make any sense. *If,*
perchance, this so-called pirate really existed, and *if* he could
actually call up and control a kraken—which seems unlikely in
the extreme—and *if* he was a Paranormal, who was forced to
retreat to the Otherworld, then why would he have suddenly
reappeared now? Those who live in the Otherworld have little
to do with the lands of the Humans."

"There is that," Beka said. "It was just a thought. Anyway,
sometimes there is a grain of truth in these old stories, so
perhaps you could ask some of your elders if any of them
remember any other appearances of a kraken, or something
that might have been mistaken for one?"

"Of course, Baba Yaga," Niall said, and they all bowed
again. "In the meanwhile, we are all grateful that you and the
Black Rider are here to help."

"I am not the Black Rider anymore," Alexei growled. But
if he was being honest, he hadn't felt this alive since the inci-

dent with Brenna. Perhaps it would not be so bad to assist a Baba Yaga one more time. Just for the heck of it.

Beka simply ignored him. "We are happy to do what we can. We will investigate, and meet you back here in two days time, to see what information we might all have gathered."

The Selkies and the Mer walked up and over a dune, and vanished into the trees like smoke.

"Well, this sounds a lot more interesting than cleaning up an oil spill or tracking an odd algae overgrowth back to its source," Beka said, rubbing her hands together in satisfaction. "A possible kraken sighting after all these years, mysterious pirates, disappearing sea life—Barbara is going to be *so* sorry she didn't come handle this one herself." She chuckled. "And that's before she finds out you're here. Ha! I can't wait to call her and gloat."

Alexei rolled his eyes. "You know, it might be best to hold off on the gloating until we have actually solved the problem and discovered whether or not the vanishing sea life has anything to do with krakens, pirates, or you know, something completely innocuous, like global warming."

"There is nothing innocuous about global warming," Beka said with a scowl, but then heaved a sigh. "Still, you might have a point there. Let's go see if we can find out anything from the other locals."

"The fishermen, you mean?" Alexei said.

Beka laughed. "No, silly, the folks who actually live in the seas where this is all taking place. Fire up the boat, big boy. We're off to talk to some dolphins. Maybe even a whale, if we get lucky."

Oh, goody. Call me Ishmael.

———

THEY STEERED *The Flora MacDonald* out into deeper waters, heading into the ocean off Chatham. They sailed for two hours in ever widening circles until finally Chewie barked at something off the port bow, pointing one paw toward a distant shape. Dragon-dogs had remarkable vision, as he never tired of explaining to Beka.

When they approached the pod of dolphins, they were greeted by eager squeaking and whistling. There were about a dozen dolphins, although it was hard to get an exact count as they swam in circles around the boat, leaping and diving in an intricate water ballet.

"Hello, my friends!" Beka yelled to the dolphins.

More excited clicks and whistles emanated from the group, although one large scarred old male came up close to the side of the boat and seemed to be directing his clicking vocalizations directly toward Beka.

"How do they know you're the Baba Yaga?" Alexei asked her without thinking. "You didn't even introduce yourself yet."

Beka's eyes widened. "A better question might be, how do you know they know? Since when do you speak dolphin?"

10

"I don't speak dolphin," Alexei said automatically. Then he thought about it for a minute, listening to all the chaotic noise. Besides the shouts of "Baba Yaga, it is the Baba Yaga!" he heard the words "boat," "big man," and something about fish.

He blinked. "Oh," he said. "Maybe I do speak dolphin. Huh. I guess I wasn't going crazy after all when I thought I was hearing Lulu tell me she wanted to go outside and dig in the dirt."

"Well, this is an interesting development," Beka said. "I can speak dolphin, but only because I did a spell for it, and it works a lot better when I am actually in the water with them. I was going to go in, but the water on this side of the country is damned cold and I'd just as soon not get into my wetsuit if I don't have to."

Alexei gave her a look.

"Hey, there's surfing on Cape Cod. Did you think I wasn't going to bring my wetsuit along? What's the point in living in a magical traveling hut turned painted school bus if you can't use it to tote along all your stuff?" She grinned at him. "We'll have to go out later. We haven't surfed together in ages, and I do so enjoy watching you fall off a board. But in the meanwhile, why don't you ask our new friends if they have seen any sign of a sea monster, or anything else unusual?"

"Um, how?" Alexei asked. "I mean, I can make out some of what they're saying, but I don't exactly speak dolphin." There was no way he was going to start making random clicking and whistling sounds. With his luck, he'd probably say something rude or obscene by accident.

Beka laughed, tossing her long hair back out of her face as the wind picked up. "When you talk to Lulu the dog, do you bark at her, or just speak normally?"

"I do *not* go around barking," Alexei said, scowling at her. As usual, the look that would have made a grown man quake just bounced off the blonde woman. The Riders had helped raise Beka and the other Baba Yagas from the time they'd each been adopted by their mentor Babas, usually around four or five years of age. Despite his strength and ferocity, they all tended to view him as a quirky kindly uncle who happened to be good in a fight. It was annoying.

"Then clearly part of your new gift, if that's what this is, makes it work both ways. You can understand animals—at least dogs and dolphins so far—and they can understand you. It seems to have worked with your pal Lulu. Go ahead, try it."

Alexei rolled his eyes, but figured if he failed, the worst that would happen was he'd get to laugh at her when she had to get into the bitter Atlantic waters and freeze her skinny butt off.

"Uh, hello," he said, gazing down over the side of the

boat. "I am Alexei, friend to the Baba Yaga. We have some questions for you, if you don't mind."

The large male looked at him, his scarred nose bobbing up and down in the water as he worked to stay in one place. "Ask questions, friend of Baba. We will try to answer, if we can." The other dolphins whistled their agreement.

"Cool," Alexei said, mostly to himself. Then thought, *wait until I tell Gregori and Mikhail,* forgetting that they weren't all together anymore, and for a moment the darkness threatened to overwhelm him again, like waves from the bottom of the sea. He pulled himself together with an effort.

"What do you want me to ask them?" This was Beka's gig —he was only along for the ride. Let her figure out what she wanted to know.

He guessed he'd spoken a little more harshly than he'd intended to when she raised both eyebrows and stared at him, but too bad. This wasn't his job anymore, and he suddenly didn't feel like being out here, trying to pretend to be useful.

Beka bit her lip, but said, "I guess you can start by asking them if they've seen any monsters."

"How the hell do you say 'monster' in dolphin?" Alexei muttered. Then said more loudly, "The Baba Yaga would like to know if you have seen any monsters."

As he'd suspected, this just got him some confused sounding whistling and nothing else.

"What is monster?" the scarred dolphin asked eventually. Alexei heard the word repeated back to him as something that translated more closely into "big not real creature."

"Oh, ah, something very large that doesn't belong in your water?" Alexei said, trying to think like a dolphin. "Scary big creature that hurts dolphins and attacks ships?"

This was met with lots of loud, high-pitched whistling and rapid clicking. Even without his newfound talent, he would have recognized agitation when he heard it.

"I'm guessing that's a 'yes,'" Beka said dryly.

Alexei hung even further over the side of the boat and held up his hand. "Slow down," he begged. "One at a time, please. It is hard for me to understand you when you all talk at once."

He was pretty sure he heard a teen-sized dolphin say something to a companion about stupid Humans. Alexei didn't bother to correct him.

"Big scary thing, yes," the large dolphin said. "Eats all that swim in ocean."

"Eats whales!" another member of the pod said.

"Pulls ships under the water!" added another. "With many long ugly flippers."

"Long ugly flippers?" Alexei repeated that, and the rest, to Beka.

"Hmmm," she said. "Maybe they don't have a word for tentacle in their language." She waved her arms at the dolphins. "Ask if these are flippers."

"Yes, flippers. Two little flippers," the dolphin who had mentioned the ships said, bobbing his head. "Big thing has many many flippers. Very long, very large, very ugly. Bad. Bad thing."

"You can say that again," Beka said in a grim tone. "It sounds like a bad, bad thing indeed."

HAYREDDIN STARED into the bottom of his glass so he wouldn't reach across the table and tear out the throat of the frustrating

Human sitting opposite him. Red wasn't sure if it was the long years since he'd last visited on this side of the doorway, or simply that this particular male was even more obtuse than usual, but it seemed as though they were speaking two different languages.

He cleared his throat and tried again. "If we are to be successful pirates, we must have a larger ship and many more men. Your boat is too small for our needs. You will get us a bigger ship. What is the problem?"

Len drank from the beer bottle he held, then wiped his full lips with the back of a slightly grubby hand. Under a black cap, his hair was overlong and stringy, and his face was narrow, with deep set dark brown eyes and a scruffy beard. Hayreddin thought Len was an unimpressive specimen, even for a Human, but this what Red had to work with, so he would simply have to make the best of it.

"I've tried to tell you," Len said. "There are no pirates anymore. Only a few Somalis in speedboats. I'm a smuggler, but it isn't the same thing at all. I told you what happened on my last trip. Until I raise the cash to pay back the Russian mob, I can't be spending money on a big ship or more men. We're just going to have to manage with what we've got."

Red held back a sigh. "And *I* have told you—with the help of the talisman and the kraken it controls—we can not only find my lost treasure, but also capture the boats of the wealthy and take the riches they hold. There will be plenty of money for a larger ship and more men, and without them, we will not be able to haul away our booty, or search for the treasure."

He did not believe this Human when he said there were no more pirates. There always pirates, although perhaps these days they went by some other name. But whenever there were those who had much, there were others who would willingly relieve them of it. It was the nature of men, as much as it was the nature of dragons to collect shiny precious objects.

It had taken more effort than it should have, but Red had finally convinced Len that yes, the talisman really was magic, and yes, Red could show him how to work it, but the stupid Human still seemed to be having trouble grasping the rest of the plan. (And of course, Red could not exactly tell Len that he needed to be the one to activate the talisman, because if Red did it, there would be Consequences.)

"We will take your small boat out today," Red finally said in a decisive tone that made it clear he would accept no more argument. "We will find a likely target and you will summon up the kraken to attack it. If we cannot find such a ship, we will send the kraken in search of treasure on the bottom of the sea. Even if it cannot find my own great plunder at first, there must be other lost ships resting on the ocean floor. We will get the money we need for a larger boat and more men. And then we will show the world that there are indeed still pirates, and ones with a fearsome secret weapon at that."

Len drank the rest of his beer in one long swallow. "Sure," he said, not sounding at all suitably excited by the prospect. "Yo ho ho and a bottle of rum."

The man was an idiot. Hayreddin was definitely going to eat him as soon as he no longer needed a Human partner.

———

THE MAN WAS AN IDIOT, Len thought to himself. Or delusional. Or both. Definitely dangerous as hell, and as far as Len could tell, perfectly serious about the two of them becoming pirates on the high seas with a crew of toughs at their command. Admittedly, this was Len's childhood dream, and if anyone could pull it off, it was probably his new pal Red.

But still, it was as though the guy had never heard of the Coast Guard, or sending money by wire transfers to a bank in the Caymans instead of putting it on a ship in the form of gold coins and precious jewels. It was as if he'd slept through the last couple of centuries, for god's sake. Crazy as a bag full of badgers, as Len's grandmother used to say. He'd never known what the hell that was supposed to mean. Until now. Mean and dangerous and completely irrational.

Unfortunately, Len needed him, crazy or not. He had to get that money for the Russians soon, or it wasn't going to matter that he'd hooked up with a guy who was just as likely to get him killed as he was to make him rich. And Len was out of any other, less insane, options.

Plus, there was that gold coin. That was real. And that huge octopus-squid thing that Red called a kraken, that had been real too. So now they were taking Len's boat (which was *not* too small, damn it) out so Red could prove to Len that he really did know how to make the talisman work, and hopefully get them enough money to rent a bigger ship and pay some lowlifes to crew it for them. Oh, yay.

Len had considered the possibility that Red would just slit his throat and steal the talisman, but he kind of figured that if the big guy was going to do that, he would have done it already. For some reason, Red insisted that Len had to be the one to do the calling—sorry, "summoning"—of the mythological beast. He'd given Len some kind of convoluted story about only the true owner being able to use the magic or something. To be honest, Len hadn't really been listening; he was just glad the large crazy man thought he needed Len as much as Len needed him. That would have to be enough, for now.

Either it was all a load of crap, and Red wouldn't be able to show him how to work the damn thing, and Len would be right back where he started (screwed and desperate), or it would turn out that all his grandfather's stories had really been true, and Len was living in some kind of freaking fairy tale. As long as it got him his money and saved his skin, he guessed he could learn to live with that.

Luckily, Len had one advantage that would work in their favor for playing pirate while they searched for Red's huge stash. As a smuggler, Len knew lots of other smugglers, and had some idea of who used which routes to carry valuable goods, drugs, or even illegal immigrants. (They definitely didn't want one of those ships. Hell no.)

Sure, in theory they all stayed out of each other's business, because not doing so could get you killed. But hey, he was going to get killed anyway, if he didn't fix his little two million dollar Russian problem, and he kind of figured that Red would have a lot fewer qualms than Len did about taking out whoever was on the ships they stopped, if that was the only way to keep their secret.

Hell, if Red was right about the kraken pulling the ships down to the bottom of the ocean and then bringing up the valuables, he and Red would never have to get their hands dirty at all. Plus any evidence would be deep underwater. Ships disappear; it happens. So maybe this wasn't such a crazy plan after all. *If* they could really get the talisman to work.

RIGHT BEFORE DUSK, they found a likely spot. Len had heard through the grapevine that one of his dubious acquaintances (smugglers didn't have friends) was going to be heading this way tonight with a load of cash and guns being smuggled out of the country. Probably for the Mexican cartel, which wasn't any healthier to mess with than the Russian mob, but hell, what choice did he have?

It probably would have been simpler to find a ship smuggling drugs—there were plenty of those. But not only did Len not have the connections to move large amounts of cocaine or marijuana, but if the mob got word of him doing so, they might decide he'd made up the story about the Coast Guard and figure he'd just stolen their drugs. That would be bad. Very, very bad.

They might be willing to let him try and come up with the money to replace their lost merchandise, but if they thought he'd stolen it, they would hunt him down and kill him slowly and gruesomely to serve as an example to anyone else who might be stupid enough to try the same thing. No thank you.

So here he was, out in the middle of the Atlantic Ocean, holding onto his grandfather's talisman and planning to call up some mythological creature to attack another smuggler's ship. When had his life gotten so crazy? He wanted to be anywhere other than here, doing this. Len wasn't a huge drinker, but right now he wanted a stiff drink so bad he shook with the thought of it.

"Stiffen your spine, boy," Red said with a sneer. "It is time. Are you ready?"

Ready to go home, hell yeah. "You bet," Len said. "So, how do I work this thing? Are there some kind of magic words or something? I said a bunch of stuff the first time, but I have no idea which one worked."

Red laughed, the sound rolling out into the encroaching darkness to mix with the noise of the waves crashing against the side of the hull. "There are no magic words, silly man. This is an amulet for a pirate, not a witch's toy. Hold out your hand, and think of how badly you want the kraken to come."

Len did as Red asked, the talisman sitting in his open palm, stretched out before him. Before he could brace himself, the tattooed man pulled out a huge knife and sliced into the fleshy part of Len's hand, right next to one of the brass tentacles.

"What the hell!" Len shouted. But then the blood oozed from the shallow cut into contact with the amulet, and that strange buzzy feeling echoed through his arm and up into the rest of his body. The amulet seemed to writhe in his hand. The stone in the middle slid open to reveal its single swirling eye.

Magic. Shit. It was real. Painful, apparently, but real.

"Find me the ship with money and guns," he whispered to the eye. "Sink it, and bring me the money."

Red nodded with satisfaction. "Now you will see," he said. "Now you will see the might of the kraken."

Len put the amulet down reverently on a storage chest nearby and wiped his hand with an almost clean rag. "You could have warned me about the blood part," he said to Red with a scowl.

"What would the fun of that have been?" the pirate said. One gold tooth gleamed when he grinned. "You should have seen your face when I pulled out my knife. Ha ha ha."

Ha. Sure. Very funny. Len settled himself against the side of the boat to wait for the kraken. After all, just because he'd gotten the strange medallion to activate, didn't mean that it would actually control the monster, or that the thing would be able to find the ship they wanted. Or that it would be able to retrieve the money, even if it did.

The more he thought about it, the less likely success seemed, and the more he longed for a warm room and a bottle of whiskey.

"Aha!" Red bellowed, startling Len so much he almost slid onto the deck on his ass. "Look!"

Len followed Red's pointing finger toward the setting sun. Just barely visible against its orange glow was the silhouette of a much larger ship, its back end tilting precariously as a giant tentacle wrapped itself around the stern. Len almost imagined he could hear the screams of the men aboard as they fell into the sea. Within minutes, the entire ship had vanished beneath the surface. Len knew he probably should have felt bad about the crew, but instead, he felt a heady surge of power. Who was the weak, skinny kid now, eh?

"Come on, kraken," he said to the empty ocean. "Bring me my money, there's a good little monster."

The big man next to him coughed. "Our money, was that not what you meant to say? And I suspect it would be best not to speak to the mighty beast of the deep as if it were a pet dog fetching a ball."

"Um, yeah, sure thing," Len agreed, gazing greedily out over the waves. Still nothing. Where was it?

Suddenly, a massive tentacle rose over the side of the boat. Len's stomach lurched; he'd forgotten how huge and frightening the damn thing was. But it was on his side...right? It wouldn't hurt him. He was its master. The hovering tentacle, larger than a ship's mast, made those probable facts hard to remember. He swallowed hard, tasting bile.

A thud made him jump, but it was just a heavy package being dropped onto the deck. The tentacle slid back down toward the sea, leaving a glistening trail of salty slime behind it on the edge of the hull.

"Uh, thanks!" Len said as the medallion's eye gave one more eerie swirling movement then blinked closed again, returning to its usual inert and benignly ugly appearance. But he waited until the rubbery appendage had completely vanished before walking slowly toward the dripping mass sitting in the middle of the deck.

"Allow me," Red said with a purr of satisfaction in his voice. He took his knife and slid it through the black plastic and duct tape as if they were tissue.

As the wrappings fell away, they revealed smaller bundles enclosed in clear plastic. Len stifled a cheer as he spotted the hundred dollar bills on the top of each stack. The kraken had done it! It wasn't Red's legendary treasure, but at least it was a start.

"This is what you wanted?" Red said, look at the money with a dubious expression. "It is not very shiny."

"It's cash," Len said, shaking his head. "It's not supposed to be shiny. But it sure as hell can buy you plenty of shiny things. I'm guessing there's about twenty, twenty-five thousand there. Not bad for a night's work."

Red still seemed less than impressed. "I would have preferred diamonds," he said. "But if you say this is good, I suppose I believe you. Is it enough to get us a larger ship and men to crew it?"

"You bet," Len said, picking up the talisman and hanging

it back around his neck. He stroked it fondly before he tucked it back under his flannel shirt. "We're in the pirate business, my friend. Let's go rent a ship."

"*Rent?*" Red said. "We're going to *rent* a pirate ship?"

"Well, sure," Len said. "I mean, it would cost a lot more than this to buy one." He had no idea what the hell was wrong with the other man. Len was doing everything he wanted, and the guy still seemed pretty bent out of shape. Still, Len knew the cure for that. "Come on. Let's go back in. The first drink's on me."

His only answer sounded strangely like a growl.

BETHANY KNOCKED HESITANTLY on the door to the guest house. It was late, and her father was in bed, but she could see by the light that Alexei was still up. He'd been strangely subdued since he'd returned from his outing with the pretty blonde girl. He was quiet at dinner, although Beka had been cheerful and pleasant, and had eaten enough fish and chips for any two sailors. After his friend left, Alexei had even helped do the dishes after dinner.

Bethany was afraid he was coming down with something or maybe wrecked her father's boat and was afraid to say so. So she figured she'd just check on him. Not that she was worried about him, or anything. Just wanted to make sure the boat was okay. That was it.

The door opened a crack and she looked up—she always forgot how tall Alexei was until she was standing right next to him.

"What?" a grumpy voice said out of the shadows. "Problem with your father?"

"No," Bethany said. "He's fine. Snoring away like an outboard motor. Can I come in for a minute?"

A sigh gusted out over her head. "Sure," he said, opening the door wider. She'd thought maybe he would be in his pajamas for the night, but he was still wearing a pair of jeans. And nothing else. The sight of his bare chest and broad shoulders took her breath away for a minute and she had to force herself not to stare. He was built as though he'd been carved out of granite, all chiseled muscles and smooth skin.

"Did you want something?" Alexei asked, raising an eyebrow.

Oh, hell yeah. It had been a long time since her last boyfriend, who had been, admittedly, boring beyond belief, both in bed and out. Bethany cleared her throat. "Ah, I just wanted to talk to you, if I'm not interrupting anything." She tried looking past him instead of at him. "Do you want to go put on a shirt?"

"Why?" he asked. "I'm not cold." She wasn't sure, but she thought she saw a glint of amusement in his eyes. If so, it vanished quickly enough.

She followed him into the living area, a small square room with a television, seating for four, and a simple desk in the corner, all decorated in classic Cape Cod—pictures of boats on the wall, vases full of seashells, and an old lobster trap that had been turned into a lamp. The couch was covered in faded chintz, not that you could see much of it under the giant dog currently taking up most of the available space.

Alexei had clearly been sitting in one of the armchairs, which was about two sizes too small for him. Bethany tried not to think about how sweet it was that he let the dog have the only decent piece of furniture in the room.

"Hello Lulu," she said, walking over to scratch the Great Dane behind one ear. "You're looking lovely this evening. Also, you're not allowed on the couch."

Neither the dog nor the man seemed overly impressed by her statement.

"It took her three tries to get up there. She's going to give birth any second now," Alexei said. "Let her be comfortable."

"I'd just as soon she didn't do it on the sofa," Bethany said, but she snuck a treat out of her pocket and gave it to Lulu anyway before she went to sit down in the chair opposite Alexei.

He was holding a half full glass of what looked like straight whiskey, and a nearly empty bottle sat on the table next to him. The lobster lamp was the only light in the room, but she didn't think the bad lighting alone was responsible for the shadows under his eyes.

"Are you okay?" she asked. "You seemed kind of quiet at dinner."

He shrugged, making the muscles in his shoulders ripple in an alarmingly attractive way. "Long day. Nothing to worry about."

"Didn't you have a good time with your friend? She seemed awfully happy to see you." Bethany reminded herself that Beka was married, and not interested in Alexei. Not that it was any of Bethany's business. She clearly needed to keep reminding herself of that, too. And, you know, stop staring at his remarkable physique. Although *damn*.

"Did something bad happen? If you damaged my dad's boat, it's not a big deal."

"I did not damage your father's boat," Alexei snarled, his face indignant. "Everything is fine."

"Then why are you sitting here in the near-dark, drinking the better part of a bottle of whiskey?"

He raised his glass in a mock toast. "The worse part, too."

Bethany rolled her eyes. "I don't know how you manage to sound so coherent with the amount you drink."

"I have a fast metabolism," Alexei said. "Also, I'm Russian."

"Uh huh. That probably explains the brooding, too." She reached out and took a sip out of his glass, hardly wincing at all as the harsh spirits burned her throat on the way down. "You know, you can talk to me. I mean, if you want to."

"Nothing to talk about," he said, grabbing the glass back. "I was just missing my brothers, that's all."

"You have brothers?" Bethany had always wondered what it would be like not to be an only child. "Where do they live?"

"Gregori is in Minnesota now, helping his lady to run an organization that helps at-risk teens, and Mikhail lives in the ass-end of upstate New York with his new wife and her baby."

Interesting phrasing, but Bethany decided that now wasn't the time to ask. "How long has it been since you've seen them?"

Alexei shrugged again. "A year. Maybe more."

"Are you close?" Bethany felt like she was hauling each answer out of him with an almost physical effort. Still, at least he was talking to her. Sort of.

"We used to be. Spent most of our time together for many, many years."

Well, that explained why he missed them, but not why he hadn't seen them in a year. "Did you have a fight or something?"

"No."

Bethany suppressed a sigh and took the glass back again for another sip. "You know, neither of those parts of the country are all that far from here. Why don't you go see one of your brothers, if you miss them so much? Are you waiting for an engraved invitation?"

"Nope. Got one. To Mikhail's wedding. I didn't go." He got up and fetched another tumbler from the kitchen and poured the last of the bottle into it. Lulu heaved herself off the couch with a noticeable effort and settled down by his feet with a sigh.

"You didn't go to your brother's wedding?" Bethany said, a little taken aback. "Why not?"

"Just wasn't going to be good company. Kind of like now," Alexei said pointedly.

"Huh. You underestimate your own charm," Bethany said, only half joking. "I think you're perfectly good company."

"Yes, but you usually hang around with your father," Alexei pointed out. "The bar is set very low."

Bethany bit back a laugh. He wasn't wrong. "Maybe so, but I'm guessing your brothers would still rather see you than not, even if you're doing your whole gloomy drunken Russian thing."

"I am not drunk," he said, not disputing the rest of her statement. "And I do not believe they *would* want to see me. I did them a great wrong. I do not deserve the honor of their company." He downed the rest of his whiskey in one gulp.

Bethany winced in sympathy, although it didn't seem to bother him at all. "I don't know what you did, or think you did, and I realize that I haven't known you for long, but for all your rough ways, I've never seen you do anything I'd consider dishonorable. Besides the pool shark thing, maybe, and even then, anyone who was paying attention could have seen how good you were at the game. But you're kind to an old man who is hurting, and you're gentle with Lulu, and you kept a woman from being taken advantage of by a predator who meant her harm."

She thought carefully before she said her next words, knowing she was overstepping the bounds of their tenuous friendship, but hating to see him in so much pain.

"Have you considered *asking* your brothers if they want to see you? They might just surprise you."

There was a moment of silence when she almost thought Alexei would either kick her out or start packing his bags. Then he reached out and took back the glass she'd snitched from him.

"Maybe I'm not ready to see them," he said. "And you are wrong—you don't know me at all. If you did, you probably wouldn't be sitting here."

Bethany gave him a crooked smile. "Oh, I don't know. I've always had a weakness for bad boys with hardly any clothes on."

Then she watched in satisfaction as he choked on his whiskey.

11

"Here," Hayreddin said to Len. He pointed at the tavern. "There is a pirate hook right on the sign, and it is called *The Hook and Anchor*. Clearly this is a good place to look for men to hire for our ship."

Len rolled his eyes in a way Red found particularly annoying. Not that there was anything about his new partner he did *not* find annoying. Even his mode of transport was foul smelling and belched, although apparently that was the way of things in this modern world. Red was finding the Otherworld more appealing by the minute. As soon as he found and retrieved his final treasure, he would happily return to his cave and never cross the borders again.

"It's just a sign. Probably something to attract the tourists," Len said, peering in the window. "On the other hand, this is definitely not a tourist bar. Lots of locals in there. So maybe you're right."

And maybe you should start with that assumption, Red thought.

But he didn't bother to say it out loud. Instead, he just shoved by Len and led the way into the tavern.

Once inside, they sat at the well-worn but gleaming bar. An attractive red-haired wench in the unbecoming man's clothing that seemed to be the fashion these days served them their beer and then left them alone. Red pulled out his pipe.

"You can't smoke that in here," Len hissed. "It's against the law."

"There is a law against pipe smoking?" Red said in amazement. Apparently the entire Human world had gone insane while he slept in his cave.

"Any kind of smoking in a public place," Len said. "It's not just cigarettes. Where have you been, France or something?"

Red sighed, wafting away stray wisps of smoke (a hazard with dragons) and wishing he could light his pipe to disguise them. Fortunately, the tavern was dark enough that no one seemed to notice. "Or something," he said. "Now, let us be subtle, and observe those who patronize this place to see if there are any likely fellows looking to hire on for adventure and glory."

Len rolled his eyes again, and Red had to resist the urge to rip them out of his useless skull.

"How about that guy?" Len asked, pointing across the room in an manner directly the opposite of subtle. "He looks like he could take on an entire ship all by himself, even without the help of our mythical friend."

Red swatted Len's hand down and gazed at the man who had caught his attention. Red had to admit, the fellow looked like a reasonable prospect. He was huge—bigger by far than any others in the place—and it appeared to be muscle and not fat. He wore his brown hair long, and his beard was neat. He lacked the earrings of a proper pirate, but Red could see the hint of a tattoo at the edge of his shirt. The man sat by himself, carving what looked like a table leg with a wickedly sharp knife.

He definitely had the look of a rough man who could handle himself in a fight, but there was something about him that made Red hesitate to approach him. Something almost…familiar.

But Red couldn't figure out why until the slim blonde woman entered the tavern and sat down beside his quarry.

A Baba Yaga! What in the name of the dragon goddess was a Baba Yaga doing here? Now he knew where he had seen the man before. That was no Human. It was the Black Rider, what was his name? Alexei Knight, that was it. A Baba Yaga and a Rider here. That could be no coincidence.

Red gnashed his teeth. *Curses.* That was all he needed, a Baba Yaga and a Rider meddling in his business. How on earth was he going to accomplish his goal with them hanging around? But then he remembered what all in the Otherworld knew, a stunning development that even he had heard about, when rising from his long rest to feed. The Black Rider was Rider no longer. More than a Human, undoubtedly, but nothing like the power he used to be. The Baba Yaga, now she might be a problem. But the former Rider, he was nothing more than an annoyance. One which could no doubt be dealt with if he got in the way.

"Well?" Len said interrupting his thoughts. "What about him?"

"No," Red said. "Not him. He is not suitable. In fact, I

suggest we look elsewhere. Now." He rose from his seat, leaving Len to throw some of his ugly paper money down on the bar and follow him out, protesting all the while. Fortunately, the Baba Yaga and her companion seemed to be deep in discussion, and paid no attention.

In theory, he should appear as any other Human to them, but it never paid to underestimate a Baba Yaga. Even if you were a dragon.

"Did you feel that?" Beka asked Alexei. They had been talking about using the dolphins as scouts, and the best way to check in with them, when she'd felt a shiver run down her spine. The kind of shiver that said *magic* and *Otherworld* and maybe *danger*. She might be the youngest of the three United States Baba Yagas, but she'd learned the hard way not to ignore that feeling.

"Feel what?" Alexei asked. He seemed a bit more cheerful tonight, and Beka wondered if it had anything to do with his new friend Bethany, who occasionally smiled in his direction from her place behind the bar.

"Hmm," she said. "I'm not sure. But something just tripped my witch-dar."

"Witch-dar?" Alexei repeated, raising an eyebrow. "Is that a thing now?"

"It is when I sense something paranormal in a room where nothing paranormal should be," she said.

Alexei glanced around, but didn't seem to see anything out of the ordinary. "Are you still feeling it, whatever it is? The place looks pretty normal to me."

Beka opened her awareness, but didn't pick up on anything other than a tiny sprite who had apparently come in to get out of the cold.

"No," she said. "Whatever it was, it is gone now. But there was something."

"I believe you," Alexei said. "Of course, it might not have anything to do with our other situation, but just in case, let me know if you sense it again."

"Will do," Beka said. "I have a bad feeling... But never mind. Let's talk about how we can have the dolphins spy for us without putting them in any extra danger. And how often you can go out and chat with them without people starting to think you're up to something."

"I *am* up to something," Alexei said with a grin. "I'm up to getting another drink, since Bethany is finally letting me have beer in here again."

A FEW DAYS LATER, Alexei wandered over from the guest house to help get Calum out of bed and scrounge a cup of coffee. An ever-larger Lulu trudged along behind him, then plopped onto the kitchen floor with a sigh.

"Still no sign of babies?" Bethany asked, patting the dog sympathetically on the head while handing Alexei a mug that sent divine caffeine-scented steam into the air.

"She says maybe today, maybe tomorrow," Alexei said absently, most of his attention focused on the dark nectar in his cup. "But I'm not sure if she really knows, or if that's just wishful thinking."

"She told you that, did she?" Bethany said, sounding amused. "I didn't know you spoke Dog."

Alexei sloshed hot coffee over his hand, suddenly much more wide awake. "Ah," he said. "Better than I speak Dolphin, but that's not saying much."

"Uh huh."

Now that he was more alert, Alexei thought he heard an odd off-note behind the laughter. Peering over his mug at her face, he saw lines of tension that weren't usually there, the skin stretched taut around her eyes and mouth.

"What's up?" he asked. "Is something wrong with your dad?"

"No," Bethany said. "I haven't even gone in to see him yet this morning. Just some bad news in the paper." She handed it to him. "I was debating about whether to tell my father or just hide it in the recycling before he got up."

Alexei drained his mug and clunked it down onto the counter so he could take a look. The newspaper was folded to the third page, where a brief article showed the picture of an older man with his arm around a young boy, standing proudly in front of a small fishing boat. The headline read "Third Generation Fisherman Lost at Sea."

"I'm sorry," Alexei said. "Someone you knew?" He scanned the rest of the article quickly and felt a gnawing in his stomach that couldn't be blamed on the coffee.

"One of my father's friends from his days on the water, although they haven't kept in touch much since my father's accident. Or, to be more accurate, my father didn't encourage anyone who tried, so they all eventually gave up and left him alone, the way he wanted." She sighed, her shoulders drooping a little.

"Henry was a nice guy. That's his grandson in the picture with him. The kid worshipped him." She wiped away a tear without noticing. "It's an occupational hazard, and the families are always prepared for the worst, but the officials can't seem to figure out what went wrong this time. The weather was fine, there was nothing wrong with Henry's boat that anyone knew about, and Henry was never reckless or careless. I talked to his daughter a few minutes ago and they're completely baffled."

"Are they sure he isn't just missing?" Alexei asked, even though he knew the answer.

"Pieces of the boat were spotted by another fisherman," Bethany said. "Small pieces. They haven't found Henry or the other two men who sailed with him, but they don't really expect to. There were sharks in the area where they found what was left of *The Maryann*."

"I'm sorry," Alexei said, handing her back the paper. She crumpled it up and stuffed it in the garbage, then blew her nose. He put his arm around her and gave her a brief hug, trying not to be distracted by the scent of her shampoo, a mix of lemon and lavender that went straight to his head. He wished he could do more, and an unwelcome echo of remembered helplessness made his muscles bunch and quiver.

"Me too," she said. "Let's go get my father out of bed, shall we? For once I might actually be grateful to hear him gripe at me about my lousy cooking."

"Do you think it was the kraken?" Beka asked him later. He was still at the house, minding Calum while Bethany was at the bar, so Beka had come over. They sat in the back yard, conversing in low tones. Calum was asleep in his recliner in front of some game show, and Lulu lay panting at their feet, occasionally shifting position in a futile effort to get more comfortable.

"Maybe. Probably. This guy was an experienced sailor and he disappeared in about the same area as the dolphins reported seeing their monster. About ten miles away, but in the ocean, that's not that far."

"Why that area of the sea?" Beka wondered out loud, more to herself than to Alexei. "It's open ocean with nothing around except fish, before the fish disappeared. Why would a kraken suddenly be hanging out there?"

"And where did it come from? I mean, if the thing had been around all this time, I'm pretty sure someone would have noticed." Alexei tugged on his beard. "Did the Merpeople and Selkies come up with anything else useful?"

"They've just got stories left over from hundreds of years ago. The elders didn't know anything more than the folks we met with," Beka said. "So if there was one, it either went away or went into hibernation or something, and now it's back."

"Huh." Alexei tried to wrap his brain around a gigantic hibernating squid-monster. "So what brought it back or woke it up again? And why?"

"All good questions," Beka said a trifle grimly. "None of which I have any answers to. I'm not even sure where the hell to look for any, but we have to do something, or I suspect people are going to keep dying, and their blood will be on my hands."

"Our hands," Alexei growled. "I don't ever want to see that look on Bethany's face again. Nor do I wish to explain to the high queen of the Otherworld if her sea-dwelling subjects start disappearing. They can't hide out in their homes forever."

Beka turned pale at the thought of telling the queen she'd failed in her mission. "We could call in Barbara and Bella, but I'm not sure what they could do that I'm not doing already. I tried a finding spell, but they don't work well with water, and all I got was a vague location, which we already had, more or less." She shook her head. "I am working on some defensive magic in case we meet up with it, especially if Chewie isn't around to go all dragon on its ass."

The Chudo-Yudos usually stayed with their Baba Yaga's traveling homes when the witch in question was out and about. The dragons (in their guises as gigantic dogs or cats) guarded the Water of Life and Death the Baba Yagas drank to increase their powers and prolong their lives; the Chudo-Yudos also kept an eye on the portals to the Otherworld that was concealed in each updated hut.

They did, on special circumstances, leave to assist a Baba Yaga with a particularly tricky situation, but Chewie especially didn't like to leave Beka's converted school bus alone for long, since one time when he had, Beka's former mentor had stolen the Water of Life and Death and caused all kinds of problems. To put it mildly.

"Going dragon only works if there are no witnesses," Alexei pointed out.

"Yeah, well, I'm not sure how we'd explain a giant sea monster either," Beka said. "Either way, we have to find the damned thing before we can worry about how we're going to take it out, although it would be wise to be prepared. And if magic can't help us, I guess we're back to taking Calum's boat out and hoping for some kind of clue to miraculously pop up out of the blue." She looked as frustrated as Alexei felt.

"I've got a better idea," he said. "That is, if you can figure out a way to persuade sharks to talk to me without trying to bite my head off. Literally."

12

"YOU WANT TO WHAT?" ALEXEI SAID.

Bethany put a foaming mug of beer down in front of him. "I want to bring my father out on the boat tomorrow," she said, giving him a funny look. "Is there a problem with that?"

A number of them, including the fact that he was going to be trying to talk to sharks. Plus, you know, man (and probably woman) killing kraken on the loose.

"Uh, I just, you know, thought you'd want to stay home on your day off."

She shrugged. "In a perfect world, I'd spend my day off sitting in front of the television watching Robert Downey Jr. and eating chocolate. But in case you haven't noticed, I don't exactly live in a perfect world. Hell, if I did, I'd be watching Robert and eating the chocolates while sitting in my old apartment in Boston and studying for the bar."

Alexei stared at the wooden surface in between them. "Why would you need to study a bar? You work at one every day."

He heard what might have been the sound of teeth grinding. "Different bar," Bethany said. "The one I'm talking about is the test that says whether or not you are qualified to be a lawyer. That's what I was doing before my father got hurt and I had to get home."

Huh. That was a surprise. Or maybe not. Bethany was clearly smarter than your average whiskey slinger, and she'd said something when he first met her about coming back to take care of her dad.

"So, you want to be a lawyer. Interesting." Okay, it kind of was, but also, maybe he could distract her from talking about going out on the boat tomorrow.

"Not really," she said. "I'd already started to have doubts about whether or not I wanted to get caught up in a system that doesn't work for most people. Now that I've been back here for a while, the idea is even less appealing, although god knows I spent enough time and money trying to achieve it. Although I had pretty good reasons for studying it when I started out, or so I thought."

"What kind of reasons?" Now he was actually curious. It was hard to envision the Bethany he knew in a suit and carrying a briefcase, living in a city and working in an office. Somehow he doubted that her motivation had anything to do with money or prestige.

Bethany tucked a stray piece of red hair behind her ear. "My mom was sick for a long time," she said, finally. "She died in misery after spending years being denied the disability and medical benefits she deserved. I thought I'd get a law degree and fight for people like her, but sometimes it seems like tilting at windmills. I'm just not sure I'm up for the fight. Some days I feel like I'd do more good just pouring drinks and easing pain that way."

Alexei winced. He hated to hear her sound so discouraged, although at least he'd succeeded in distracting her.

She turned away to pour a drink for a customer and then turned back. "About tomorrow…"

Or maybe not.

"Beka and I already had plans for the boat," Alexei said apologetically. "And your father did say we could use it. How about next Sunday? Maybe."

"Look, Alexei. Going out the last time really cheered my dad up, and he's been in a terrible funk since he found out about his friend Henry. I think it would make him feel better, and tomorrow is supposed to be a really nice day." Bethany polished the already clean bar. "Unless, you know, you and Beka have something romantic going on. I mean, I know she said she's married, but it's none of my business if she and her husband have some kind of understanding."

Alexei almost choked on his beer. "No! Ew. I practically helped raise Beka. I look at her like a daughter. Or a niece or something. And she and Marcus are madly in love with each other. So no, yuck. Nothing like that."

Was it his imagination, or did Bethany actually look relieved?

"Well then, why shouldn't my father and I come along wherever you're going tomorrow? He won't care where it is, as long as he's out on the water." Now she looked puzzled. With maybe a hint of annoyed thrown in for good measure.

"Don't you think it is a little too dangerous?" Alexei thought he'd try a different tack. "What with Henry's boat disappearing and the other odd incidents the local fishermen have been reporting?"

Bethany narrowed her eyes. "If you think it is so dangerous, then why are you and Beka still taking the boat out? Wouldn't it be just as dangerous for you as it would be for us?"

Alexei had never missed his brothers so much. If they were here, Gregori would think of something clever to say or Mikhail would dazzle her with his charm. Alexei couldn't do either, so he resorted to desperate measures: the truth.

"Well, maybe, but we're going out to look for the monster. You don't want to be along for that."

"Wait, you're *what*?" Bethany stared at him. "You mean you're going out searching for a giant squid? Why the hell would you do that?" She lowered her voice when a few heads swiveled in their direction. "Please don't tell me that you actually believe it's a kraken, like you told Duke. I figured you were just looking for an excuse to get into a fight."

She wasn't wrong there. Too bad she was wrong about the kraken. A giant squid would have been a piece of cake, comparatively speaking. Or a piece of sushi.

"Beka is kind of a monster hunter," he said more or less honestly, avoiding the second part of Bethany's question. "I'm just helping her out. That's why she came here from California."

"And you two think you're going to find some mythological sea creature that eats ships?" Bethany shook her head. "The insurance company told Robbie they had documented one other case of an attack from a giant squid, off the coast of Japan, so they paid on his claim. It's pretty freaky, but they think it must have been attracted by something on the boat that reminded it of prey. The oceanographers from Woods

Hole are having a field day, but neither they nor anyone else has caught a glimpse of the thing. It has probably headed back out to deeper waters."

"So you're not worried about being out there? Bringing your poor defenseless father?" Alexei was running out of ways to talk her out of it. Crap.

"Oh, please," Bethany said. "I'd like to see a giant squid try and take on my father, wheelchair or not. We're coming out with you tomorrow, and that's all there is to it. If it is safe enough for your friend Beka, it is safe enough for us. Monsters. Ha." She went down to the other end of the bar to fill a drink order for three craggy old men sitting together and playing cards.

Well, SHIT. That was going to pose a bit of a problem, wasn't it?

"I CAN'T BELIEVE you let them come along," Beka said out of the corner of her mouth as she guided the boat out to sea. Bethany and her father were sitting toward the front of the boat, and Alexei and Beka were in the small cabin, but Beka still kept her voice down, just in case. The ocean breeze could play funny tricks with sound, snatching it away and carrying it where you least expected it. "What were you thinking?"

Alexei scowled at her. He'd been in a crabby mood since they'd all arrived at the docks that morning. Probably because he'd lost an argument. He hated that.

"I was thinking it is their boat and I couldn't exactly keep them from coming if they wanted to," he said, glaring out at the innocent waves. "Besides, I tried to talk her out of it. She wouldn't listen to me."

"No wonder you're so grumpy," Beka said with a grin. "You always used to pout like this when one of your brothers got the better of you."

"I am *not* pouting," Alexei muttered. "Grown men do not pout."

"Could have fooled me," Beka said. "Are you really worried we'll run into the kraken while they're onboard?" She fingered the spell pouch she'd tucked into her waterproof jacket. In theory, the magic she'd worked up would pack enough of a punch to scare off a kraken, although she doubted it would kill one. And she'd just as soon not have to test the theory out one way or the other, thank you very much. Besides, it was her job to protect Paranormal creatures, not kill them, if at all possible.

Alexei shook his head. He'd pulled his shoulder-length hair back with a leather strip so the wind wouldn't constantly blow it in his face. Beka thought it was a good look for him, and she was pretty sure Bethany thought so too, from the glances she kept sneaking at Alexei when she thought no one was watching. But there didn't seem to be much point in mentioning it, since they were both so set on ignoring their obvious attraction to each other. Idiots.

"I doubt it. We probably won't get that lucky."

Beka shuddered, but he sounded quite cheerful about the prospect of encountering a gigantic legendary monster. The Riders had always been a little more adventurous than was probably wise, but that was when they were immortal. She wasn't sure if Alexei had really processed what a difference this meant to how he should approach risk. Or maybe the problem was that he had, and didn't care.

"I know we need to track it down," she said. "But I don't

really want to do it with innocent bystanders around. Especially ones who don't know about magic and the paranormal."

"It's not exactly optimum for my plan of trying to talk to the sharks that were at the site of Henry's wreck, either. Assuming we can even find them," he added glumly.

"Ah, that I think I can help with," Beka said, a little smug at finally being able to do *something*. "This isn't the time of year when there are many sharks in the area. They mostly show up in the summer when the seal population is larger. So I got one of my Selkie scouts to ask our dolphin friends from the other day to meet us out here. If anyone knows where the sharks are, it is them. If only so they can avoid that area, if nothing else."

"Great," Alexei said. "Now all we have to do is figure out how I'm going to talk to them without Bethany and her father figuring out there is something strange going on. Hopefully they will stay at the front of the ship. I've got Calum set up with a fishing pole and bait, so with any luck that will keep both of them occupied."

"I guess we're going to find out," Beka said, spotting something off the port side. "Because I think we've got company."

She slowed down to a crawl and put the ship on autopilot after double checking that there were no other vessels in the area, and the two of them hurried down to the stern. The scar-faced dolphin Alexei had talked to the other day waited for them impatiently, whistling a rapid series of tones when they finally came into view over the edge of the boat.

"He doesn't like being out here," Alexei said, although she didn't really need the translation. The dolphin swam back and forth restlessly, occasionally peering back over its shoulder. "His pod is staying in closer to land than usual as long as the big scary thing is out here. But they're hungry, because the fish are gone."

Alexei's brows drew together, concern written across his open face. "He says they're afraid of Humans, but more afraid of the big scary thing. Their little ones are starving. We need to find the big scary soon and kill it." He shook his head. "Sorry, I added that last bit myself."

"Oh, I don't disagree," Beka said. "Ask him if he knows how to find the sharks that were nearby when the fisherman's boat got attacked."

Alexei relayed her question and got more agitated whistles in return. "He thinks we're crazy for wanting to talk to sharks, but they were spotted not long ago off an island to our south. So I guess we head there." He hesitated. "Do you think there is anything we can do to help his pod in the meanwhile?"

Beka thought about it. "Tell him to meet us with his family tomorrow. Um, at sunset, I guess." She tried to pick a time the dolphin would understand, since they didn't exactly wear watches. "If you can't get off Calum duty by then, I can come out on my own and bring a few barrels of fish."

"Great," Alexei said. "I'm sure one of the guys I've met at the bar will be able to sell us some, or we can get them at the fish market." He swiveled around suddenly. "Did you hear something?"

Beka had been focused on the dolphin. "No, I don't think so. Look, I'd better get back up to the cabin and start steering us in the right direction. Tell our friend that the Baba Yaga says thank you, okay?"

"Will do. I'll be back up to join you in a minute."

Bᴇᴛʜᴀɴʏ ғᴏᴜɴᴅ the sight of multiple sharks circling the boat highly disconcerting. In theory, they were perfectly safe, but that didn't stop the hair from standing up on the back of her neck at the sight of the triangular gray fins cutting through the water.

Only slightly less disturbing was watching Alexei and his friend Beka trying to act as though they weren't trying to get Bethany and her father out of the way. She might have been amused by their antics if she hadn't already been so freaked out.

"Why would I want to go take a nap?" Calum was saying. "It's a boat, not a hotel. And I'm not tired." He glared at Alexei. "Not to mention that there are sharks swimming around *the Flora MacDonald*. That hardly makes me want to go take a nice little snooze. In all my years at sea, I've never seen anything like it."

"Maybe they're attracted to the fish guts," Beka suggested.

Calum snorted. "I caught one fish worth keeping, and its guts are still inside its belly. I'm telling you, there's nothing to make the sharks that interested in us. It just doesn't make sense."

Bethany cleared her throat, so the other three turned their heads to look at her.

"Maybe they're waiting for Alexei to talk to them, like he did to the dolphins earlier," she said in an even tone.

Beka and Alexei exchanged worried glances.

"What's that now, girlie?" Calum said. "You think Alexei talks to dolphins? Maybe you should put on a hat. The sun seems to be getting to you."

Bethany just stared at Alexei. "Dolphins, and maybe dogs. Seems to me that you and Lulu have a lot of pretty intense conversations. I heard you talking to the dolphins before. What are you, some kind of animal whisperer? Is this a new scientific breakthrough you don't want to make public yet?"

Beka choked back a laugh, covering her mouth with her hand. "Does Alexei look like a scientist to you?" She snorted, then shrugged apologetically in Alexei's direction. He shrugged back.

"Well, then what is it? I know what I heard. Alexei was *talking* to that dolphin. I mean, he was speaking English, but he clearly understood what the dolphin said, and the dolphin understood him. You even had him ask the dolphin questions, so you know he can do it. If it isn't a technical gizmo, then what is it?"

Alexei and Beka looked at each other, then at her and Calum. They had a moment of silent communication, the kind that only happens when people have known each other a very long time. Then Beka raised one shoulder in a "what the hell" motion.

"It's not science," she said. "It's magic."

"RIGHT," Bethany said. "Magic. Ha." Then she looked at the expressionless faces around her. "Oh, *come on*. You don't seriously expect me to believe you can do magic, do you?"

Alexei cleared his throat. "If you want to get technical, only Beka does magic. What I do is more of an innate gift of paranormal origins. You know, technically."

"Right. Technically," Bethany repeated. "You do realize you're not making any sense. Technically."

Beka smothered a laugh with one slim hand. "Sorry," she

choked out. "But you have to admit this is a pretty funny conversation."

When Bethany continued to glare at them, the blonde woman shook her head. "Okay, it probably isn't all that amusing from your end. This isn't something we tell people about often, so we aren't either of us very good at explaining it."

"Why don't you start at the beginning and speak in small words so I can understand it," Bethany said through gritted teeth. She didn't enjoy feeling like the only one in the room who didn't get a joke, and for some reason, her father didn't look nearly as confused as she felt.

She swung around to focus her glare on him instead, which had about as much effect as it usually did. Which is to say, none whatsoever.

"Why aren't you jumping in here?" she asked him. "You don't like unanswered questions any more than I do."

Calum flashed her one of his rare smiles, one of the kind that made his eyes twinkle. As a little girl, she'd lived for those smiles. After her mother had died, she couldn't remember ever seeing one again. "Probably because I believe in magic."

"You what?" she said, wondering if her head was going to actually swing around on her neck like that girl in *The Exorcist*. "Has everyone on this boat lost their minds except me?"

Her father chuckled. "Not at all. But you grew up here in the New World, where everyone is obsessed with facts and science. I grew up in Scotland, where my grandmother took me out into her garden on my fifth birthday and introduced me to the little sprites that lived in the old apple tree. I never saw them, mind you, but she believed they were there, and so did I."

He turned to Beka. "So what kind of magic are you? A mermaid?"

Beka laughed. "Well, I *am* a very good swimmer, but not a mermaid. More of a surfer, really."

"A witch, then?"

Bethany would have thought he was kidding around, except he was more animated than she'd seen him in months. What the hell was going on here?

"More like *the* witch," Alexei said with a grin. "Well, one of *the* witches. She's a Baba Yaga."

"Pull the other one," Calum said, his eyes wide. "She never is."

"What's a Baba Yaga?" Bethany asked. Besides blonde, pretty, and a pain in her ass.

"Don't you remember the books your mother used to read you?" Calum asked. "Her mother loved the fairy tales, she did," he explained to Beka and Alexei. "She had that whole series of books by Lang: *The Red Fairy Tale Book, The Blue Fairy Tale Book, The Yellow Fairy Tale Book.* I'm pretty sure there was a tale or two about the Baba Yaga in one of those."

He turned back to Bethany. "Remember? The Russian witch who lived in a wooden hut that traveled around on chicken legs through the forest?"

This time it was Bethany's time to laugh. "You mean the ugly old crone with the iron teeth that rode around in a mortar steered by a pestle? That Baba Yaga?" She pointed at Beka. "She doesn't look much like the witch in those stories. Really, dad. You're going to have to do better than that. Did the three of you all get together and decide to play a joke on me? That's what this is, isn't it? Alexei can no more talk to animals than I can."

"This is always so much easier when Chewie is around," Beka said to Alexei rather mournfully. "A dragon is instantly convincing."

"Still," he said. "It will save a lot of time if you just show her, don't you think?"

Bethany was starting to get mad. She opened her mouth to tell them all off when Beka's outline began to waver oddly. Bethany blinked rapidly, wondering if the sun really *was* starting to get to her. When she opened her eyes again, Beka was gone, and an old woman stood in her place, her hair gray and wild, her nose long and crooked, her back bent. Only the laughing blue eyes remained the same, gazing back at her with benign good humor.

"*What the everlasting hell?*" Bethany gasped.

The old woman wavered again, as if surrounded by fog, and then she was young and blonde again, albeit with a more serious expression than before.

"Sorry," Beka said. "I know it is kind of startling the first time you see it, but we could have talked forever and you would never have believed us."

Bethany turned to her father. "Did you see that?"

"Told you so," he said smugly. "I knew I should have brought you home to the Old Country more often, but there was never enough money, and then your mom got sick. There are tales of the Baba Yagas in Scotland, although they're not as common as some other stories. Never thought I'd get to see one in person, though."

Bethany's head was spinning. "But…I thought the Baba Yaga was a Russian fairy tale." She was still trying to grasp that it wasn't a fairy tale at all. Or that fairy tales were real.

She wasn't sure which one was worse. Or better. Argh, she was so confused!

"Oh, it is," Beka said. "But we're everywhere, really. We just take other names in some countries. There's a Baba Yaga who is in charge of all of the British Isles, including England, Ireland, and Scotland, and three for the United States, of which I am one. The youngest," she added wryly. "You should see Barbara's crone. It's *way* more convincing than mine."

"Oh, I don't know," Bethany said in a faint tone. "I thought yours was plenty realistic." She gazed at Alexei. "Are you a Baba Yaga too?" If so, his disguise was insanely good. And she was about to be really depressed. Leave it to her to develop a crush on a witch masquerading as an incredibly attractive man.

He guffawed, a low deep sound that bounced out over the waves. "Goddess, no. Can you imagine me traveling around the country righting the balance of nature and helping worthy seekers?"

Beka rolled her eyes.

"I know!" Calum said, his face alight. "In the stories my grandmother told me, the Baba Yagas had three companions called The Riders, who helped them with their tasks. Especially when they needed a strong arm or someone to have their backs in a fight. That makes perfect sense. You're a Rider, aren't you?"

Alexei's smile slid away like the sun going behind a cloud and he regained that distant, shuttered look he'd worn when he'd first walked into the bar. Even the normally cheerful Beka got quiet, a strangely haunted expression flitting across her face almost too fast to see.

"Not anymore," Alexei said. "I was once, but not these days, no."

"Then what are you now?" Calum asked, for a change sounding as puzzled as Bethany felt.

"Nothing," Alexei muttered, at the same time Beka said, "My friend."

Bethany swung her head from one to the other, her heart hurting at the aura of pain emanating from Alexei. "You're still helping her, though," she said quietly. "What does it matter what you call it?"

Alexei just grunted. "I'm not helping much standing here talking to you when I'm supposed to be talking to these sharks, am I?" He gestured at the gray shapes still circling the boat. "So now that we've gotten the whole 'magic is real, not everyone is who they seem' conversation out of the way, maybe I can get down to work?"

He turned his back on her and leaned over the side. "Yo, sharks! What can you tell me about a boat that got wrecked near here a few days ago?"

Beka gave her a sympathetic look, patting her on the shoulder as she went to stand next to Alexei.

Calum, on the other hand, pulled out a stub of cigar he wasn't allowed to smoke anymore and stuck it in the corner of his mouth to get even more noxious than it was already.

"How about that, girl? We've got a real life Baba Yaga on our boat. And the guy who has been taking me to the bathroom can talk to dogs and sharks and who knows what else. How about that."

Bethany's knees suddenly felt like they were made out of rubber. How about that indeed.

13

ALEXEI HAD A MOMENT'S TEMPTATION AS HE LEANED OVER THE side of the boat. He could lean just a little further and the sharks would probably be able to tear him to bits before Beka could stop them. Of course, that wouldn't be fair to the sharks, since not only would Beka blast them to kingdom come for something that wasn't their fault, but then she wouldn't get the answers she needed. Still, getting gnawed to death by sharks might be preferable to seeing that stunned, appalled look in Bethany's eyes again.

Of course, this wasn't the first time a Human had figured out their secrets, or had to be told the truth for some reason. It was just the first time he'd ever cared about the response.

He growled under his breath at nothing in particular, which the shark below him apparently took as some kind of greeting.

"What? What you want?" it asked, jaws gaping open. "Who talks to sharks?"

Alexei repeated what it said for the benefit of Beka and their unplanned audience.

"Ah," Beka said. "I've talked to sharks back home a few times, although I try to avoid it if I can, for obvious reasons. They're not nearly as smart as dolphins, so you will want to keep your side of the conversation as simple as possible."

"Ought to be easy for him," Calum said with a snort. "Most mornings he only talks to me in grunts anyway."

"Ha," Alexei said, without taking his eyes off the shark. "Not everyone is a morning person. It's not like you're Mister Cheerful first thing in the day." He cleared his throat. "My name is Alexei. I am a friend of the Baba Yaga."

The shark swam in a circle, its powerful tail bringing it back around to where it started with seeming effortlessness. The whole time they talked, it never stopped moving.

"Baba Yaga here?"

Beka moved closer to the edge and bowed slightly. "I am the Baba Yaga," she said. "Thank you for your help."

Alexei translated for the shark, whose name, apparently, was White with Big Teeth. Alexei wondered if all his friends had the same name, or if there was one called Pale Gray with Big Teeth. He decided not to ask.

"What Baba Yaga need?" White asked.

"We are looking for the sharks who saw a ship like this one get destroyed recently." Alexei also had no idea if sharks had any idea of time. "Near here. Lots of pieces. Three Humans died."

The shark opened its mouth wide, showing multiple rows of very sharp teeth. Alexei had the uncomfortable feeling this was its equivalent of a smile.

"Boat in pieces. Dead Humans. Yes. We were there. We saw."

"Ask him if he saw what caused the boat to go down," Beka suggested. "An explosion, or something else?"

"Big boom make boat sink?" Alexei asked. "Large wave?"

The shark bumped its head against the side of the boat, making the whole thing shudder slightly. "No boom. No wave. Was Too Large to Be Prey thing. Very big Too Large to Be Prey."

Great. "He calls it a 'Very big Too Large to Be Prey thing,'" Alexei reported. "Sounds like our friend the kraken all right."

"Kraken?" Calum said, eyes wide.

"It's a giant squid," Bethany corrected. "Probably. Shush up and let him finish talking to the shark." She bit her lip in a way Alexei always found particularly adorable. "Damn it. I can't believe that sentence just came out of my mouth."

"If you believe I can talk to sharks, maybe you should believe me when I say there is a kraken," Alexei pointed out crossly before turning his attention back to White with Big Teeth.

"Do you know where the Too Large to Be Prey is?" he asked.

The shark swam in another circle. "Followed Human boat because they followed fish. When Too Large to Be Prey took boat to very deep, it ate all fish. No fish, no stay."

"Crap," Alexei said. He'd brought along a cask of fish to use to bribe the sharks if necessary. Now he wished he'd given it to the scarred nose dolphin, since it didn't seem as though they were going to get anything helpful here.

"Maybe Baba Yaga ask Humans in other ship," White said.

"Wait, what? There was another ship out there that day?" Alexei and Beka exchanged startled glances.

"Ask it if the kraken attacked the second ship," Beka said, gripping his forearm in an iron clasp worthy of one of his own.

He asked.

"No," was the answer. "Too Large to Be Prey swim to other ship. Give something to Humans. Swim away toward place where sun sets."

"Son of a bitch," Alexei breathed. "Someone is controlling the kraken. How is that even possible?"

"It shouldn't be," Beka said. "Although I remember some-thing...I can't quite put my finger on it. I need to call Barbara and Bella when we get back to land. Maybe they can shed some light on this."

"At least you know it headed west," Calum added. "Maybe it has a cave or an underwater cavern in that direction it holes up in."

"Even if this doesn't help us find it, it does give us an important piece of new information," Beka said. She suddenly looked a lot less like a cute California surfer girl and a whole lot more like a dangerously powerful legendary witch.

It made Alexei nostalgic for the old days. "So what do we do next?" he asked.

"First we give the sharks the barrel of fish we brought with us, and thank them politely," she said. "Then we head back to port so I can make some calls. If the others can't remember whatever it is I'm thinking of, I might have to take a trip to the Otherworld."

She set her jaw. "After that, I am going to track down whoever thought it was a good idea to set a kraken loose off Cape Cod and stop him. Even if it means I have to feed him to his own creature." For a moment, her eyes gleamed with an unearthly light. "*Especially* if it means I have to feed him to his own creature."

"Hell," Bethany said. "She's pretty fierce when she gets riled."

"Damned straight," Alexei said. "Atta girl."

BETHANY SAT at her kitchen table nursing a cup of cold coffee and ignoring the paperwork piled up in orderly stacks in front of her. It was late, and Calum had been in bed for hours. The house was silent and peaceful.

If only that could be said for the inside of her head.

A thousand aimless thoughts swam inside her skull like a school of minnows. She was still trying to wrap her brain around the fact that there really was such a thing as a Baba Yaga, even if the mythological witch was nothing like the stories. Okay, *especially* because the wicked witch was nothing like the stories. Oh, and there were dragons, and sprites, and yes, unfortunately, a kraken. But that was all right, because the witch was here to deal with the kraken.

Jeez Louise.

Oddly enough, the part Bethany found the least difficult to accept was that Alexei was something more than—or at least different than—Human. Maybe it was because he was such a huge presence, impossible to ignore once he walked into a room. Maybe it was because he'd affected her in ways that no other man ever had. She'd always thought there was something out of the ordinary about him. Silly her, she'd just figured it was charisma or something.

But no, the only man she'd been attracted to in years was…well, she didn't know what he was. Except leaving, sooner rather than later, probably. And he was everything she despised in a man, from watching her father fight and drink his way through life. The universe clearly had a strange sense of humor, since neither of those things kept her from thinking about him constantly, even before she found out he was a mythological hero.

Once Alexei had picked up the heavy barrel of fish in a seemingly effortless movement and dumped its contents over the side of the ship, he and Calum had settled in together at the bow, leaving Bethany and Beka to head up to the cabin and get them under power and heading back to port.

Beka could have done it on her own, of course, but Bethany had some questions and she figured she was more likely to get answers from Beka than she was from Alexei, who had lapsed back into a sullen silence as soon as he stopped talking to sharks.

"Is he okay?" Bethany asked, once they were underway.

Beka sighed. "Define okay. If he were a Human being, I'd say he was suffering from post traumatic shock. He and his brothers went through something awful. It not only robbed them of their positions as The Riders, which was all any of them had ever known, but left them broken in ways I don't think anyone can really comprehend. His brothers Mikhail and Gregori had their own struggles too, but they eventually found their way to new paths and to women who loved them. I'm not sure Alexei is even trying to find anything to replace the life he once had." Her blue eyes looked immeasurably sad. "I'm not sure he ever will."

"He does seem to be working rather hard at drinking and fighting," Bethany said

Beka laughed, but it lacked her usual humor. "Well, you could say that used to be a hobby for the three of them when they were together. I hope he hasn't decided to turn it into a full time career now that he's alone."

"I hope not too," Bethany said. "I've only just started letting him back into the bar again since he wrecked it the last time. I'd hate to have to ban him for good."

"What seemed like over-exuberant high spirits when it was the three of them just seems desperate and unhealthy when he is on his own." Beka gazed out over the wide expanse of ocean in front of them as if it might hold some elusive answer. "I wish I knew what to do to help him."

"He misses his brothers," Bethany said. "Maybe you could figure out some way to get them back together?"

Beka's head swiveled around. "He told you that?" She sounded stunned.

"He did. He doesn't talk about himself much, but one day when I could tell he was feeling down, he told me he was missing his brothers. But when I asked him why he didn't visit them, he told me they wouldn't want to see him, because he'd done something terrible to them and wasn't worthy of their company."

"Huh. He probably said more to you than he has to anyone he knows since the incident," Beka said, looking bemused. "None of us has seen him since he left the Other-world, and the only communication we've had, if you could call it that, are the occasional postcards from across the country, usually smelling like beer. He didn't do anything terrible, of course. Just didn't do the impossible, which they all seem to have expected of themselves. I'm surprised he told you that much, though. He must really be comfortable with you."

Bethany shrugged. "I don't know why he would be. I'm usually bitching at him about something and I twisted his arm into taking care of the grumpiest, most uncooperative man in the world."

This time there was actual amusement in Beka's chuckle. "I suspect that makes him feel right at home. You should meet Barbara, the eldest of the Baba Yagas. She's turned cranky into an art form, although less so since she met and married Liam, a Human sheriff."

Bethany's heart stuttered for no obvious reason. "Oh?" she said in a casual tone. "So you magical folks can marry Humans?"

"I did," Beka said, flashing a fond smile as she thought of her husband. "Marcus is a fisherman and a former Marine. He's as Human as they get. For that matter, so did my sister Bella, and both of Alexei's brothers. But it isn't exactly the usual thing."

She gave Bethany's face an intense perusal. "Not that it is any of my business, but you're not falling for Alexei, are you? I mean, I wouldn't blame you if you did, he's a terrific guy. And I can tell he is attracted to you too. But this is the longest he has stayed in one place since he came across the portal from the Otherworld in California and started drinking his way across the county. I'm not sure he's ever going to settle down anywhere. He's too busy trying to outrun the ghosts of his past."

"Oh, I realize that," Bethany had said in a breezy manner,

as if she'd never even considered the possibility of anything else. "I'm not looking for a man. Believe me. I had my share of going-nowhere small town boys and big city guys who think they're god's gift to women. I haven't met one yet who treated me like I was his equal. Besides, I've more than got my hands full looking after my dad and running his damned tavern."

But now she sat at her kitchen table and realized that somewhere in the back of her mind, some small sneaky part of her subconscious had been visualizing a future that still had Alexei in it; helping her with her dad, hanging around each night at the bar, spoiling Lulu, and…well, being around. Preferably with his shirt off. But none of that was going to happen.

One of these days he was going to pack up his few belongings, climb onto that huge Harley of his, and drive off to somewhere else. He'd probably never even think of her, of them, again. Besides, she'd seen enough of her parents' relationship growing up to know what happened to women who tried to build a life with a man whose idea of coping with difficulty was fighting and drinking instead of actually trying to make anything better.

She shook her head, trying to clear it of such maudlin and unproductive thoughts. She needed to either work on the damned accounting papers or go to bed. Morning would come soon enough, whether or not she sat up brooding over things she couldn't change. The last six months should have taught her that, if nothing else.

A knock sounded at the kitchen door, and Bethany glanced at the clock on the wall, startled. *Who the hell would be knocking on the door at midnight?*

It opened on creaky hinges and Alexei stuck his head inside, as if her thinking of him had summoned him.

"Hey there," he said. "I saw the light on and figured I'd come tell you."

Shit. "You're leaving, aren't you?" A part of her brain wondered if he would stay if she threw herself at him. Naked.

His dark eyebrows shot up. "Why would you say that? No, Lulu is having her puppies. I thought you might want to come watch."

Bethany practically fell over getting out of the chair. "What? Now? Is she okay? Should I call the vet?"

The corner of Alexei's mouth twitched but he considerately didn't laugh at her. "She's fine. Dogs have puppies all the time and there's no reason to think she's going to have a problem. You don't need a vet, but you do need to hurry up if you don't want to miss it."

"Holy crap, we're having puppies!" she said, following him out the door. *And he's not leaving. Thank god, he's not leaving.*

ALEXEI HAD SEEN baby animals born before, of course. Hard to avoid when you live as long a life as he had, much of it spent in rural Russia. But never to an animal he'd been as close to as he was to Lulu. To be honest, although he would never have admitted it out loud, he was a little worried. There were so many things that could go wrong. Lulu seemed calmer now that Bethany was here, and he kind of felt that way himself.

He had made a nest of sorts on the floor for the dog, figuring that Bethany wouldn't be thrilled if a Great Dane gave birth on the couch in the guest house. Still, it was as cozy and comfortable as he could manage, and he was quite pleased with himself when he guided Bethany into the corner he'd set up in the small bedroom.

"Are those the sheets and blanket off your bed?" Bethany asked in a choked voice. "I had a stack of old towels set aside in the closet."

"Don't worry," he said. "I don't mind going without them for the night. I brought in the bedroll from my bike."

"Terrific," Bethany said. "I hope you like doing laundry." But she knelt down by Lulu and stroked her on the head. "Aw, honey, you're going to be fine."

The dog whimpered, and Alexei translated. "She says she just wants to have these babies now. She is tired of feeling like a big sausage." He laughed. "I think sausage is the word she means. What she actually said was 'silly fancy hot dog.'"

"Yup, that's probably a sausage. She always sniffs at them and makes a face before she takes a bite, when we offer her one. I think she is a hot dog snob." Bethany sat between the bed and the window, next to Lulu's pile of bedding. "Is she okay? She's panting a lot."

"That's normal," Alexei said. "It means she's in labor. The first pup should make an appearance pretty soon."

"Oh my god, this is so exciting," Bethany said. "I've never seen anything born before. When I offered to foster her, I didn't really think about this part of it."

Alexei chuckled. "Pregnancy does usually lead to babies," he said. "I can tell you this fact based on my years of experience."

"Thank goodness I have you to explain these things to me," Bethany said. Her cheeks were flushed and her eyes bright, and Alexei tried to remember it was nothing to do with him and everything to do with a pregnant dog. No one should be that attractive at a time like this. It was damned distracting.

Lulu barked at him and he laughed.

"What did she say?" Bethany asked. Then, "I still can't believe you can talk to dogs."

"Better than I can talk to women, sometimes," he muttered under his breath. "She said, wait, let me make sure I get this right, okay, she said… OW."

"Oh, poor baby." Bethany stroked Lulu's ears, just the way the dog liked it. "I wish there was something we could do."

Alexei watched the dog's sides heave. "I think you can say hello to the first puppy," he said, as a slippery mass slid out onto the sheets.

Bethany peered at it doubtfully. "That's a puppy?"

Lulu twisted around and licked the sack off and then started to eat the afterbirth.

"Ugh," Bethany said. Then leaning in to get a closer look at the baby, "Oh. Oh, Alexei, look at it. It's so tiny."

The small, squirming creature made its way unerringly to one of Lulu's teats and started sucking. Bethany turned away to blow her nose and Alexei pretended not to be affected, although he leaned in to give Lulu a big kiss.

"Nice job, mama. Now only another six or seven to go."

"Six or seven more?" Bethany said. She looked down as another puppy came into view. "Oh, good." But she sounded a little faint.

———

BY TWO AM, it was all over. Lulu was resting as comfortably as possible, given that she'd just given birth to eight puppies. The puppies themselves were snuggled up against Lulu's side, their little bellies distended with milk. Alexei had cleaned up the area as much as he could without disturbing the new family and he and Bethany had retreated to the living area to give mama her well-earned rest. Bethany had a large box she'd been saving that they'd move the puppies and Lulu into in the morning.

"That was amazing," Bethany said, beaming at him happily over a small glass of whiskey as they sat on opposite ends of the couch. "Thanks so much for coming to get me. I wouldn't have missed it for anything."

Alexei gazed at her. Fatigue from a long day showed in the tiny lines around her eyes and the slump of her shoulders, but she still seemed to fizz with pleasure over the birth of the puppies. He didn't know how she did it. Despite everything she dealt with, most of the time she remained upbeat and positive. And beautiful, but never mind that.

"Lulu was glad to have you there," he said. He grinned at her. "You're her foster mother so I guess that makes you a foster grandmother to her puppies, right?"

"Shut. Up." Bethany threw a pillow at him. "I am so not a grandmother."

He threw it back, avoiding the glass in her hand. It wouldn't do to spill good whiskey. "Puppy Grandma. You look pretty good, all things considered."

Bethany narrowed her eyes at him and put the glass carefully down on the table. Then she whipped the pillow back at him, followed by the other two that had been sitting next to it. "I wouldn't provoke me, if I were you. I'll have you know that I was the Greater Cape Cod All State Pillow Fight Champion three years running. I seriously considered majoring in it in college."

Alexei roared with laughter, suddenly feeling freer than he had in months. Something about the light-hearted banter reminded him of hanging out with his brothers, but instead of making him sad, the way it usually did, it just made him remember how good it had felt to goof around with them. And they weren't nearly as cute as Bethany was.

"Don't be so cocky," he said. "I've had a lot more years to practice than you have."

She winked at him. "Yes, but I know something you don't know."

"What's that?" he asked.

"I cheat," she said, and whacked him over the head with the pillow she'd had hidden behind her back.

"Hey!" he yelled. "Who keeps extra pillows under the couch?" He threw two of them back at her.

"Former Pillow Fight Champions, obviously," Bethany said, ducking. "You never know when you're going to need extra ammunition."

The next few minutes were a blur of laughter and pillows, until somehow they both ended up on the floor, with Bethany kneeling over Alexei's prone body as he pretended to cower away from the dangerous paisley bolster she held in one hand.

Their eyes met and something shifted. Suddenly the air was heavy with potential. Alexei felt as though he couldn't catch his breath. In the dim light from the lamp on the wall, Bethany seemed like some ethereal creature, her red hair floating around her fair-skinned pixie face, flannel shirt riding up to reveal a smooth midriff.

"I think you win," he said. "I should have known better than to take on the champion."

"Yes, you should have," she said, putting down the bolster. But she sounded a little breathless too, and her eyes darkened. "I'm afraid you're going to have to pay the penalty now."

"And what would that be?" he asked, wondering if he should end this now, and knowing he really didn't want to.

"A kiss, of course," she said, as if it was nothing. But when he rose up to meet her and their lips touched, it was something. It was everything. It was as if the past year just dropped away, leaving him weightless, his heart near to bursting with some emotion he didn't want to put a label on.

"Bethany," he said, whispering her name as if it were some magical word that could unlock the mysteries of the universe. He ran one hand up under her shirt in the back, reveling in the feel of her smooth soft skin, pulling her closer to him. "This probably isn't a good idea."

"Probably not," she whispered back. "We're doing it anyway though, right?"

He kissed her again, harder. *Hell yes.*

Suddenly he wanted, no, needed to have her next to him. All of her. Next to all of him.

"Are you sure?" he asked. He didn't want to risk regrets later. Not on his part, because he couldn't imagine any universe in which he could regret being intimate with Bethany. But he wanted to give her the chance to change her mind.

"Oh, *hell yes*," she said, unconsciously mimicking his thoughts. She pulled her shirt off over her head without unbuttoning it, revealing a silky camisole, which quickly followed.

Alexei cupped her breasts in his large hands, losing what

little rational thought he'd managed to hang on to. Her creamy flesh felt like silk, the pink tips inviting him to nibble and suck and lick until Bethany gasped and collapsed on top of him.

He rolled her over and quickly pulled off his own shirt and jeans before sliding hers off too. Now, their positions reversed, he reveled in the feel of skin on skin, while carefully holding the mass of his body up so he wouldn't crush her smaller form.

She writhed underneath him as he teased her with lips and hands until she bit his shoulder and said, "I want to feel you, Alexei. All of you. Now." And grasped him with greedy fingers, in case he had any doubt of her meaning, guiding him to her center.

Then there was only heat and pleasure, low moans that turned to cries of ecstasy, and a rush of joy so heady he thought that everything that had come before was merely a faint shadow of the reality of this moment.

ALEXEI WOKE in the morning feeling more cheerful than he had in a long time, and it took him a minute to remember why. He stretched out in the too-small bed, peering over the edge to check on Lulu and her babies. Bethany was gone, but there was a stack of pillows where she had ended up, and a piece of paper with a note on it that said, "Still the champion." So apparently she was okay about what had happened between them the night before.

That was good, since they had to spend a lot of time together. On the other hand, he hoped she wasn't thinking it meant something it didn't. He was still leaving as soon as they'd found and vanquished the kraken. He wasn't the settling down type, and he wasn't going to risk letting someone else important to him down the way he had his brothers. Not that Bethany was all that important. Nope. They'd practically just met. Just because he could actually breathe when she was around, that didn't mean she was important. Just really, really amazing.

"Outside," Lulu whined, bringing him back to reality. He let her out, then moved her and the babies into the box (lined with old towels, as promised) that Bethany must have put in the living room at some point after she left his bed. Then he wandered over to the house, his need for coffee overwhelming his desire to put off seeing Bethany.

The dazzling smile that greeted him almost made him forget his resolve, his wanderlust, and everything else that wasn't her.

"Morning," she said, handing him a mug. "How are Lulu and the puppies doing?"

"Great," he said, gulping the coffee too fast and burning his tongue. "I put them all in the box you brought over."

"Great," Bethany repeated. "Can you get my dad up on your own? I want to peek in on the babies, then run a few errands and then get to the bar early so I can catch up with some paperwork."

"Uh, sure," Alexei said. "Um, are we okay? I mean, you're not upset with me, are you?" He didn't know what he'd been expecting, but this calm, normal, cheerful attitude wasn't it. Not that he was disappointed. He was happy not to have to deal with a fuss or clear up a misunderstanding. But Bethany was acting like nothing had happened at all. He hadn't actually dreamt the whole thing, had he?

"Why would I be?" she asked, grabbing some folders off the table and sticking them in a tote bag, not even looking at him. "We were both emotional after the puppies were born and got a little carried away. It was fun, but it's not like it changed anything, right?"

"Right," Alexei said as she walked out the door. He wasn't sure which one of them was lying. Or if they both were.

14

HAYREDDIN HATED TO ADMIT IT, BUT THAT DAMNED LEN HAD been right.

Being a pirate in this new world was just no fun.

So much had changed during the time Red had been away, and his kind of piracy just didn't work anymore. Len had been right about the lack of ships to attack. Wealthy men still sailed the seas in expensive boats, but during the month of April, they were all someplace warmer, like the Caribbean, and no one sent their fortunes by ship anymore. Except drug dealers, apparently, and Red saw nothing worth stealing in piles of white powder.

To be sure, they occasionally attacked a yacht or a tanker just for fun, but Len was surprisingly squeamish about all the killing, and the supposedly tough men they'd hired to be their pirate crew were a disappointment, one and all. Half of them, panicked after one glimpse of the kraken, took off as soon as they came back to port, swearing this wasn't what they'd signed on for. The rest had to be paid extra to keep them from blabbing to everyone they knew.

Without booty to amass, the larger ship Len had procured was mostly just wasted space, and not nearly as maneuverable as one of Red's old sloops. There were no cannons mounted on it, and just as Len had said, today's weapons were smaller and more portable. In the end, he had grudgingly allowed Len to return it, and get rid of most of the extra men, retaining the three most bloodthirsty to work on Len's battered fishing boat.

Hayreddin told himself it was a better disguise anyway, since no one would suspect a mundane fishing boat of piracy, but really, it was all so disappointing. He longed for the day when the kraken found his long-lost treasure and he could return to the Otherworld. This was all taking much longer than he had expected it to, and sooner or later word would get back to the queen, and she would summon him home.

Even though dragons were given a bit more leeway than other Paranormals due to their extreme power and longevity, not even they could disobey a direct command from high queen of the Otherworld. The trick was to stay on this side of the portal until he had accomplished his task. If she forbade him from returning after that, he did not much care. He hated this new world, with its technology and its lack of swashbucking adventuring. He would be happy never to come back here again.

So he had been having Len send the kraken out more and more often, searching for where his ship had gone down on its final voyage. The beast had found a few other wrecks, even some with riches and gold aboard, although nothing to compare with what he'd lost. They had a nice little stash of booty for Len to drool over, but it was not what Hayreddin had come here seeking.

And then there was the added complication of the attention the kraken's presence was drawing. In the old days, anyone sensible would have run in the opposite direction. Now, they sent out *scientists*.

"I have an idea," he told Len over a breakfast of rum and sandwiches.

"Oh, god," Len said, putting his head in his hands. "Not another one."

Red missed the days when people who irritated him could simply be made to walk the plank. This stupid little vessel did not even have a plank. But no, he still needed the Human, both to control the kraken without violating the technicalities of the queen's rules and to help Red navigate this confusing and uncomfortable modern world. But later, oh yes, later, there would be a reckoning.

"We need to scare people away from the area we are searching," Hayreddin explained in what he believed was a calm and even tone. One of the hired men turned white and helped himself to more rum in a hurry.

"Yeah, okay," Len agreed cautiously. "I mean, it makes sense that we don't want anyone to figure out that the kraken is under our control, or stumble across us when we find my, I mean your, treasure."

Red puffed on his pipe furiously to mask the smoke coming out of his nostrils. He closed his eyes and counted to ten dead bodies until he could be sure he had himself back under control. "Yes, exactly. So I have come up with a cunning plan."

"Uh, huh." Len rolled his eyes. "You mean like all the other cunning plans you've come up with so far?"

The youngest and stupidest of the men guffawed, and Red casually took out the knife he kept tucked into his boot and stuck it into the annoying Human's chest, then picked him up in one smooth motion and heaved him over the side of the boat.

Silence settled over the remaining crew and Len opened and closed his mouth like a fish on the end of a spear.

"Would anyone else care to make a comment about my leadership skills?" Red asked mildly, wiping his knife off on the leg of his trousers. "No? Excellent. Then I assume you are ready to hear my idea?"

Three heads nodded up and down in unison, Len's bobbing the hardest of all.

Good. It was about time the little twit remembered who was in charge here. The kraken was only the second most dangerous thing on this ocean.

"People are still afraid of ghosts, are they not?"

Len's usual blank look became even blanker. "Uh, sure. Most people. Why?"

"I will start appearing as the ghost of Blackbeard, the fearsome pirate," Hayreddin declared, quite pleased with the cleverness of his idea. (After all, he had *been* the man known as Blackbeard, along with many other famous pirates, so it was not as though he would have any difficulty taking his semblance.) "These scientists will be so frightened, they will stop chasing the kraken and leave us in peace to pursue the treasure." He waved his tattooed knuckles in the air to reinforce his point.

"Uh, I'm not sure that will work," Len said, albeit in a more cautious manner than before. "People probably won't believe you are really a ghost, his ghost especially. I mean, he wasn't known for operating in this area, was he? I thought he ended up mostly in North Carolina."

Red waved away his protestations. "I can take on the guise of Blackbeard as easily as you can pull on your boots," he said. "Just you wait and see. And it matters not where he sailed in life, since all is different now anyway. It is only important that I am fearsome and strike terror into the hearts of those who see me, so they run away and stay away."

"You sure as hell strike terror into my fricking heart," one of the men muttered.

Red beamed at him. "Exactly. So we will await the next passing vessel and I shall appear to them as if out of nowhere. They will spread the word and before long, we shall have peace to continue our search."

"Or end up on the Internet," Len said. But he said it quietly, and so Red was happy to ignore him.

"OH, COME ON," Bethany said. "You saw *what?*" The last couple of days had been difficult enough without her having to deal with idiots. And this particular idiot wasn't even drunk yet, unless he'd started in another bar.

"Blackbeard's ghost," a fisherman named Clyde said, with complete seriousness. His face was ashen and he'd tossed back his first whiskey like it was water. "I swear to god. Scariest thing I ever saw in my life. And you've met my mother in-law."

The two men who crewed for him nodded their heads in unison, looking equally unsettled.

Bethany *had* met his mother in-law. It was hard to believe there was something out there that scared him more. (Her

Christmas fruitcakes had been known to make grown men cry.)

"How did you know it was Blackbeard?" she asked, her skepticism clear in her voice. Alexei, who was sitting at the bar with the three sailors, took a sip of his beer and perked up, like a man whose favorite reality TV show had just come on. A group of regulars gathered around.

Bethany often thought sailors gossiped more than any dozen women in a hair salon. Her father said it was because of the long, boring hours out on a boat with nothing to do but talk. He was going to be really cranky that he missed *this* particular conversation.

"How did I know?" Clyde said. "He freaking told me, didn't he? Said, 'I am the ghost of Blackbeard the pirate. Fear me, puny mortal!' Plus, you know, it was tattooed on his knuckles, one letter on each finger."

"Puny mortal?" Alexei choked back a laugh. "He actually said 'puny mortal'?"

Clyde glared at him. "Oh yeah, it sounds silly now, sitting in a brightly lit," he glanced around, "well, a reasonably well lit bar. But out on the ocean, miles from land, with the sun going down, it sent a chill right down my bones."

His shipmates nodded mutely, and pushed their empty glasses across the bar for a refill.

Bethany poured them each some more whiskey and set the bottle down within reach. She could tell it was going to be that kind of night.

"Okay, so how do you know he was really a ghost?" she asked. "Not to mention, how did he appear to you if you were in the middle of the ocean?"

"And why were you out so late?" One of the other fishermen asked from a nearby table. "You're usually in by afternoon at this time of the year."

Clyde held up a hand for them to wait and slugged down the rest of his whiskey. "Let me just tell the whole story from the beginning, will ya? It will be a lot faster."

He swiveled on his stool so he was partially facing Bethany at the bar, but could still address the others gathered around to listen.

"As for why we were out so late, well, we were trying to make a buck, weren't we? There's hardly any fish out there—" this got nods of agreement from everyone else—"so we took out a boatload of those damned thrill seekers who wanted to try and catch a picture of the sea monster."

"Giant squid, not a sea monster," one of the scientists from Wood Hole said from a table off to the side. "Much more interesting, really, given the rarity of giant squid sightings."

"Like sea monster sightings are common," Alexei muttered, but for a change, he kept his voice down so only Bethany heard him.

She was grateful for that, since the last thing she needed was for him to create another riot. But he'd been strangely quiet since their night together a few days before, and she wasn't sure what to make of it.

She knew she was faking pretending she didn't care about their crazy (wonderful/amazing/holy crap that was the best ever) sexual encounter, but she had no idea how he felt. And she wasn't going to ask him, either. They both knew he was leaving soon, and not the type to settle down. What would be the point? Other than to have more wildly satisfying sex. But she wasn't going to think about that either. More than twenty or thirty times a day.

"Sea monster, giant squid, Moby Dick's second cousin twice removed, I don't care what it is," an old-timer named Mike said glumly. "It's either eating the fish or scaring them away, and we're all going to go broke and starve to death if someone doesn't find the damn thing and kill it."

"Exactly," Clyde said. "So with no fish to catch, I figured, why not rent out my boat and my services for the day to people with more money than sense. Right? So we picked up this bunch at noon and spent hours hanging around the waters where this creature has supposedly been seen. Or where boats have disappeared, or whatever."

"Weren't you afraid your boat would be next?" Bethany asked.

Clyde shrugged. "My family has to eat. I mostly figured it was a fool's errand, but even if it wasn't, and there is some giant creature out there, I'm not going to sit at home while my kids go hungry."

There were lots of nods around the room. Bethany's heart ached for these men, who worked so hard in conditions that were already difficult enough without having to contend with a kraken. She bit her lip and glanced at Alexei. He narrowed his eyes and nodded, a silent promise that he would deal with it. His friend Beka had left a couple of days ago for the place they called the Otherworld to try and find some answers. Alexei said time worked differently there, so there was no telling exactly when she'd be back.

This all just got weirder and weirder.

"So what happened?" one of the guys asked. "Did you see the monster?"

"No," Clyde said. "Not a glimpse. The folks who hired me kept insisting on going a little further, but I finally told them we had to head back when it was starting to get dark. Then, out of nowhere, this other ship appears."

"What kind of ship?" Mike asked.

"We couldn't tell," Clyde said. "It was freaking spooky, I'm not kidding you. One minute, there was nothing there, and then there was this strange fog, and all you could make out was the vague outline of some kind of ship. We couldn't even tell how big it was. But it was flying a big black skull and crossbones flag, and this huge guy suddenly steps to the end of the prow, almost on top of us. Luckily, we weren't going very fast, since the picture people were still hoping to see something."

"Did anyone get a photo of this Blackbeard guy?" Bethany asked.

Clyde shook his head. "Most of them didn't even think to try, we were all so startled, but the couple who did just got a blur that looked much bigger than this guy—who was pretty damned big—that seemed like it was surrounded by smoke."

"So how did you know he was a ghost?" Bethany asked again.

"Because Nicky the genius here tried to shoot him with a spear gun, and it went right through him." Clyde glared at the man sitting next to him, who turned red and took another drink of his whiskey. "He coulda gotten us all killed. But this Blackbeard guy just laughed."

Alexei raised an eyebrow. "He laughed?"

"Damn straight," Clyde said with a scowl. "Like we were amusing little runts trying to take out a giant with a flyswatter. Which wasn't much off, probably, but still. Then he turned around, picked up the spear, and threw it back at us so hard, it is still stuck in the side of my damned boat."

"So he was real enough to pick up a spear and throw it," Alexei mused. "Interesting."

Bethany narrowed her eyes at him. She could tell he was thinking something, but she couldn't tell what. She'd wager a year's earnings that whatever it was, it was going to cause trouble, though.

"What happened next?" Someone else asked.

"You mean after he skewered my boat like it was an olive in a martini? He told me he was going to let us all live so we could bring back a message to anyone else who might be foolish enough to venture into his waters. His words, not mine."

Duh, Bethany thought. No fisherman she knew talked that way.

Clyde went on. "He said I should tell everyone I knew that Blackbeard's ghost had come back to claim his rightful treasure, and that anyone who got in his way would be sent to their rest on the bottom of the ocean, where their bones would turn into sand and their flesh be eaten by the creatures of the sea." He shuddered.

"Flowery sort of guy, wasn't he?" Alexei said. "That's quite a turn of phrase."

"You should have heard him," Clyde said. "I swear, it's like every word was etched into my memory with acid." He swallowed the rest of his whiskey and stood up, followed by his two men, who did the same. "Well, I delivered his message. Hopefully that will satisfy the freaky bastard and I'll never see him again."

"So you're not going to take monster hunters out in your boat tomorrow?" Bethany said, genuinely curious.

"Oh hell yeah I am," Clyde said with a lopsided grin. "I'm

not turning down good money. I'll just take them in the other direction from where the thing actually might be. I'm guessing one piece of ocean will look pretty much the same as the other ~~as another the same~~ to anyone not from around here." He grimaced. "I wish I'd thought of that this morning."

After Clyde and his crewmen left, everyone returned to what they were doing before things got interesting, leaving Bethany alone at the bar with Alexei.

"Fascinating story," Alexei said. "Do you think he was telling the truth?" He stroked his beard, which looked both neater and softer now that he'd cut it.

She'd always liked her men clean shaven before she met him. Of course, she'd never liked men who were huge and muscular, either. Mostly, she just liked Alexei. Damn it.

Bethany laughed, looking down at the glasses she was washing so she'd stop staring at Alexei. "You mean, do I think he actually met Blackbeard's ghost? Of course not. Do I think something strange came out of an unexpected fog and frightened him? Yeah, that I believe."

"What do you suppose it was, then?"

"I have no idea," Bethany said. "Somebody playing a practical joke? Another fisherman who had the same idea he did and was trying to scare off the competition?" She stared at him. "Why? You don't seriously think it was a ghost, do you?"

Alexei looked thoughtful. "I've met a ghost or two in my time. Never met one who could throw a spear hard enough to imbed it in the side of a wooden boat, though. I think I might wander down to the docks and take a look at Clyde's boat, just for the heck of it."

"And if there really is a spear sticking out of his boat? What then?" Bethany was almost afraid to ask.

"Then I might decide to take your father's boat out to see if I can meet this Blackbeard fellow." He tugged on his own beard and grinned at her. "Maybe if I can find him, we can compare facial hair."

"That sounds like a terrible idea," Bethany said, glaring at him.

"Okay," Alexei said with a shrug. "We can compare tattoos instead. Whatever makes you happy."

Bethany bit her tongue so she wouldn't tell him what would make her happy. That would be an even worse idea than trying to chase down a bloodthirsty pirate ghost.

"If you're set on doing this," she said, knowing him well enough to tell that he was, "why don't I get the neighbor to come in a little early tomorrow, and I'll see if I can get my day bartender to cover for me until I get back."

The eyebrow went up again, quirking in a way she found ridiculously attractive. Damn it.

"You're coming with me?"

"If you're taking my father's boat out at sunset to try and confront a ghost, I'm not letting you do it by yourself. Somebody needs to steer the boat while you're being all dangerous and fierce." She grinned back at him. "Of course, if your friend Beka is back by then, I'm happy to let her do it."

She didn't know which one of them was crazier. Oh, wait. Yes she did.

HAYREDDIN WAS FEELING QUITE proud of himself. He had put on a masterful performance the previous night, if he did say so himself. (And he had, repeatedly, to the increasing annoyance of Len and their remaining two pirates. Dragons were not known for their modesty.) A little simple dragon magic to create the illusion of an eerie mist and mask the sound of their approach, plus his own innate ability to change his form, and suddenly Blackbeard was back from the dead.

He could tell his appearance had had the desired effect. Those poor fools had nearly wet their breeches with fear. Red rather admired the one man who had kept his head enough to fire a spear at him, although of course it simply glanced off his tough dragon skin without doing any harm. He might take on the guise of a man, but he was still a nearly indestructible dragon under it all. Still, it did do rather a fine job of reinforcing his "ghost" impression.

The seas had been pleasantly empty all day. No fishermen or foolish gawkers to intrude upon his treasure hunt. He was getting close; he could feel it in his bones. And a dragon's bones never lied about treasure. Another day or two without distractions and surely the kraken's search would finally bear fruit and Hayreddin could leave this dreadful place and return home to his lovely, peaceful, *Human-free* cave.

His plan had been brilliant. If he did say so himself.

"I told you so," he said to Len, who was sullenly wrapping his hand, bloodied again after another turn at summoning the kraken. "My plan was brilliant."

"Oh yeah?"

The man was an imbecile. "Indeed. We have been left alone all day. The Humans are so afraid of this area now, we probably won't see another ship out here until after we have completed our task."

"What about that one, then?" Len said, pointing with his

bandaged hand. "Maybe it is another ghost ship, come to get in on our act?"

Red spun around. He could not believe his eyes. The imbecile was, incredibly, correct. A small fishing boat was moving slowly in their direction. What in the name of all the gods was wrong with these Humans? Could they not understand the simplest of messages? Fine, then. He would simply send it again. This time, it would be written in blood.

15

"THAR SHE BLOWS!" ALEXEI SHOUTED IN DELIGHT.

Bethany couldn't bring herself to be quite so thrilled. What the hell was she doing out here anyway? Did she really believe she could somehow keep this giant warrior safe if he couldn't do it himself?

"Isn't that for whales?" she asked dubiously, slowing the ship down to a crawl as they approached the strange foggy spot in the middle of an otherwise clear sea. The sun was going down, and its orange glare lit the mystery boat with an additional ominous aura. As if it needed one.

Alexei gave one of his huge, booming laughs. The crazy man was actually enjoying himself. "Probably," he admitted. "But I don't know the proper term for sighting a supposedly haunted pirate ship."

"Probably 'this blows,' would be sufficient," Bethany muttered.

"You just don't know how to have a good time," Alexei said.

"You have a very short memory," Bethany countered.

"Ha," he said. "But that's different. This is dangerous and uncertain."

Bethany thought back to their wild coupling. "And I say again, you have a very short memory."

Alexei scooped her up and kissed her, then put her down with a thump. "Oh, I remember every moment of that night, believe me." He grinned. "Perhaps we'll repeat it once I have dealt with our supposed pirate."

"Don't bet on it," she said, glaring at him.

"Which?" he asked. "The pirate or the repeat?"

She smacked him on the arm, which only hurt her hand. "Either. Both. Now, what's the plan?" It occurred to her that she probably should have asked that question before they left port. Oh well, too late now. A grim, darkly bearded figure was striding toward them out of the mists, their boats so close to each other they were almost touching. Alexei strolled down to meet him.

"Foolish churls, you are trespassing on the waters claimed by the ghost of Blackbeard the pirate. Be gone and never return, lest I send your bones to the bottom of the sea to become food for oysters!" The figure brandished a long, curving broadsword.

Alexei leaned casually against the side of the cabin. "No, I don't think so."

"What?!" roared the bearded man. Smoke wreathed his head and mingled with the eerie fog.

"Well, for one thing, oysters don't eat people. That's just silly. For another, you're no more a ghost than I am a ballerina." He straightened up. "So I'm kind of curious as to what you're up to here and why you want people to stay away. Care to enlighten me?"

"I am the ghost of Blackbeard the pirate!" the man thundered. "How dare you speak to me that way, you miserable failure? You are the laughingstock of the Otherworld. You are nothing but a shadow of your former self. You should abase yourself before me and run away in terror."

From her vantage point above him in the raised cabin, Bethany could see the muscles in Alexei's neck and shoulders tighten as the other man taunted him. For a minute, she was afraid he would lose control, but instead, he simply responded with a soft drawl that belied the tension that coiled in his body.

"Well, which is it?" he asked. "Abase myself or run away? It's kind of hard to do both at the same time."

Despite the seriousness of the situation, Bethany had to try and smother a laugh. Dark piercing eyes followed the sound and glared at her with a hatred that made them seem to glow red around the edges.

"You bring your Human whore with you to confront me?" the purported Blackbeard said. "What kind of fool are you? Her bones will lie beside yours, twenty fathoms deep."

Alexei's hand tightened on the side of the boat so hard, Bethany could hear it creak. But when she expected him to respond with anger, he surprised her by smiling.

"Not as big a fool as you are, whoever you might be. You just told me that you know who I am. Very few people on this side of the doorways would, so I'm guessing you're from the Otherworld. I'm also guessing that you are here without the queen's permission. Now that really *is* foolish."

The figure took a step back, suddenly less aggressive. "This is none of your business, Rider. Leave this place now and I will let you go in peace." He made a gesture to someone unseen behind him and his boat slowly began to move away. His voice, thick with malice, drifted to them over the widening gulf of water. "But I warn you, Rider. If you do not stay out of my way, I will make you and yours suffer in ways that made what that insane Baba Yaga did to you seem like a gift. Heed me in this, or pay the price."

The pirate boat drifted away, taking its strange fog with it. It faded into the growing darkness within minutes, as soon as it was out of range of *The Flora MacDonald's* lights.

"Well, that was interesting," Alexei said, rolling his shoulders in a way that revealed that he'd been much more tense than he would ever have admitted. He rejoined her in the cabin as they headed back.

Bethany realized her hands were trembling as she fired up the engine to take them home. "Interesting? That's what you want to call it? I don't know about you, but I thought that guy was scary as hell, even if he wasn't a ghost." There was something about the man's casual malice that frightened her to her core. No wonder Clyde and his men had been so shaken. "I sure as hell wouldn't want to meet him in a dark alley. Hell, I don't think I'd want to meet him in a sunlit park."

"Mmm," Alexei said. "A thoroughly unpleasant character, I agree. But coming out here was well worth the trouble. I learned something very important about our friend Blackbeard, something that Beka needs to know as soon as possible."

Bethany thought back to the confrontation. "Wait, you said he was from the Otherworld. That's how he knew who you were. How can that be?"

"Some Paranormal folks do visit from time to time, as long

as the queen consents to allow it. Or if they keep a low profile and happen to have access to one of the portals that lead to this world; although most of them are guarded, there are always random doorways if you know where to look," Alexei admitted. "But this fellow didn't strike me as a casual traveler. You saw how he reacted when I accused him of being here without the permission of the high queen. No, he's not supposed to be here. I'd bet my Harley on it. And that means that whatever he'd after is important to him and probably valuable.

"Plus, I'm guessing from the way he talks that the last time he was here was some time ago. That may help us to narrow things down nicely, especially if Beka gets an answer to whatever it was that she couldn't quite remember."

"I'm glad it was helpful," Bethany said. "But I'd still just as soon never see that man again."

"Oh, no worries. I don't see any reason why you would," Alexei said.

But Bethany wasn't so sure.

———

HAYREDDIN WAS SO FURIOUS, it was all he could do to hang on to his Human shape. Inside, his dragon roared and raged, wanting to breathe fire at the sky and torch this fragile wooden boat until it burned to a crisp, taking its insignificant and annoying occupants with it.

How *dare* that Rider laugh at him, Hayreddin the mighty, the glorious, the renowned? A fallen hero, pathetic and useless, dared to put himself in the way of Hayreddin's plans? This could not be allowed to stand.

But what was he to do? Killing the one who insulted him would be temporarily satisfying, but the queen had a ridiculous soft spot for the Riders, even in their current reduced state. And the Baba Yagas...those witches would hunt him to the ends of the earth. So killing Alexei was out of the question, alas. But there were other alternatives.

Red knew the Riders of old. They were well known throughout the Otherworld. Everyone knew Alexei was restless, always wandering (his brothers had been too, and Red had no idea where they had ended up, being simply grateful they were not here for him to deal with in addition to Alexei). It was passing strange that he had stopped in this tiny port town for long, although less so that he pretended to be helping the Baba Yaga as he once had. Still, as far as anyone Red talked to could tell, the only thing keeping Alexei here was his apparent infatuation with a barmaid. A Human, whose father he was caring for. It was beyond Red's comprehension.

But he supposed that when one was a former Rider, with no real useful occupation, anything at all might seem worth doing. Or perhaps it was the free beer. Either way, it was unlikely that Alexei would stay around for long. Hayreddin intended to see to it that the Rider moved on sooner rather than later.

One of the men Red had hired had been at *The Hook and Anchor* the night Alexei had wrecked the place. The whole fishing community talked of little else for days. So Red knew that the woman who ran the bar had told Alexei that if it happened again, he would be forbidden to return. If Alexei angered her, she would no longer wish him to care for her father, and he would leave town.

Simple enough.

"I have another brilliant plan," Red shouted back to where Len was sitting, as far away as possible.

A groan was his only answer.

ALEXEI SAT at the bar and watched Bethany through half-shuttered eyelids as he pretended to listen to a drunken sailor tell some long, rambling story about a sea monster that turned out to be a lost Russian submarine.

About a tenth of Alexei's attention was focused on the story—enough so he could grunt in the right places. Another third was focused on the door, hoping that Beka would walk through at any minute. Now that he knew their mysterious fake pirate was from the Otherworld, it shed an entirely new light on the whole matter.

Alexei really needed to talk to Beka and compare notes. Assuming she had learned something worth sharing, of course.

The rest of his attention was in the same place it had been for days, studying Bethany and trying to decide what she was thinking. She hadn't shown any change in attitude since the night they'd spent together or any indication that she expected their relationship to have altered because of it.

That was good. At least, he was pretty sure it was good. Of course it was good. Wasn't it? After all, it hadn't affected him at all. Other than the fact that he couldn't stop thinking about the way she looked in the heat of passion, like a wild and glorious valkyrie. Or the glow of the sun on her creamy skin when they were out on the boat together, or the fierce glint in her eyes when she was mad at him…which admittedly, was pretty often.

She glanced in his direction and he nodded enthusiastically at the man next to him, trying not to seem like he was watching her. Unfortunately, the sailor launched into an entirely new story, encouraged by Alexei's supposed interest. Great, this one had something to do with inappropriate tattoos. Please, gods, let there not be pictures.

It wasn't as though there was anything wrong with Bethany not wanting to jump back into bed with him, although it made him worry a little that their encounter hadn't been as wonderful for her as it had been for him. After all, she knew he was just passing through, and she wasn't the kind of woman who went for casual relationships.

Unless she just didn't want to be with him in particular. Not that he wanted to be with her. He didn't do relationships at all, casual or otherwise, his attachment to his brothers and the Baba Yagas aside. Of course, he also didn't brood over women, and look at him now. What the hell was wrong with him?

Bethany brought him over another beer, nodding at the guy next to him, who had pulled up his shirt to show off a tattoo of…what the devil was that, anyway? A mermaid and a dolphin? Alexei grimaced, pretty sure that the act depicted in the tattoo was not only physically impossible but unlikely to be considered desirable by either party.

Unlike the adorable redhead currently winking at him, who was absurdly desirable on multiple levels.

"Put that away, John," she was saying to the sailor. "And if you drop your trousers to show him the other one, I'm calling your wife."

"How do you know what he's got under his trousers?"

Alexei asked, curious (but not at all jealous, because he'd never been jealous a day in his life).

She rolled her eyes at him. "Not that way, you big oaf. Everyone in town knows what he's got tattooed on his left butt cheek. The tattoo artist who did it was so proud, he has a photo up on the wall in his shop." She gave a mock shudder. "Believe me, you don't want to know. You'll never sleep again."

Bethany turned to John. "Speaking of which, you need to go home and sleep it off, buddy. I've called you a taxi. You can come get your car tomorrow." She held out one hand and he dropped a set of keys into it meekly and staggered off in the direction of the door.

Bethany sighed, resting her elbows on the bar and her chin in her hands. "It was nice of you to let John blither on at you. I know he can be kind of annoying, but today's the anniversary of his mother's death, and he always gets drunk and tells ridiculous stories. You were kind to listen to him."

"I am *not* kind," Alexei growled, out of sorts for reasons he couldn't quite put his finger on. Probably just tired of waiting for Beka to come back so they could solve this damned kraken problem and he could get back on the road.

Bethany blinked at him. "Well, *you're* grumpy tonight. And you're not fooling me, either. You're kind to my father, and you're kind to Lulu. Once or twice you've even been kind to me. Probably accidentally."

Alexei opened his mouth to apologize when a deep, gravelly voice said, "I'll bet lots of men are kind to you, pretty lady."

A strange-looking guy slid onto the barstool vacated by John. He had an odd haircut, with one side of his head shaved a third of the way up, and the remaining hair combed up and over, so it fell in one straight gray sheet down to his chin on the other side. He had a tangled salt and pepper beard, a hooked nose, cold gray eyes, and wore gold hoops in both ears. Something about him seemed familiar, but Alexei was sure he'd remember having met someone so distinctive, so perhaps he'd simply seen the guy in the bar on a previous occasion.

Bethany ignored the compliment, although she raised an eyebrow in unspoken commentary in Alexei's direction. "Hi, I'm Bethany. What can I get you?"

The man gave Alexei a sideways glance, then stared rudely at a spot well below Bethany's face. "How about a whiskey, neat, and a night with you?"

"How about a whiskey and you stop ogling my boobs?" she countered. "Any particular brand you prefer?"

"Yours will do quite nicely," the man said with a smirk. "As for the whiskey, I am not particular."

Bethany seemed to be dealing with this asshole with her usual patient forbearance, but Alexei had had enough.

"You don't seem to be too particular about your manners, either," He said, swinging around to face the man. "I'm going to have to ask you to stop being so rude to the lady. She's a friend of mine."

"It's fine, Alexei," Bethany said. "I think the gentleman would be happier drinking in some other bar, that's all."

The man reached over and grabbed her arm. "The gentleman is quite happy right where he is, thank you, darling. Although we might have a more enjoyable evening if you would tell your large ugly friend to go elsewhere so we can get to know each other better in peace."

A red cloud seemed to descend over Alexei's vision.

"Remove your hand," he said through gritted teeth. "Or I will remove it for you. Possibly permanently."

Alarm crossed Bethany's face. "Alexei, don't."

But it was too late. The stranger gave him a grin that glinted gold at one edge. "I will enjoy seeing you try," he said, and let go of Bethany to stand up. "Shall we have at it?"

"Oh, yes, why don't we?" Alexei stood up too, so the two of them were almost toe to toe. The man was larger than he'd thought—almost as tall as Alexei himself, although not quite as broad in the shoulders. Of course, he was a Human, so he wouldn't have nearly the strength and endurance. Alexei might be a former Rider now, but his father was the god Jarilo and his mother had been the daughter of the legendary warrior Svyatogor, whose name meant *Sacred Mountain* because he was so large—no normal man could match him.

"Alexei," Bethany said warningly. "Not again."

Crack. The stranger struck Alexei so hard, it flung him across the room and into the wall.

Alexei straightened, shaking his head. *Son of a bitch. That actually hurt.* He roared as he raced back over and swept the man off his feet, barreling him a few yards before throwing him down on the ground with a thud.

The man bounced back up, seeming unshaken. He aimed another roundhouse punch at Alexei's head, but this time Alexei was expecting it and ducked under the blow. He plowed into the man again, ramming his shoulder into the stranger's gut and making him grunt as all the air left his lungs. They shot forward another couple of yards before the man dug in his booted feet and they screeched to a halt.

"Open the door!" Alexei yelled to one of the regulars who

was sitting next to it. The guy stopped staring and jumped up with alacrity, suddenly figuring out what Alexei was doing.

A meaty fist connected with the side of his head, but Alexei just shook it off, although his ears rang a little from the impact. He took one step back to gather himself and then hit the man with all his strength. The stranger flew out the door and landed in the parking lot on his ass.

"The lady asked you to drink elsewhere," Alexei said, folding his arms over his chest. "I suggest you do as she says."

The man stood up, making a low growling sound of mixed frustration and anger. His eyes seemed to glow red in the reflection from the neon beer signs in *The Hook and Anchor*'s window. "Fight me," he said. "Come back inside and fight me like a man."

Alexei shrugged. "No thanks. I seem to have lost my taste for brawling. Besides, I promised not to bust up the bar again. So I'm afraid you'll have to find your entertainment elsewhere."

"I could keep striking you," the man hissed. "You would have to fight me then."

"Sure. If you insist." Alexei shrugged again and gestured around them. "If you feel like rolling around in the dirt in a parking lot. I suspect all these cars and trucks are insured. But I *will* beat you to a pulp eventually, and what would be the point?"

The stranger scowled. "What would be the point indeed?" He glanced back at the doorway, where Bethany stood looking out at them. "Very well. But this is not over."

"I think it is," Alexei said mildly. "Go home."

"Soon," the man said. "But not soon enough." He turned and stalked away into the night.

A small crowd spilled out of the bar and applauded. Alexei just grinned and waved them off. He couldn't believe he was being hailed for *not* fighting. His life was getting odder and odder. The Baba Yagas would never believe it.

But then Bethany ran over and jumped up into his arms, kissing him soundly before sliding back down to the ground. "You were amazing!" she said. "You purposely moved him out of the bar so it wouldn't get wrecked. And then you chose not to fight." Tears seemed to glimmer in her eyes. "You crazy, wonderful, amazing man."

She kissed him again, to more applause from the regulars, and suddenly Alexei didn't care how odd his life had become. If not fighting got him this kind of reward, he might just give it up forever.

Once it was clear the excitement was over, everyone went back inside and got back to their drinking, although not without a heightened buzz of conversation as the entire fight was recapped and discussed from every angle. Bethany and Alexei followed the pack, but she surprised him by grabbing his hand and steering him toward the storeroom instead of the bar.

"Hey!" he protested. "I thought I'd at least get a free beer for not wrecking the place."

Bethany closed the door behind them and shoved him up against a stack of wine crates. The bottles clinked cheerfully as she stood on her toes to whisper against his lips, "I thought I'd give you a different kind of reward," and kissed him with so much passion, it made him tingle down to his fingertips.

"Just so you know, you have never been sexier to me than you are right at this moment," she said in a husky voice.

Naturally, he kissed her back. He liked drinking, but the

buzz that came from having his body pressed up against Bethany's was better than the most expensive champagne.

"Not that I'm complaining," he said hoarsely a few minutes later when they both came up for air. "But there is an entire bar full of thirsty sailors out there waiting for their drinks. And I'd rather not have that big a cheering section for this kind of activity." He'd been holding her up with both hands on her bottom and set her down reluctantly until her feet touched the floor again.

Bethany sighed, but took a step backward. "You're probably right," she said. "But you'd better believe you're going to get lucky when I get home tonight."

"I'll be counting the minutes," Alexei said. "And possibly the seconds." That was, if he got enough blood flow back in his brain to count anything.

***

THAT HAD NOT GONE AS PLANNED. NOT at all. Hayreddin could not believe that the Black Rider of all people had refused to fight him. Had the man completely lost his nerve when the wicked Brenna tortured him and his brothers? Or had he lost his mind over that silly, flame-haired Human? Either way, yet another brilliant plan had failed miserably.

Hayreddin had had enough. It was time for more drastic measures. If a direct attack could not achieve his goal of getting the former Rider out of his hair, then something more underhanded would be required. Fortunately, Red excelled at devious and malicious schemes. With the help of Len and the two remaining pirates, he would do something that would force Alexei to do as he was told. Or else.

16

BETHANY HUMMED TO HERSELF AS SHE PUT THE CHAIRS UP ON top of the tables for the night and shut down all the lights. The bar closed at one AM at this time of year, and the last customer had left ten minutes ago. As usual, Alexei had gone back to the house around eleven thirty to help Calum into bed, and as usual, the place had seemed quiet and a bit empty without his overly large presence. She didn't even want to think about how it would feel when he was gone for good.

Alexei. She couldn't believe what he'd done tonight. She would have bet a substantial amount of money that nothing he could do would surprise her, but it turned out she would have been wrong.

When that creep had started in with her, then kept pushing and pushing, she was certain Alexei was going to flip out and go into what she privately thought of as "Hulk mode." She'd seen it coming, and could already visualize the damage the two huge men would wreak as they battled back and forth across the bar.

When Alexei stood up, she knew she was doomed. She'd have to ban him from *The Hook and Anchor* for good, get everything repaired again, and maybe even kick him out of the guest house, even though she still hadn't found a new aide for her dad. Her stomach had clenched so hard, she was afraid she was going to throw up.

Then he'd done the completely unexpected. It had taken her a minute to understand what he was doing, but she'd almost cheered when she realized he was purposely driving his opponent in the direction of the door. When he'd shoved the guy out into the parking lot and then refused to fight, she'd been overcome with a rush of emotion—part stunned amazement, part gratitude, and part sheer unadulterated lust. She always found him ridiculously attractive, but in that moment, he had been almost irresistible. The impulsive kiss in front of an entire bar full of customers was probably a mistake, but she couldn't bring herself to regret it.

He was definitely going to get lucky when she got home.

She hefted the last chair up and turned off the lamp behind the bar, then made her way down the hall past the bathrooms to the back exit. She couldn't wait to get into her truck and go give Alexei his reward for not wrecking the place again.

As always, she turned around once she was outside to jiggle the old brass doorknob and make sure it was really locked, a habit her father had instilled in her when she was still in her teens. But this time, when she turned back to go to her truck, she saw a silhouette standing under the lone light in the parking lot next to the bar. Before her brain could even process what she was seeing, someone came up behind her and grabbed her, sticking a nasty-smelling cloth over her nose and mouth.

Bethany struggled briefly, her heart stuttering with panic, pulse racing as she struggled not to breathe in. But despite her best attempts, her vision blurred and her knees buckled, and then the world went away.

———————

ALEXEI SAT at the kitchen table and tried not to worry. After all, Bethany was a grown woman who had been managing for years before he ever came along, and who would undoubtedly manage just fine when he was gone. Still, it was unusual for her not to be back by now. The hands on the old crooked clock pointed at two; she should have been back at least a half an hour ago. He'd been looking forward to collecting his reward when she got home...now he just wanted to know that she was all right. He could almost hear his brothers teasing him about becoming a mother hen, but he couldn't help it. Something was wrong. He could feel it in his bones.

He could hear the faint sounds of Calum's snoring echoing through the house, and thought about taking a quick run to the bar to check and make sure everything was okay. But he'd promised Bethany not to leave her father alone—she worried about things like fire, or medical emergencies, or anything else where Calum wouldn't be able to manage without help.

Alexei figured the old man would probably be fine for ten minutes on his own, but he'd made a promise, and if he broke it, Bethany would kick his ass. Assuming she was okay.

She had to be okay. He was just being paranoid. But if she hadn't shown up by two thirty, he was going to wake the neighbor and go to the bar and check, even if he got yelled at for his efforts.

He'd even gone so far as to try calling her cell phone, much as he hated the things, but there had been no answer. No doubt there was a perfectly reasonable explanation, and she'd walk in any minute and laugh at him for worrying. That would be okay with him.

A knock at the back door made him jolt up in relief. Finally. But then he realized that Bethany wouldn't be knocking at her own door, and the relief morphed into a sharp stab of concern. So it was with a mix of pleasure and anxiety that he opened the door to find Beka standing there instead.

"Hey," he said. "You're back." He motioned her into the kitchen and she sank into a chair with a sigh.

"Yeah. Finally. This search took a lot longer than I anticipated. I kept chasing down rumors and finding people who had bits and pieces of 'Gee, that sounds like something I might have heard a hundred years ago,' or 'Have you asked Symon the blacksmith who lives under the enchanted mountain?'" She took the cup of tea he handed her and smiled at him gratefully.

"I know it's late, but I parked the school bus in the street out front so I could talk to you first thing in the morning, and when I saw the light on, I figured you might still be up." Beka glanced around the kitchen. "Is Bethany here? I thought you two were probably sitting here gabbing." She winked at Alexei. "Mind you, I was hoping I wouldn't be interrupting something else. Like something that involved whipped cream and nakedness on top of the table."

She thought a second. "Or maybe I hoped I would be. How are you two doing, anyway?"

Alexei ignored her second question to answer the first, more pressing one. "No, Bethany isn't here. And she should be. I'm starting to get worried."

Beka raised one blonde eyebrow. "Really? It isn't like you to worry about other people. Gregori once vanished for six months and you just said, 'He's probably staring at his damned navel.'"

"And I was right, wasn't I?" Alexei mocked, although his heart wasn't in it. "When he finally turned up, he'd been at a Buddhist monastery in Tibet, helping the Abbot there solve some kind of weird Paranormal mystery."

"Oh, right. I'd forgotten that," Beka said. "But still, my point is, you weren't at all worried. And he's your brother."

"He was also a Rider, and better equipped to take care of himself than some small armies," Alexei reminded her. "Bethany, well, Bethany is tough, but she is still a Human, and therefore fragile. What if she has been in an accident or something?"

Beka stood up and gave him a hug. "You're really concerned, aren't you?" She gazed into his eyes. "I can't believe it. You've finally fallen for someone." Her grin could have lit up half of Broadway. "It's about damned time. I like her, too. She may be tiny and Human, but I think you've met your match."

Alexei shook his head, not even bothering to deny it. "It's impossible, Beka, and you know it. We're too different. And I don't stay in one place. It could never work out between us."

"Seems to me like you've been in one place for a while now," Beka said softly. "I don't see any signs that you're suffering, either. As for differences, I don't think anyone could be more different than a powerful witch who is also a California surfer chick and a former Marine turned fisherman, and Marcus and I have made it work. I've never been happier. Maybe you should give yourself a chance at that same happiness, Alexei."

He stared at the clock again. "I'd be happy if she would just walk in the door. I have a bad feeling, Beka." Fear clenched at his belly, making it feel as though his entrails were on fire.

"She probably just has a flat tire or something," Beka said, laying a gentle hand on his arm. "You went through some pretty terrible things, and I know it was awful not to be able to help your brothers when you were all suffering at Brenna's hands."

Lines formed around the sides of her mouth and she suddenly looked much older than her usual carefree appearance. Brenna had been her mentor, the one who had raised and trained her, all the while subtly undermining Beka's confidence so that Brenna wouldn't have to give up her position as Baba Yaga.

"I hate what that bitch did to you all. But I especially hate that she left you all so broken that you felt as though you couldn't be a part of each other's lives anymore, or of ours. I can't tell you how wonderful it has been to be able to reconnect with you, and I know the others will feel the same when you're ready to reach out again." She blinked back tears that tugged at his heart.

Then she sniffed and punched him on the arm. "But don't wait too long, okay? Your brothers have finally come back to us, and you need to too, you big jerk."

Alexei bit back a smile. "This was the point you were trying to make?"

Beka wiped her eyes. "No, sorry. I kind of got side-tracked there. What I meant to say is that you're still raw from the experience. Humans would call it PTSD—post traumatic stress disorder—and say it is normal that you're jumping at shadows that aren't there. I'm sure Bethany is fine."

Alexei felt his shoulders relax a little bit. Beka was probably right. It was probably something perfectly benign, like a problem with the truck, or something minor that had needed to be dealt with at the bar. Maybe her cell phone had run out of whatever it was regular cell phones were powered by, since they didn't have magic.

"Yeah," he said. "I guess. But look, since you're here, would you mind staying with Bethany's father so I can run over to the bar and make sure she doesn't need help with something? I'd feel a lot better if I could go check. Even though she'll probably give me hell for not trusting her to be able to take care of herself."

Beka laughed. "Oh, she definitely will. But I don't mind staying. You run off and check on your woman."

Alexei rolled his eyes. "She's not *my* woman."

Beka just snickered and settled back into her chair with her cup of tea. "If I'm asleep when you get back, just roll me out to the bus, will you?"

"With pleasure," he said and headed out the door at something that wasn't quite a run.

ANXIETY PRICKLED up his spine when he saw that the bar was shuttered and dark. Alexei drove around to the parking lot, figuring she might be in the tiny office in the back, but there were no lights on anywhere that he could see. He hopped off his Harley and went to check the door.

Locked. But his foot kicked something that jingled when he hit it, and he bent down to retrieve a set of keys he recognized from the tiny metal anchor that hung from the ring. Bethany's keys. But no Bethany. He couldn't seem to draw air into his lungs, and he had a sudden flashback to the moment he'd awoken in a dank, dimly lit cave to see his brothers bleeding, locked into cages where he couldn't reach them.

If someone had harmed Bethany...

He glanced around the area and his eyes fell on her father's beat-up old truck, parked at the far end of the otherwise empty lot. He raced over to check it, but it was as empty and abandoned as the bar.

A small white square tucked under the windshield wiper caught his eye, and he forced himself to stop and breathe before plucking it out from underneath the rubber wiper. He walked slowly to stand underneath the light, tilting the paper so he could read it. It felt strangely heavy in his hands, like old-fashioned parchment, and the message appeared to be written with a fountain pen. The writing was flowery and bold, and the nib of the pen had bitten so deeply into the paper it had left grooves that could be felt with Alexei's trembling fingertips.

In contrast to the elaborate delivery system, the message itself was quite simple:

Leave town immediately and never return. Or the woman dies.

17

BETHANY WOKE SLOWLY, HER HEAD FILLED WITH FOG, HER mouth dry and nasty tasting. Nausea threatened to overwhelm her, and it took her an immeasurably long time to get to the point where she was certain she wasn't going to throw up. Reasonably certain, anyway.

Unfortunately, that was about the only thing she was sure of. The space she found herself in was completely unfamiliar, tiny and claustrophobic, with only a dim light coming from a lantern hanging from a hook far overhead and no windows that she could see. She seemed to be lying on a folded mass of white cloth than smelled damp and moldy, and the vague shapes of boxes, crates, and bags surrounded her on all four sides.

Bethany thought she could just barely make out the outlines of some kind of hatch in the ceiling. It was that and the subtle swaying motion of the floor underneath her that finally registered in her groggy brain as something she could put a name to: she was on a boat, somewhere at sea. Probably locked in the hold.

Shit.

She dug into the fog, trying to find the last things she could remember, looking for a clue as to how she had ended up here. She could remember being eager to head home to Alexei; that brought a pang of loss and sorrow so powerful it threatened to swamp her like the waves she could hear brushing up against the hull. But she pulled herself together. There was no time for emotion now. Nobody knew where she was. No one, not even Alexei, would be coming to rescue her, although if she knew him, he would probably be moving heaven and earth to try to do so.

No, she was going to have to rescue herself. And for that she needed all the information she could get. *Think, Bethany, think.* Hard to do when your head throbbed in time with the swaying of the ship, but eventually she recalled locking the back door, then turning around. She'd seen something…someone.

That man. The one from the bar. The one who had tried to pick a fight with Alexei. He'd been standing there by her truck, right before someone had grabbed her from behind. But why?

A cold hand of dread grabbed her by the throat. Was the man stalking her? Had he locked her up so he could rape and torture her for weeks without interference? You heard about those kinds of things on the news. All women lived in fear of it happening to them. Was she going to join those horrible ranks?

She forced herself to breathe again. Thought about the way he'd looked at her across the bar. No, that hadn't been lust, for all that he'd made such a production of staring at her breasts. Not lust. Not even interest, really. But if it hadn't been about her, then what? Where had his real interest lain?

Alexei. He'd come for Alexei. She'd seen him purposely try and provoke Alexei into a fight, although it hadn't really dawned on her until later that that's what the stranger had been doing. So his goal probably wasn't rape and murder. She tried not to sob in relief, suddenly aware that she'd been biting her lip so hard it had bled.

But why kidnap her if he really was after Alexei?

The thought of Alexei being in danger made her try to sit up, only to be thwarted by the thick ropes that tied her wrists and ankles. It took her ages to struggle into an upright position, but she was motivated enough to ignore the discomfort the movement caused in her head and stomach. She had to get out of here. She just had no idea how she was going to do it.

An eternity later, the hatch creaked open and a slim figure clambered awkwardly down the ladder into the hold, carrying something in one hand and clinging to the rails with the other. Not the huge stranger. There was something about that guy that was…sinister. An old-fashioned word, but one which seemed to fit. Bethany felt a rush of tension leaving.

The man who approached her was slightly scrawny and sallow, with a scruffy three-day beard and a haunted look in his brown eyes. He wore a typical sailor's gear of a waterproof jacket and a dark woolen hat, and a net bag swung from one callused hand.

"Oh, good," he said. "You're awake." There was relief in his voice as he knelt down in front of her. "I was worried I'd given you too much chloroform. You've been out for ages."

Bethany craned her neck to look up at the crack of sky revealed by the open hatch. "What time is it?" she said, her voice raspy. Her mouth felt as though she had been crawling through the desert, and despite her best efforts, she felt a surge of gratitude when the man handed her a bottle of water.

She grasped it the best she could between her bound hands and managed to get some of it down her throat without spilling it. But she'd be damned if she'd say thank you.

"You. You were the one who grabbed me," she said, when she had enough saliva to speak. She recognized the familiar odor of fish mingled with cheap cologne. "You son of a bitch."

"Hey," he said, holding up a hand as if to keep her from attacking him. As if she could. "It wasn't my idea. Red made me do it." A pout rendered his homely face even less attractive. "It was another one of his brilliant ideas." An eye roll accompanied this statement, but he looked over his shoulder at the hatch as if to be sure he wasn't overheard.

"Who the hell is Red, and why on earth would he have you kidnap me? I haven't done anything to either one of you." *Yet.*

Her captor just shrugged his narrow shoulders. "Red, he's, well, he's my partner. We're treasure hunters."

"Partners, huh?" Bethany raised an eyebrow. "Sounds to me more like he's the boss and you're the flunky, if he's the one giving the orders." She figured she'd better learn as much as she could as long as this guy was willing to talk.

He straightened up, scowling at her. "He doesn't give me orders. I told you, we're partners. He just, well, he's kind of um, forceful. So sometimes it's easier to do what he says."

"Red wouldn't happen to be a big man with a weird haircut and gold earrings in his ears, would he?" she asked. "If so, I think I met him. Not impressed."

"Yeah, well you should be," the man said. "He can do things you would never believe. And he's going to make us both rich."

"Sure," Bethany said with mock patience. "With this imaginary treasure of yours."

"Ha. Shows what you know." The man looked over his shoulder again. "We're *this* close to finding his lost pirate treasure." He scowled again, dark eyebrows drawing together. "But your damned boyfriend is getting in our way, so Red figured that if we grabbed you, he'd have to leave us alone." He started walking back toward the hatch. "You'd better hope your guy does what he's told. Red is a bloodthirsty bastard, and he doesn't have much patience when his plans don't go the way he wants them to."

On that cheerful note, he scrambled back up the ladder and shut the hatch with a thud. Bethany could hear the sound of a bolt being thrown.

As if being tied up wasn't enough, they had to lock her in. Apparently they had more faith in her ability to escape than she did. She thought of the way Red had looked at her across the bar, as if she were an object, not a person, and shuddered. Maybe she was going to have to prove them right. She sure as hell wasn't going to sit down here and wait for Alexei to do something this Red didn't like, since that was almost a guarantee that sooner or later, that's exactly what would happen.

She didn't like her odds if it did, either. She took one more swig of water and then started looking around for something to use to cut her ropes. Barring that, she'd settle for a weapon of any kind. Unfortunately, she doubted her captors had been kind enough to leave a nice sharp knife lying around, so she was probably going to have to improvise.

———————

ALEXEI PULLED the motorcycle into the driveway so abruptly it skidded on the gravel, probably only staying upright because at heart it was a magical steed and not mere metal and gears. He slammed in through the back door, startling Beka into dropping the book she was reading at the kitchen table, and let loose with a string of Russian curses which thankfully, she couldn't understand.

"He took her. The bastard took Bethany." Alexei handed Beka the note. "I found this under her windshield."

Beka read the few, not very helpful words and visibly restrained herself from hugging him. Just as well, since he probably would have exploded at the smallest touch, no matter how well intentioned.

"Who took her?" Beka asked. "The note isn't signed."

"It has to be Blackbeard," Alexei said with a growl. "Or the man calling himself that. I'm pretty sure he is the one behind the kraken, and I got right in his face the other day. Laughed at him. Bethany was there. I thought I was being so clever, baiting him into showing his true colors." He sagged, leaning against the doorframe so hard, the whole house groaned. "Now he's taken her, and it is all my fault."

"Blackbeard?" Beka said. "As in Blackbeard the famous pirate?"

Alexei nodded. "Impossible, I know. But he was appearing

to the local sailors as the ghost of Blackbeard, and I don't know what else to call him."

Beka raised an eyebrow. "Actually, it might be more possible than you think. I found out some interesting tidbits in the Otherworld, although it took me a lot longer to chase them down than I expected." Her normally cheerful expression took on an unusually grim tinge.

"First, somebody better tell me where the hell my daughter is and what the devil has happened to her," Calum said, rolling into the kitchen. He was still wearing his pajamas and his forehead was damp with sweat, but he'd gotten there under his own power.

"How did you get out of bed by yourself?" Alexei asked, once he'd closed his mouth.

Calum scowled. "Apparently all those damned exercises you've been making me do finally paid off," he said. "Now, what the hell is going on? Where is Bethany?"

Alexei and Beka exchanged glances. There was clearly no way they could keep the truth from him, no matter how much they might want to, and besides, she was his daughter. He deserved to know. Alexei braced himself for the recriminations he assuredly deserved.

"She's been kidnapped. Grabbed outside the bar after she closed up, as far as I can tell," Alexei said as Calum wheeled himself up to the table. Alexei sank into a chair, telling himself it was so that they could all be on the same level, and not that it was because his legs wouldn't hold him up any longer.

"The door was locked, and I found these on the ground next to it," he said, tossing her keys onto the table in front of Calum. "The truck was still parked in the lot, and this note was under the windshield wiper." He pushed it over so Calum could read it.

"Huh," Calum grunted. "Not much to go on. I take it you have an idea who did this?"

"Probably. Maybe." Alexei sighed. "I've pissed off a few people since I've been in town. But there is only one I can think of who would want me to leave badly enough to kidnap Bethany to force me to do it." He waited for the yelling.

"So where do you think he's holding her?" Calum asked.

"You're awfully calm about this," Beka said, leaning forward. "Aren't you freaking out? I'm kind of freaking out and she's not my daughter."

"Yeah," Alexei said. "Go ahead and yell at me. It's all my fault. I got her involved with this. It's my fault she's in danger."

To his surprise, Calum actually laughed. "I know my girl. There's no way you pulled her into anything she didn't want to be caught up in, and there was no way to keep her out of it if she decided she wanted in. She's as stubborn as her father, and makes her own decisions."

He stared at Alexei. "But I expect you to find her and bring her back to me in one piece, or chair or no chair, I'm going to make you sorry."

Alexei nodded. "Oh, I intend to, believe me. As for where he's holding her, that's a problem. I'm guessing he took her to his boat, and that could be anywhere." He restrained himself from banging his head on the table—just barely, and only because he didn't have time to mend another piece of furniture.

"Not just anywhere," Beka said, furrowing her brow. "If he's the one who has been controlling the kraken, and I think he probably is, then we know he has been sighted in a certain area. It's a big ocean, but we can narrow it down a little bit."

"You said something before, about how it wasn't impossible that he was Blackbeard's ghost," Alexei said. "Want to explain that?"

"Not Blackbeard's ghost," Beka said, a small smile playing at the edges of her mouth as she dropped her bomb. "Blackbeard himself."

"What?" Calum sputtered. "Blackbeard lived and died hundreds of years ago. Are you suggesting this guy is some descendent of the original pirate?"

"Not at all," Beka said. "Let me start at the beginning. When I got to the Otherworld, I started asking questions about how it would be possible for a Human to control a kraken. There were a few folks who had vague memories of hearing about something like that, but they were long enough ago that no one was sure where they'd heard them."

"I'm not sure it is a Human," Alexei interjected. "When I confronted this guy who calls himself Blackbeard, or Blackbeard's ghost, he knew who I was. So he had to have connections with the Otherworld. I'm pretty sure he was a Paranormal, because he didn't look happy when I threatened to tell the queen he was here."

Beka waved her hand at him. "Oh, I believe it. I'm getting to that part. Give me a minute." She waited for him to settle back down.

"So I finally tracked down a slightly shady centaur who specialized in growing exotic herbs for, shall we say, less than savory magical users. He told me that years ago, he traded some herbs to a witch for a handful of gemstones and a golden goblet. Kyler, that was the centaur's name, still had the goblet, and he showed it to me. It was definitely from this side of the doorway. Spanish, maybe."

"What does this have to do with our supposed pirate?" Alexei grumbled. He'd never had much patience with long stories, unless he was the one telling them.

"I'll tell you, if you let me finish," Beka said. "So I asked him what the witch wanted the herbs for, pretending that I didn't believe she would have trusted him enough to have told him." She grimaced. "Centaurs have huge egos and they are *so* prideful. Anyway, he swore that the witch bragged to him about being hired by—wait for it—a dragon."

"What?" Alexei sat up straight. "You're kidding."

Calum's eyes grew even wider. "A dragon? Seriously? How is that possible?"

"It's possible," Beka said. "They used to live on this side of the doorway, long ago. There's a reason there are stories about them in just about every culture. But most of them retreated to the Otherworld long before the queen issued her decree forcing all the other Paranormals to move there, because it is a lot harder to hide a twenty foot dragon than it is a two foot tall sprite." She shrugged. "Of course, they can change shape, so in theory they could have lived among Humans as long as they wanted to. But they're much more comfortable in their own skin, for the most part, and even more proud than centaurs."

Calum blinked a few times, digesting this. "Alexei told me that your dog, I mean, the one you travel with, is really a dragon. But I thought he was kidding."

Beka laughed. "He is. But he's a Chudo-Yudo. They're dedicated to spending their lives living here and traveling with their own chosen Baba Yaga. You might say they are a breed unto themselves. And they're used to staying in disguise most of the time, either as extremely large dogs, like mine, or occasionally a really, really large cat like my sister Bella's Koshka."

"Never mind that," Alexei said, impatient to hear the rest of the tale. "What does this dragon and his witch for hire have to do with Blackbeard and Bethany?"

"According to Kyler, the dragon in question had hired the witch to create an enchanted amulet. One which could be used to control a kraken. Mind you, this was before the queen's edict, back when Paranormal folks lived on this side of the doorway and traveled back and forth freely between the worlds. Kyler said the witch, who was apparently a regular client, bragged that this dragon was famous for taking on the guise of various Human pirates, including…"

"Blackbeard!" Alexei and Calum cried in unison.

"Exactly so," Beka agreed. "The witch said that this dragon wanted a way to control a kraken so he could use it to attack ships carrying treasure. Dragons are big on treasure," she explained to Calum. "It's kind of their thing. They're seriously into shiny objects."

"So the witch made this amulet for a dragon," Alexei said. "Dragons don't leave the Otherworld much these days, although the queen gives them a little more leeway than most of her other subjects, as long as they stay within the rules. Did your new centaur pal know where the amulet ended up?"

"No," Beka said. "He barely remembered the entire transaction until we started talking about it. That's one of the downsides to a very long life. Lots of memories, and it is easy to misplace ones that aren't important. The last he knew, the witch had given the dragon the amulet, gotten paid in gemstones and treasure, some of which she used to pay the centaur for his herbs, and that was it. And before you ask, he said the witch died years ago, so we can't ask her either."

"Crap," Alexei said. He thought for a moment. "So according to the centaur, the amulet that controlled the kraken belonged to a dragon who perhaps used to disguise himself as a pirate. Is it possible that our Blackbeard is this dragon? They can do small magics, so that might explain the illusion of a ghost ship."

Beka shrugged. "This is the Paranormal we're talking about here. Anything is possible. You met this ah, person. What do you think? Could he have been a dragon in Human guise?"

Alexei clenched his fists. He just wanted to get his hands on whoever this guy was and make him give Bethany back. "He was arrogant enough. Could have been. I'm sorry, I just don't know." He grimaced. "If I'd known it was a dragon, I wouldn't have provoked it. Dragons aren't exactly known for their even tempers."

Beka laughed. "Alexei, you would have provoked this creature if it had been the queen of England." She sobered. "But if it is a dragon, that does put a different spin on things. We're pretty tough, but we're not really equipped to take on a dragon in a direct fight. Especially not in the middle of the ocean, where my powers are at their weakest."

"What about your dog?" Calum asked. "I mean, he's a dragon, right?" He grunted. "I can't believe I'm having this conversation."

"He is," Beka said. "But although Chewie is a very large dog, he is actually a pretty small dragon. All the Chudo-Yudos are, since they have to be able to take on reasonable size forms. If our mystery pirate really is a traditional dragon, Chewie would be way out of his weight class. But I sent word to an old friend—well, an old friend of my sister Barbara, to be more exact. We'll see if he shows up. In the meanwhile, we'll just have to do the best we can, and pray that the dragon who commissioned the amulet lost or sold it years ago, and it is currently in the hands of someone more manageable."

"And what do you think the odds of that are?" Calum asked, sounding discouraged.

Alexei and Beka exchanged glances. "Not great," Alexei admitted. "It would be out of character for a dragon to give up anything valuable. But you never know. Denizens of the Otherworld do a lot of barter and swapping, so anything is possible." He ground his teeth. "Either way, it doesn't matter. I'm going after Bethany."

"We're both going after her," Beka said, crossing her arms and looking determined as only a Baba Yaga could. Even one who was blonde and perky.

"I'm going too," Calum said. "I know I probably won't be much help in a fight, what with these." He patted his useless legs. "But she's my daughter, and if there is any chance she might need me, I'm not staying behind."

"Neither am I," said a deep voice from the doorway. An extremely large black Newfoundland stood there, the door still swinging behind him. "If you're up against a dragon, and Beka's backup doesn't show, I'm your best chance at coming out on top."

"Chewie," Beka said, affection and admonition warring in her voice. "How many times have I told you that it isn't polite to eavesdrop?"

The dragon-dog gave a barking laugh and came the rest of the way into the room. "About as many times as I have told you not to leave me out of important discussions. So which one of us isn't teachable?"

Calum's jaw was open so wide, Alexei thought he might accidentally unhinge it.

"I can understand what he's saying," Calum said with amazement. "Holy shit. I'm hearing a dog talk. Have I lost my mind? Or have I caught whatever it is that Alexei has that lets him understand animals?"

Beka laughed. "You're hearing a dragon talk. That's completely different. Only Alexei can actually hear dogs talk, as far as I know. It's probably something to do with the huge dose of The Water of Life and Death he got." When Calum looked like he was going to ask her what she meant, she waved a hand in his direction to stop him. "Sorry. We don't have time to get into that. Chewie can make himself understood by anyone he chooses. Obviously, he has decided it will save time if I don't have to constantly translate for him."

"Speaking of time," Alexei said. "We should get going. We don't know what that bastard is doing to Bethany while we're standing around talking about who or what he might be."

"Going where?" Calum asked plaintively. "We don't even know where to look."

"I have a couple of ideas about that," Beka said. "Do you have a map of the local waters?"

"Of course," Calum said indignantly. "I'm a fisherman." He pointed Alexei toward a drawer in the living room, and Alexei went to fetch it. He unrolled it on the table in front of them and Beka grabbed a pen.

"Alexei, do you have any idea where this so-called Black-beard's boat was when you confronted him?"

He nodded. "Around here somewhere," he said, circling a spot on the map.

"I see what you're doing," Calum said, holding his hand out. "I should be able to add in most of the spots where the local fishermen saw the kraken, or said they spotted this pirate."

When they were done, they had about a dozen places indicated on the nautical chart, in a rough triangle.

"That narrows it down quite a bit," Alexei said, tugging on his beard. "But it still leaves us a lot of ocean to cover." The thought of Bethany waiting for him to come and rescue her, while her captor was doing who knew what to her, was making him crazy. He wanted to tear the room apart with his bare hands and acid churned in his stomach.

"I had a thought about that too," Beka said. "Once we get close to the area where this mystery ship might be, hopefully we can find a dolphin or a shark or some other sea creature who has seen it, and can direct us to where it is."

Alexei took a deep breath. "Oh. That might even work." It had never occurred to him that his new gift might end up being so vital.

Calum blinked. "I forgot about Alexei being able to talk to sharks. It's such a bizarre thing."

"It's an Alexei thing," Beka said. "He's still figuring it out. But it may come in very handy under these circumstances." She stood up decisively. "Well, if we're going to do this, I should go out to the bus and get some supplies. No point in going up against a pirate without a few swords."

She grinned happily at Alexei, who gave her a ferocious smile back. Beka might look like a harmless California surfer girl, but the walls of her reconditioned bus were decorated with an extensive and completely usable sword collection. Along with the shells and driftwood, of course. The Baba Yagas didn't much like guns, but they were quite fond of sharp pointy objects.

"Uh, I hate to point out the obvious," Calum said, gesturing at his chair. "But we're not all going to fit on the back of Alexei's motorcycle. Or in my truck, even if it weren't still parked in front of the bar."

"Hmmm. Good point," Beka said. "Besides which, we want whoever left that note to think that Alexei might have done what he was told and left town." She turned to Alexei. "You should probably put the Harley away in Calum's garage, out of sight."

"How are we going to get to the boat then?" Calum asked. "Call a taxi?"

"I think a taxi driver might object to a bunch of people carrying swords, accompanied by a talking dog," Alexei said. "I've had problems with things like that before."

"Of course you have," Calum said in the tone of a man whose credulity has been stretched to its limits for one night.

"We'll just have to take my bus," Beka said. "It's not exactly inconspicuous, what with having mermaids and ocean scenes painted on the outside, but once we get to the docks, I can use a 'don't look over here' spell to make it blend in better. And it will carry all of us, plus Bethany once we get her back."

Alexei heard the words she wasn't saying: no matter what kind of shape Bethany was in when they found her.

"What are we waiting for, then?" he said, grabbing up the map.

Beka bit her lip, looking at Calum's wheelchair. "The bus

might be magical, but it isn't exactly handicapped accessible. Sorry," she said to Calum.

"No problem," he answered. "This big bear has been carrying me around for weeks. He can carry me and the wheelchair onto the bus, and back off of it onto the boat." He swallowed hard. "I might have let my pride get in the way of my pulling my weight around here up until now, but I'll be damned if it is going to get in the way of my going to rescue my daughter."

18

BETHANY WAS DOZING LIGHTLY WHEN SHE HEARD THE HATCH
door swing open with a slam, jolting her fully awake. Her
wrists jerked, making them sting where she'd been trying to
work her way out of the ropes. All that her efforts had gotten
her were bloody wrists alas; the ropes were too thick and tied
too well. Note to self: never get kidnapped by sailors. They
really knew how to tie knots.

She was hungry and tired and thirsty, although she had
tried to make her water bottle last. She hoped they were
coming down to let her go. Barring that, she hoped it was time
for breakfast. Or lunch. She wasn't sure what time it was.

But any hopes she had of a semi-innocuous visit were
dashed when she looked up and saw the strange bearded man.
Red, the other one had called him. He was wearing a strange
pirate costume, for some reason, although she had to admit it
suited him.

The skinny guy who had given her the water skulked

behind his so-called partner and didn't make eye contact with her. Instead, he carried a bulging, lopsided bag that clanked like it was full of some kind of metal, which he deposited against the side of the hold with a number of other anonymous and similarly odd-shaped parcels. The smell of fish was faint, as if the hold hadn't been used to store its usual cargo for a while.

"What ya got there?" she asked, probably unwisely. "Lost pirate treasure?"

The big man laughed, the sound booming in the restricted echo chamber of the hold. "Exactly that, my lady," he said, strolling across the floor to stand over her. He held a large pipe in one hand, puffing on it contentedly and wreathing his head in smoke.

"I do apologize for your less than stellar accommodations," he said. "I am not usually so bad a host. My name is Hayreddin. Welcome to my ship, Miss McKenna."

His less impressive companion came over to join them. "I think you mean my ship, don't you Red?" He looked at Bethany's bloody wrists and winced, but didn't say anything.

"Of course, of course. This fine ship actually belongs to my friend Len here. Both he and it are quite indispensable."

Bethany saw a glint in his eye that made her think that neither boat nor man were nearly as valuable as Len might suppose. There was something about this Hayreddin that made her skin crawl, although she couldn't have said what exactly it was. Some atavistic instinct that screamed "danger" at her, despite the fact that he wore an old-fashioned sword buckled around his broad waist, and Len had a gun tucked into the back of his pants.

"Not that I don't enjoy the smell of old fish and tar as

much as the next girl," she said. "But I don't suppose there is any chance of getting out of this hold." She hadn't been able to find anything within reach that could help her escape. She hoped that there might be more opportunities up on deck in the open.

Hayreddin shrugged. "I do not see why you should stay down here. I have merely been waiting to see if your paramour the Black Rider would be sensible and leave town as I suggested, or if I would have to drag your dead body out to show him the error of his ways, should he be foolish enough to ignore my directions."

There was so much wrong with that sentence, Bethany didn't even know where to start. The dead body part, of course, but also, Alexei was most definitely *not* her paramour, and really, who the hell talked like that anymore? As for the possibility of Alexei being sensible? She ranked that up with little green men living on Mars and the fact that the polar ice caps were melting being a fluke that had nothing to do with global warming. Alexei, sensible. Ha. And also, HA. If he hadn't shown up yet, it was only because he hadn't been able to find her.

But if her host hadn't figured that out yet, she wasn't about to enlighten him. Probably it wouldn't be smart to tell him that she meant nothing special to Alexei, either, since her value to her captors seemed to depend on that misconception.

She liked to think that their friendship would be enough to make him come after her. But she sure as hell wasn't going to sit around like some damsel in distress and wait to find out.

"Thank you," she said meekly. "I'm a little claustrophobic. And I think I might have heard a rat." She gave a fake shudder and tried not to laugh when Len glanced around a little wild-eyed.

Hayreddin reached down and hauled her to her feet with no discernible effort, although she noticed he didn't offer to untie her hands. He left it to Len to undo the rope around her ankles and then help her up the ladder to the deck, although once up top Red offered her a mug of tea, which she gratefully accepted.

"So," he said, drawing on his pipe hard enough to make its interior glow cherry red. "It would appear that the Rider's reputation was exaggerated. Or possibly it is true what some said, that losing their immortality under torture made Alexei and his brothers much less than they once had been."

Immortality? Torture? Somebody was going to have some explaining to do when she saw him again. If she saw him again. The thought that that might never happen hit her like a fist to the gut, much stronger than any fear she had of her own death at the hands of those holding her. She shook it off, needing all her focus to keep either of those possibilities from happening.

This Hayreddin obviously assumed that she knew every-thing about Alexei's past. She remembered seeing Red in the bar once or twice before the incident with the aborted fight, she thought maybe with Len in tow, although the big man was a lot more memorable. He must have been spying on them, and thought he'd seen an intimacy that didn't exist.

Unless he had seen something she'd missed… She shook that off too. No time to pine over what might have been.

"Can I ask you something?" she said, more to keep his attention on her while she looked around for something useful than out of a real desire to make conversation. She saw two other men, tough looking sailor types with tattoos and grim expressions, working at various shipboard tasks. Great. Four against one. No problem at all. Damn, she wished Alexei was here.

"Certainly," Hayreddin said. "No doubt you are curious as to how the ghost of Blackbeard came to be sailing the seas again."

Bethany nearly choked on her bitter black tea. "Uh, no. Not really. I was actually wondering if you had something to do with the kraken that has been attacking ships in this area." It seemed unlikely to her that there were two completely unrelated mysteries afoot, but considering that she'd met a Baba Yaga and a man who could talk to dolphins recently, she wasn't making any assumptions.

Hayreddin preened, smoke rising up toward the sky. It was only a little before noon, from the look of it. Less time had passed than she'd thought. It had felt like much longer, stuck down in that hold waiting for someone to come kill her, or worse. Bethany didn't want to die at all, but if she was going to, she'd much rather it was up here, in the open air, with the sea all around her.

"Indeed, that is my doing," he said proudly. At a cough from Len, he added, a touch reluctantly, "And that of my young friend here, without whom it would not be possible. As I said, he is indispensable.

"After all, what is a pirate without a ship?" He pointed up at the Jolly Roger flag flying proudly in the breeze. "Mind you, these modern vessels are nothing like the schooners of old. No grace to them at all, alas, although it is somewhat convenient not to be dependent on the whim of the winds." He shook his head. "In truth, being a pirate is not what it once was."

"I *told* you so," Len said, rubbing one hand, which bore a slightly grubby bandage wrapped around it.

Hayreddin sighed, his pipe suddenly billowing even more smoke than before. "Yes," he said in the almost patient tone of someone who has had the same conversation multiple times before. "You were quite correct when you told me that being a pirate was no longer a grand profession ruled over by men of grit and steel." The glare he directed at Len seemed to go right over Len's head.

"And I was right about it not being a good idea to pretend to be Blackbeard come back to haunt the high seas, wasn't I? It didn't scare anyone away for long. It might have rattled the local fishermen, but they're a superstitious lot. Hell, we've spent most of our time dodging thrill seekers with cell phones trying to catch a video to put up on YouTube." Len leaned over and spit on the deck, his face etched with exhaustion and discouragement.

Bethany noticed Red's fingers tighten around the hilt of his sword and thought perhaps Len would be smart to keep his mouth shut.

"So, ah, how does the kraken figure into all this?" she asked, both to distract Red and because damn it, she really wanted to know. "I never heard of a pirate having a pet sea monster before."

Hayreddin chuckled, his volatile mood switching back to benign amusement. "No one else was ever clever enough to harness such a creature," he said. "Mind you, I had resources not available to most, as well as the cunning to use them. But the kraken is hardly a pet, my dear. It is a dangerous creature, unless one has the means to control it."

He gestured in Len's direction. "Go ahead and show her."

Len straightened up and pulled a large amulet out from underneath the sweater he wore. It was odd and unattractive, but it drew the eyes strangely.

Len saw the face she made. "I know. It's butt ugly, ain't it? It's been in my family for years, but I was the first one to be able to make it work." He swung it to and fro a little on its brass chain. "It's magic. Real magic. I can use it to summon the kraken, and command it to find us treasure. We're gonna be rich."

"Rich?" Bethany said. She didn't see how having a kraken would make anyone rich, unless you sold people tickets to come see it. And as far as she knew, there wasn't a lot of treasure lying around off the shores of Cape Cod. Some, probably, but not a lot. Nothing famous, anyway.

"Indeed." Hayreddin gave a smug smile, sharp white teeth glinting in the sun. "I sailed these waters long ago, and I was returning home with one last great load of booty when my ship ran afoul of a mighty storm. When young Len activated the ancient talisman which I had given up for lost, I returned so that he might help me reclaim this treasure."

Len nodded. "I use this thing to call the kraken, and then I send it out to look for Red's treasure. We're getting really close." His sullen face lit up as he pulled a handful of old gold coins out of his pocket. "Look. It brought these back the last time. Red says they're definitely from the ship he lost!"

"Very impressive," Bethany said, edging closer to a tall gaff, a pole ending in a hook most often used to land large fish. "I don't suppose this kraken of yours has anything to do with the boats that have been wrecked or disappeared recently?"

Len stared at his boots, but Hayreddin just gave a booming

laugh. "What do you expect from pirates? An invitation to a tea party?"

Bethany glanced over his shoulder and felt her heart jump in her chest. "Some kind of party, anyway, although maybe not the one you were expecting," she said. Her father's boat was closing on them as fast as it could move, and she could see Alexei standing on the bow, a huge sword in one hand. She had never been so happy to see anyone in her life.

Red swiveled around to see what she was looking at and uttered a series of foul curses that turned the air as blue as the smoke from his pipe. "Stubborn Rider," he said through gritted teeth. "I should have known he would show up and try to ruin everything." He swung back around and pointed at Len.

"Call it. Call the kraken. Now!"

A pained expression crossed the younger man's face but he didn't argue. As Bethany watched in amazement, he quickly pulled the talisman off his neck and placed it on the deck, then unwrapped his bandaged hand, exposing a series of red and irritated-looking cuts. Wincing, he pulled out a knife and sliced through the skin again, dripping the blood onto the amulet at his feet.

For a moment, nothing happened, then the center stone blinked open and became a swirling eye, and the water around the boat began to churn.

SHIT. Bethany cast a frantic eye at the distance between her father's ship and the one she was on. She had to do something to buy them some time. Something to distract Hayreddin and Len so they couldn't order the kraken to attack Alexei.

Swiveling, she grabbed the gaff in both hands, still tied in front of her, and swung it as hard as she could toward Red's face. The hook on the end caught his pipe and tossed it through the air to land in a pile of cleaning rags someone had left sitting against the hull. The rags immediately burst into flames, which in turn ignited the container of cleaning fluid, which went up with a surprisingly loud *whoosh.*

The blaze ran up some nearby ropes and suddenly that side of the boat was engulfed in flames.

"Son of a bitch!" Len yelled. "My boat! She set my boat on fire!" He grabbed a nearby bucket, but the rope he would have used to lower it into the ocean was currently burning merrily.

"You can do magic," he shouted at Red. "Do something!"

The light of the flames seemed to be reflected in Hayreddin's eyes. "I am actually much better at starting fires than at putting them out," he said with something that sounded suspiciously like a laugh. "You deal with it. I, on the other hand, will deal with our unwelcome guests."

He turned his back on the conflagration and on Len, glaring out toward the other side of the boat where the *Flora MacDonald* was rapidly closing in on them. "And I'll deal with you, my pretty little troublemaker," Red said to Bethany as he drew his sword. "Permanently."

As they stood in the bow, they could hear Calum yelling into the radio as he steered the *Flora MacDonald* toward Len's boat. Alexei had carried him up to the captain's chair so Calum could drive while Alexei and Beka fought; a reasonable division of labor that had the side benefit of hopefully keeping Calum out of harm's way. Alexei didn't want to ave to explain it to Bethany if anything happened to her father.

Alexei didn't even want to consider the possibility that he might not have the chance to explain anything to Bethany at all. Being too late was simply not an option. He'd already lost so much. He couldn't stand it if he lost her as well.

"If he's harmed one hair on her head…" he said through gritted teeth.

Beka patted him on the arm, trying to hide the worry she clearly shared.

"Bethany's tiny, but she's tough," Beka said. "I'm sure she's fine."

"But Humans are so fragile," Alexei said. He leaned forward, as if he could make the boat move faster through sheer force of will. He'd been standing in the front of the boat since a pod of helpful dolphins had pointed them in this direction; if he'd thought it would get him there any quicker, he would have jumped in the water and swum the rest of the way.

"You're nearly Human yourself these days, barring a strange gift or two and some enhanced endurance. You need to start giving Humans a little bit more credit," Chewie said from where he stood next to Beka. The dragon-dog was so large, his head was high enough to look over the side.

Chudo-Yudos were supposed to guard their Baba Yaga's supply of the rare Water of Life and Death, created in the Otherworld by the queen herself. The last time Chewie had broken that rule to aid Beka, her supply of the Water had been stolen, so this time he'd brought it with them, tucked safely into a cask tied around his neck. Alexei had mixed feelings about the stuff, since it had saved his life and that of his brothers, but not his immortality. And the huge doses it took to do so might have been at least partially responsible for the strange gifts they'd all developed since.

"Ha," Alexei said. "Not close enough to Human to be with one. Not with my history."

"She seems to have done a pretty good job of dealing with all the weird stuff we've thrown at her so far," Beka noted.

"That's because she's amazing," Alexei said. "And smart. And brave. And beautiful. And amazing." He strained his eyes as the ship in front of them grew closer.

"I think you said that one already," Chewie said. "Maybe you should tell her, not us."

"I hope I get the chance," Alexei said. Alexei stared at the vessel they were rapidly approaching. "Is that boat on fire?" he asked no one in particular.

Beka laughed. "It looks like your girlfriend got tired of waiting to be rescued and decided to rescue herself." She tested the edge of her sword on a strand of long blonde hair and grinned when it sliced through cleanly.

"I am not so sure that setting the ship you're on ablaze is the best way to rescue yourself," Chewie rumbled. "All things considered."

"That's my girl," Alexei said proudly, ignoring the dragon-dog. He hauled himself up onto a precarious perch atop the front edge of the bow, ready to leap onto the kidnappers' boat as soon as Calum brought them in close enough. "Let's go kick some pirate booty."

A WILD SIGHT awaited him and Beka as they made the almost-impossible leap from *The Flora MacDonald* to the deck of the other ship. Two burly men and one skinnier one battled a conflagration that threatened to take over half the port side. The odd-looking yet still imposing fellow with the gold earrings who had tried to cause a fight in the bar was waiting for them with a huge curved sword raised over his head and a fiery glint in his eyes.

Alexei swallowed hard when he saw Bethany lying in a heap on the ground near a trio of barrels, a broken gaff near one limp hand.

Damn it. Too late after all. Well, if nothing else, he'd make the bastard pay.

"You killed the woman I love," Alexei bellowed, and raised his own sword high as he ran across the deck. "Prepare to die!"

Their swords clashed with the sound of ringing fury as they danced back and forth across the deck, dodging obstacles and each other. Alexei saw Beka race toward an object that lay on the worn boards, gleaming dully, but Blackbeard—or whoever he was—spotted her movement and changed course to intercept her.

For a moment, he fought them both, sword weaving effortlessly and darting out to land a glancing blow on Beka's left bicep. A thin slice appeared in her shirt sleeve and blood flowed down her arm.

"Beka!" Alexei yelled.

"It's nothing," she yelled back. "I've got this!"

"Call the damned kraken, Len, you useless twit!" Blackbeard bellowed at the skinny man. "Order it to sink their boat to the bottom of the ocean. Let's see how they like that!"

The scruffy man turned from where he was frantically trying to empty a fire extinguisher at the flames. "You call it,

Red," he suggested with a hint of hysteria. "My fucking boat is on fire, in case you hadn't noticed. I'm a little busy here."

"I cannot call the kraken. It breaks the one rule I dare not cross," Red sputtered. "If I could, I would never have had to put up with your idiocy. Now *focus* and command it to do your will. Focus, damn you!"

Even in the blur of rage that subsumed him, Alexei thought it was probably unreasonable to demand a man focus while his livelihood was burning up around him. He redoubled his efforts to attack the pirate while his attention was distracted.

At the same time, Beka dived for the amulet and scooped it up triumphantly. She had prepared a spell ahead of time that she thought would negate the ancient talisman's ability to control the beast. But before she could recite it, a huge bulbous head rose above the side of the ship, followed by two massive tentacles that spattered sea water on the ship below.

One of the pirate's men shrieked as the tip of a tentacle wound around him and plucked him off the deck. The other thug took one look and fainted dead away, rolling slightly as the ship tilted from the waves caused by the kraken's movement.

"Command it, ye swarthy bastard!" Red yelled at his remaining henchman. "Focus and command it to kill our enemies!"

Another tentacle dropped a rotting bag on deck, where it split open to spill out dozens of gold coins. Len glanced wildly from the coins to the fire and back again.

"Focus!" Red screamed, his face suffused with fury.

Beka held up the amulet and recited the spell, but nothing happened. A sucker-tipped tentacle waved through the air dangerously close to her head and she cast a wild-eyed look in Alexei's direction.

Then he heard the sweetest sound in the world—Bethany's voice, shaky but most definitely alive, saying, "Blood, Beka! You have to activate it with blood!"

He glanced over to where he'd seen what he thought was her dead body, and caught a glimpse of her propped up on bound hands, gazing in his direction. Then he had to duck out of the way of another flash from Red's sword. He heaerd Beka reciting the spell again. This time anointing the bizarre talisman with some of the blood from the cut on her arm.

"Monster risen from the deep
Return now to your watery sleep
I free you from enslavement vile
And send you back to your exile
So mote it be!"

As soon as Beka spoke the last words, there was a shuddering vibration that could be felt across the entire boat. It almost knocked Alexei off his feet, it was so strong, and even Red staggered. The amulet dropped to the ground, inert, and the kraken sank below the waves without a sound, disappearing from sight as suddenly as it had appeared.

"You cursed *witch!*" Red screamed. "Now I'll never find the rest of my treasure!" His eyes gleamed with an unearthly light and his form shimmered, expanding and growing until in his place there stood a gigantic black and yellow creature with leathery wings and smoke coming out of its nostrils.

"Holy shit!" Len said, gaping. "You're a dragon."

The dragon turned its head toward Beka and shot a great gout of fire in her direction. She ducked and rolled, barely getting out of the way in time, and another section of the hull went up in flames.

"MY BOAT!" Len shouted, practically crying.

"Oh, shut up," the dragon said, and casually knocked him into the sea with one huge clawed rear foot. "Now, about the rest of you," he said turning back toward Beka, Alexei, and Bethany. "Who wants to die first?"

19

BETHANY STARED UP AT THE DRAGON GROGGILY. HAYREDDIN had hit her pretty hard, but she was pretty sure she wasn't hallucinating. In which case there was a huge dragon standing over her and she was about to be eaten...or maybe fried. On the whole, she thought she preferred the concussion option. That would explain why she could swear she heard Alexei say he loved her. Either way, she wasn't going down without a fight. She staggered to her feet, the hooked end of the broken gaff clenched in between her hands.

"How about me? I set your boat on fire. I'm pretty sure that means I've pissed you off the worst," she shouted. "You big, overgrown lizard."

Alexei gave a huge, bellowing laugh, whirling his sword in the air. "No, no, that won't do at all. I insist on going first. I'm the largest. And the oldest, come to think of it. Kill me first."

The dragon's massive head swung back and forth between the two of them as if confused.

"I'm the blondest—kill me first!" Beka yelled. When

Bethany and Alexei stared at her, she shrugged. "Hey, that should count for something, right?" She did a fancy figure eight move in the air with her own, narrower sword, and then bowed gallantly in the dragon's direction.

"Or you could try fighting someone a little closer to your own size," a deep, melodious voice said from above as a shadow fell over the ship. "Why don't you try and kill me first and see how that goes for you?"

Bethany looked up and had to suppress a squeak as another dragon swooped down, so close to her head she could feel the breeze from its passage ruffle her hair.

The second dragon was smaller than the first, but still impressively large. His wedge-shaped head was a vivid royal blue that shaded down his body into an iridescent aqua and then deep green. It dove at the dragon that had been masquerading as Human, causing it to take to the sky in evasive maneuvers. Bethany held her breath as the blue and green shape ducked and wove through the clouds, shooting flames at its black and yellow adversary. It was as though some primal battle raged for possession of the earth itself.

"Bethany!" Alexei said as he ran over and grabbed her up in a huge bear hug. "You're alive."

"OW," she said as his welcome but over-exuberant embrace practically crushed her. "I'm happy to see you too, you big oaf, but you're bruising my bruises."

"Oh, sorry," he said, dropping her.

"Ow again," she said with a sigh from the wooden deck. "How about you help me up—gently—and untie my hands? We can congratulate each other for being alive later, you know, if we still are."

Alexei glanced around at the flaming ship and at the

conflict being waged overhead and gave her a crooked smile as he eased her to her feet. "You have a point. It's just I thought, well, I'm glad you're okay. When I saw you lying there…"

"Yeah, well, Hayreddin hit me pretty hard. I nearly passed out. I thought he was going to kill me, but then you and Beka arrived and started poking at him with pointy swords. Nice timing." She rubbed her wrists.

Beka came running up. "Not to ruin the party, but I think we'd better get out of here. I'm not sure how long Chewie can hold Hayreddin off."

Bethany peered up at the sky. "Chewie? Like your dog, Chewie?"

"Dragon-dog," Beka explained. "One and the same. But he's really outclassed. The only reason he's lasted this long is because he is smaller and more agile. If Hayreddin can get close enough to do some real damage, Chewie is toast." Her normally cheerful face was etched with worry, her blue eyes clouded. "He's buying us time, so we'd better make the most of it. Besides," she gestured around them, "if we don't get off this ship, we're going to be toast too. Literally."

Alexei handed a still shaky Bethany off to Beka. "I'll be right back," he said, and ran toward the flames. Bethany saw him reach down to scoop something up and then he raced back. "Here," he said, thrusting the amulet into Beka's hands. "If we get out alive, I suspect the queen is going to want to take a look at this."

Bethany looked around. "I don't see a lifeboat or a dingy. Any suggestions?"

"We swim for it," Alexei said grimly. He pointed at a ship hovering at a safe distance from the inferno the one they were currently on had become. "That's your father's boat. Do you think you can make it that far?"

Bethany shuddered at the thought of how cold the ocean water was going to be at this time of the year, but she hadn't grown up as a fisherman's daughter for nothing. "Race you," she said, and dived off the side of the boat. Beka dove in gracefully to join her, and a moment later, Alexei yelled "Geronimo!" and cannonballed into the ocean with a huge splash that almost swamped the two women.

"You're an idiot," Beka said in a fond tone. Then they all swam like hell.

ALEXEI LET Beka climb the ladder up the side of *The Flora MacDonald* first, then boosted Bethany a little more forcefully than he intended ("again, OW") before heaving his own chilled wet body onto the deck. Damn, that water was cold. Teeth chattering, Bethany grabbed them all some blankets from a metal locker and slung hers over her shoulders.

"Is that my father?" she asked, looking up at the sound of cheering from the cabin. "What the hell is he doing here?"

"His daughter, his boat," Alexei said with a shrug. "Where else would he be?" He fought the impulse to enfold Bethany's shivering body in his own, rapidly warming one. He might not be a Rider anymore, but he still had the metabolism of one. It should be good for something besides drinking massive quantities of beer. But he didn't want to hurt her. Again. And he wasn't sure he could let go of her once he got his arms around her for real.

"Besides, he earned the right. He actually got himself into

his wheelchair and came charging in to join us when we were planning your rescue. The only way we could have left him behind was if we had tied him down." Alexei glanced at Bethany's bloody wrists and cursed himself for his choice of words. He was an idiot, as usual.

But she didn't seem to notice as she gave him a huge grin and ran up to see her father.

Beka gave him an affectionate smack on the shoulder. "Dude, I didn't think you could be any more socially awkward than you were already, but it turns out I was wrong. You're cute when you're in love."

"Oh, shush," Alexei said, feeling his face heat. "Anyway, we have bigger problems." He pointed at the sky, where Chewie was clearly beginning to lose the battle. Hayreddin's larger size and sheer power were starting to wear down the smaller dragon. Burn marks marred the aqua blue wing on Chewie's right side, and his swooping dives were becoming slightly off-kilter.

Beka clenched her fingers into Alexei's arm. "Hang on, Chewie," she whispered. "Hang on." Tears mixed with seawater on her face.

"It's not going well, is it?" Bethany said quietly as she rejoined them, moving to stand on Alexei's other side.

He just shook his head, peering up into the clouds as he tried to make out the two opponents as they flew intricate maneuvers around one another.

"What happens if your dragon loses?" she asked Beka.

Beka drew her blanket more tightly around her shoulders. "I try and remember all the anti-fire spells I know while Hayreddin does his best to burn us to a cinder." Her normally cheerful attitude seemed to have been washed away by their swim, or the circumstances, or both.

But Alexei spotted something he was pretty sure would bring it back. "Hey, look! I think your help arrived just in time."

Bethany's mouth gaped open as she saw yet a third dragon flying overhead, this one a vivid ruby red creature so large, he dwarfed even Hayreddin. The new arrival arrowed in from the direction of the Cape, then dive-bombed the black and yellow dragon, hitting it so hard it pin-wheeled through the sky.

"Who the hell is that?" Bethany said. "He's...glorious."

"Koshei," Beka and Alexei said in unison. Beka sounded positively gleeful.

"He's an old friend of my sister Baba Yaga, Barbara," Beka explained. "I knew he'd come if I asked him to; I just wasn't sure he'd get the word in time."

"Friend," Alexei said with a wink. "And occasional lover, until Barbara met her husband Liam. He's always had a soft spot for the Baba Yagas."

There was a thud and the boat shook as a blue and green dragon half-flew, half-fell out of the air. Its shape shimmered and flowed until a large, somewhat battered black Newfoundland dog stood in its place.

"Crap," he said. "Do you think he could have cut it any closer?" But his mouth lolled open in a doggy grin, and he reached up to lick Beka's face when she ran over to check him out. "I'm fine, I'm fine. Honestly, it's the most fun I've had in a century." He winced as her hand found a sore spot. "You know, now that it's over."

And it was definitely over. Chewie had already done a good job of wearing Hayreddin out; Koshei pressed his opponent relentlessly, pursuing him with claws and teeth and sheer overwhelming mass until finally the crimson dragon bore the black and yellow one down to hover helplessly over the deck of *The Flora MacDonald.*

"Change," Beka demanded, her long blonde hair whipping back and forth in the wind created by the wings of two dragons. She suddenly sounded like the powerful witch she actually was, her voice resonant with threat. "Change into your Human form, Hayreddin, or I will let Koshei tear your throat out."

One ruby-tipped silver claw set itself not-quite-gently in the black dragon's thorax, in case it hadn't gotten the message.

The dragon shimmered, its outline wavering and blurring until the mythical beast disappeared and the man with the uneven gray hair and golden earring stood in its place, one arm still held in the grip of red dragon's talons, and blood dripping from a dozen small wounds.

"Curse you, Baba Yaga," the pirate said with a grimace. "You damn witches are always interfering."

"Well, that's kind of in our job description," Beka said in a milder tone. But she pulled a set of handcuffs out of the bag she'd brought on board and snapped them around Hayreddin's wrists with a decisive click that belied her calm exterior.

"What good is that going to do?" Bethany asked. "Can't he just turn back into a dragon and break them?"

"Not these handcuffs," Beka said triumphantly. "They used to belong to Barbara's husband, who is a sheriff, but I put a spell on them that would force anyone wearing them to stay in the form he or she was in when I put them on. I thought they might come in handy in this particular situation. Should make it a lot easier to get this guy back to the queen without a fuss."

As soon as he heard her, Hayreddin started to struggle in earnest, but Alexei reached out and whacked him upside the head, and the erstwhile pirate fell to the deck with a thud.

"Feel better?" Bethany asked, eyebrow raised.

"I do," Alexei said. "You have no idea how long I've been waiting to do that."

"Well, it looks like my work here is done," the red dragon said, and landed lightly on the boat to become a devilishly handsome man with curly dark hair, a close-cropped beard, and light blue eyes.

"Baba Yaga, you are as ravishing as always." He bowed in her direction, then leaned in and kissed her lightly on the cheek. "Black Rider, it is good to see you looking so well."

His eyes glowed as he examined Bethany. "I don't believe we've met. I am Koshei. A friend of the family, you might say. And you are?"

"Off limits," Alexei said with a growl.

Koshei blinked. "I see. Indeed. So that's how things are. Lovely." He bowed at Bethany too. "A pleasure to not meet you, my lady. Now, if you would be so kind as to steer this vessel back in the direction of Beka's hut—I mean, school bus —she and I can take this miscreant back to the Otherworld to face the queen's justice. That should prove to be an entertaining afternoon."

"You're going to drive Beka's school bus to the Otherworld?" Bethany said, her face scrunched up in a way Alexei found irresistibly adorable as she tried to envision it.

Beka smiled. "Not at all. There is a magical doorway inside my bus. I assume that's how you got here in the first place," she said with a nod toward Koshei.

"Naturally. Kind of you to leave it unlocked for me," he

said. "I came through in Human guise, since my dragon self is not only too large to fit through the door but also would undoubtedly have caused something of a stir if it had been spotted. Once I was out of sight of any innocent bystanders, I changed forms and flew to you as quickly as possible."

"But how did you know where we were?" Bethany asked.

Koshei gave a wicked grin. "I can always sense a Baba Yaga. As I said, something of a member of the family. Besides, dragons are very territorial; we can perceive each other from miles away."

He glared down at the seeming Human at his feet. "Mind you, most of us have better manners than this one seems to have displayed. I knew him in the Otherworld, of course, but we dragons rarely socialize with others of our own kind, so I can't say I could have predicted his bad behavior." Koshei scowled. "Greedy fools like this give dragons a bad name. It will be a pleasure to watch the queen make an example of him."

Koshei turned to Alexei, a wicked glint in his light blue eyes. "Perhaps her majesty would like to meet your lady. I'm sure she would be interested in your testimony as well. You have been much missed at court."

"I don't think that will be necessary," Alexei growled. "The word of the Baba Yaga should be more than enough. I am not ready to return to the Otherworld. You two can take Hayreddin back without me. Bethany still needs me to help with her father."

Bethany gave him a look he couldn't quite decipher. "Once you get us back to the truck, I'm sure I can manage," she said. "If you want to go back."

Alexei glared at her. Was she trying to get rid of him?

Maybe this whole adventure—dragons and all—had been too much for her. He couldn't blame her if she just wanted to go back home and forget all about the Paranormal. Or maybe she was just sick of having him around.

"You got kidnapped and knocked out," he said. "I can stick around for another couple of days." And he stomped off to the cabin to check on Calum, before anyone else tried to make him do something he didn't want to do.

20

In the end, of course, he went anyway. As Beka pointed out, the queen had been waiting for some time to get word that Alexei was okay. If Beka and Koshei went back and reported they'd had an adventure that involved the former Black Rider and Alexei didn't even bother to make an appearance, there would be hell to pay.

Besides, as Bethany said somewhat acerbically, she and her father had managed without Alexei before he'd shown up, and no doubt they would continue to do so after he was on his way to wherever he decided to go next.

So that was him told. And she wasn't wrong, but for some reason the statement made him grumpy anyway.

Not so grumpy that he couldn't appreciate the unearthly beauty of the Otherworld when they arrived back at the place where he'd spent so much of his time. Including the six months he'd spent recovering from his torture at the hands of the evil Brenna, but he was trying hard not to think about that.

As far as he was concerned, he'd be happy never to think about that time again.

The sky was various tones of lilac shading into indigo, so the queen must have been in one of her purple moods. Bright pink grasses lined a path made of sparkling white stones and willow trees sang quietly as they walked by, accompanied by a satyr on a lyre who was serenading a pretty green-haired nymph. A part of his heart he hadn't realized he'd walled off seemed to open up again, leaving him feeling lighter than he had in a long time.

"It's good to be back, isn't it?" Beka said perceptively. "Even if you wouldn't want to live here."

Alexei had to smile. "Yes, I suppose it is. I've probably been avoiding the place for too long."

"You had a really tough experience," she said as they rounded a corner to see the dainty spires for the castle up ahead. "You just needed some time to heal and figure out what you were going to do next."

"Besides," Koshei added as he shoved a scowling Hayreddin down the path ahead of him, Chewie helping with the herding by nipping at his heels. "It never hurts to return bearing gifts."

THE QUEEN always knew what was going on in her lands, if she was bothering to pay attention, so it was no surprise when they arrived at the castle grounds to see an elaborate pavilion prepared for high tea, with extra plates set for guests. But clearly she hadn't anticipated the addition of a handcuffed and disgruntled dragon-in-Human-form, since she raised one silvery eyebrow in mild surprise as their group came to a stop in front of the throne-like chairs she and her consort sat upon.

As always, the queen was stunningly beautiful. Her ethereal grace and poise marked her as royalty even if the diamond and amethyst tiara perched atop her carefully braided and twisted white hair wasn't enough of a clue. Today she was dressed in a flowing purple silk gown that matched the color of her eyes, and her consort the king was attired in a coordinating deep purple tunic over dove gray leggings. They both wore matching expressions of benign curiosity, although the surrounding courtiers were less subtle, whispering behind fans of peacock feathers or staring openly.

The queen actually rose from her chair to greet Alexei, kissing him lightly on each cheek before returning to her seat and inclining her head regally at Beka, Chewie, and Koshei.

"My dear Black Rider, welcome back to Our court. I cannot say how pleased We are to see you looking so well." She gazed down her elegant nose at the rest of the party. "Baba Yaga, it is a pleasure to see you and your Chudo-Yudo as well, although you are hardly properly attired for tea. We assume this means you have some interesting tale to tell?"

The king stroked his dark, neatly trimmed beard. "A tale involving multiple dragons and the Black Rider promises to be fascinating indeed. Do proceed, Baba Yaga."

"It is mostly Alexei's tale to tell, Your Majesties," Beka said. "Although Chewie and I played our part in it. When I was Called to the east coast by the local Paranormal peoples, I discovered Alexei already there, on the trail of the same mystery I had come to solve. So naturally, I persuaded him that it would be more efficient for us to work together."

"Of course," the queen said, eyes twinkling. She might no

longer rule on the Human side of the doorway, but she had plenty of contacts there still among the Paranormal creatures who had been unable to make the move to the Otherworld. Alexei was fairly certain she knew exactly how he had spent his time since he'd left, and how hard he would have resisted being dragged into any purposeful task.

"Beka did most of the hard work," Alexei said, trying not to sound too brusque. "I just talked to some dolphins and sharks, and fought a pirate."

There was a moment of silence. "You can talk to dolphins now?" the queen asked. "How interesting."

"And dogs," Beka put in helpfully. "I mean, not just Chewie. Regular dogs."

"Ah." The king nodded sagely. "That must be your new ability. I confess, after your brother Mikhail turned out to be a shapechanger, and Gregori developed strong psychic abilities, I would have expected your own gifts to be something more...flamboyant."

Koshei smothered a laugh. "He always did tend to be the most dramatic of all the Riders. Makes this a bit ironic, doesn't it?"

Alexei ground his teeth. "I am perfectly happy with something a little less difficult to handle and potentially life-threatening than what my brothers ended up with, thank you very much. Besides, I'm much less dramatic these days."

"Did you not just say something about fighting pirates?" The king asked, his lips twitching.

"Oh. Right. That." Alexei shrugged. "But the pirate was really a dragon, so it doesn't count." He nodded at Hayreddin, who so far had been successful avoiding attention.

"One of Our dragons was in the Human world, playing at

being a pirate?" The queen sat up even straighter than before, although her posture was always perfect. "Hayreddin, isn't it?" she said, staring at him. "Would someone care to tell Us why Hayreddin has been trapped in Human form in bonds that smell of Baba Yaga magic?"

Beka looked at Alexei, but when he didn't speak up, she took up the story. "The Paranormals who *Called* me were complaining that the fish they depended on for food had been disappearing. There was also talk of some kind of monster being sighted, although nothing definitive. In the meanwhile, the fishermen at the local bar where Alexei was hanging out had the same issue, plus something had been wrecking their boats."

The king leaned forward. "A curious story, but what has this to do with the dragon? Or pirates, for that matter. Do get to the part with the pirates."

"It turned out that the monster that was scaring away the fish and destroying boats was a kraken," Beka said. "And the kraken was being controlled by an old talisman once owned by Hayreddin, back in the days when his kind still lived on the other side of the doorway. Apparently he took on the guise of a succession of famous Human pirates, and used the kraken to sink other ships and take their treasure."

The queen made a moue of distaste. "And My people ask why they were forced to leave those lands and hide out in these. Really, Hayreddin, how short-sighted and inappropriate." She made a tutting noise, and turned back to Beka. "I do not approve of such actions, of course, but that was then, and the rules were quite different."

"When there were any rules at all," Chewie muttered.

The queen ignored him. "So who was controlling the

kraken now and causing all the disruption?" She paused for a moment. "One would think such a thing would be beyond the skills of a mere Human."

Alexei opened his mouth to protest her use of the word "mere," but thought the better of it. Instead, he took up the rest of the story. "It probably would have been, if that Human hadn't had help. It would seem that Hayreddin sensed that his talisman had been found and activated, and he returned, taking on the guise of a pirate again and guiding a fisherman named Len in the controlling of the kraken."

The queen's austere features grew even sterner as she held out one slim finger to beckon Hayreddin closer. "Is this true, dragon? Did you instruct a Human in the use of a magical tool to the detriment of Our Paranormal kindred still living on the other side?"

Hayreddin executed as polished a bow as was possible while wearing handcuffs. "The issues affecting the local Paranormal community were accidental and unintentional, Your Majesty," he said in a smooth tone. "The fish would have returned as soon as I had reclaimed my final treasure, which was all I sought on the other side. Then the kraken would have gone back to its rest, with no permanent harm done."

"No permanent harm done!" Alexei sputtered indignantly. "What about the harm to the fishermen whose livelihood you ruined? The ones your kraken killed left families behind."

Hayreddin shrugged one shoulder. "As Her Majesty said, mere Humans. What does it matter?"

"It matters to them," Alexei said. "And some of those Humans are my friends, so it matters to me."

The king and queen exchanged looks at this, undoubtedly

intrigued by the thought of Alexei having Human friends, but Alexei ignored their unasked questions and went on.

"It was your talisman and you were responsible for Len using it to call the kraken. You're not going to just walk away from the mess you made."

"Ah, but my dear Rider," Hayreddin smirked. "Oh, I am sorry, it's former Rider, isn't it? Either way, I did not control the amulet myself, so I broke no laws. Making suggestions to the weak-minded is hardly a crime."

"Your Majesty," Alexei protested. "He's just splitting hairs. Yes, technically he wasn't the one controlling the kraken, but surely that doesn't matter since he was the one behind the whole thing."

The king tugged on his beard. "You know how the laws of the Otherworld work as well as any, Black Rider. His actions were despicable, yes, but if he was able to trick someone else into doing his dirty work for him, he has not, as you say, *technically* broken Our rules. We can forbid him to return to the other side in future, but for what he has done, there will be no other repercussions."

Alexei started to argue, something which would undoubtedly have gotten him into considerable trouble, but Beka put a hand on his arm to stop him and winked reassuringly.

"I assume, however, that there will be some form of penalty for threatening a Baba Yaga and injuring her Chudo-Yudo?" she said in a deceptively mild voice.

Hayreddin's ruddy face turned pale as the queen turned her basilisk stare on him. She had, in fact, been known to turn people to stone, often for much smaller offenses than the one he had just been accused of.

"Is this true?" the queen asked in a tone so frosty, the small blossoms under her chair all withered and died. "Did you dare to interfere with one of Our Baba Yagas and her faithful companion?"

"I was just trying to reclaim the treasure that belonged to me," he said, chin held stubbornly in the air, and wisps of smoke eddying about his head in silent witness to his already evident annoyance. "They should have minded their own business."

"They were minding *My* business," the queen reminded him. "As the Baba Yagas are tasked with answering the calls of those in need and keeping the balance of nature. Having a kraken loose in the ocean is most certainly not my idea of balance."

"It was only temporary," Hayreddin said sullenly. "If they had just left me alone, I would have finished collecting my treasure and been back in my cave with no one the wiser. As it is, I was only threatening to hurt the Baba Yaga. I would never have done it."

"And me, Hayreddin?" Chewie stepped closer so the queen and king could get a good look at his injuries. "Did you mean to harm me, or are these wounds simply accidents as well?" He limped on three paws and blood still ran sluggishly from a cut above one furry eyebrow, the injuries incurred in his dragon form transferred to his canine one.

Alexei had to choke back a laugh. And they called him dramatic. The truth was, Chewie could have used a tiny dose of the Water of Life and Death he still carried safely in a small cask around his neck and it would have healed his wounds instantly. He and Beka had clearly known that Hayreddin might get away with his other crimes and made sure they had proof of even worse transgressions to show the queen. He had never loved them more. It paid to have clever friends.

The queen looked from Chewie to Hayreddin, her gaze darkening to the purple of a horizon just before a storm. "Did you do this?" she asked in a voice that echoed with power.

Hayreddin dropped his eyes, but Koshei stepped forward to break the silence he had kept up until that moment.

"He did, Your Majesty, and I can bear witness to it," Koshei said, bowing gracefully. "Had I not arrived when I did, in answer to Beka's request for assistance, her Chudo-Yudo would most assuredly have died at the hands of this ill-mannered oaf. He gives dragons a bad name, and I am ashamed to be of the same race."

"I have heard enough," the queen said, rising from her seat. "You are found guilty of crimes against the crown, Hayreddin, and We will enjoy coming up with an appropriate punishment." The surrounding courtiers applauded, enjoying the entertainment, but Alexei just felt a deep sense of satisfaction that the man who had kidnapped and hurt Bethany would pay for what he had done.

"First, since this debacle was caused by your pursuit of treasure, all your existing treasure shall be confiscated. It is forfeit, and will be dispersed to others."

Hayreddin let out an anguished cry, but he clearly knew better than to voice a protest.

"Might I make a suggestion, Your Majesty?" Beka said.

The queen nodded her head regally.

"Such treasure is of little real value here in the Other-world," Beka said. "Unless you are a dragon or one of the other races that cares about having gems and gold simply for the sake of having them. But back on the other side of the doorway, they are worth a great deal. As Alexei told you, there were a number of fishermen—folk who work hard to make an honest living to feed their families—who suffered from Hayreddin's actions. Perhaps I could take some of the treasure back with me and use it to establish a fund to compensate those men and women for the losses they suffered?"

The queen returned to her seat, sinking back down with a graceful flurry of skirts. "A very wise proposition," she said, looking at Beka thoughtfully. "You have truly grown into your position in the last year, despite the unusual challenges you faced. We are aware that your mentor, whose name We no longer speak, may have led you to believe that you were unsuitable to be a Baba Yaga. We would like to say, in case there is still any doubt in your mind, that We believe that you are, in fact, eminently qualified. We shall do as you propose."

Beka turned a becoming pink and gave a deep curtsy, despite the fact that she was still wearing jeans. "Thank you, Your Majesty. I can't tell you how much that means to me, coming from you."

"No need," the queen said, waving one languid hand. "We are aware."

Alexei chuckled, which had the unfortunate effect of drawing the queen's attention to him instead.

"And what of you, our faithful Rider? Have you no requests of Us in this matter? Nothing for these," she gave a delicate cough, "*friends* of which you speak?"

Now it was Alexei's turn to blush, something most would have guessed he was incapable of doing. He dug his hand into one pocket and pulled out a dozen large gold coins. He'd scooped them up off the deck when he'd gone back for the talisman. Hell, they were just going to go down with the ship anyway.

"I had thought I'd give her—I mean them—these coins, which were part of Hayreddin's lost treasure. The kraken brought them up right before Beka sent it back to the deep. Bethany, that is, my friend, isn't very good about taking help from anyone, but I thought she might use the money from these to help her father."

"Bethany was kidnapped by Hayreddin, and fought quite valiantly," Beka said.

"She set his boat on fire," Chewie added with a wide doggy grin.

"Did she?" the king said with a chuckle. "She sounds quite remarkable."

"She is," Alexei said. "Quite remarkable." He hoped he wasn't blushing again.

The drama seemingly over, most of the courtiers drifted away in search of something more entertaining. The queen sent a few lackeys off to fetch Hayreddin's treasure, then dealt with the erstwhile pirate, giving Beka back her handcuffs when she was done. Then the queen gestured Beka, Alexei, and Koshei to their seats at the table.

"Such thirsty work," the queen said. "It is definitely time for tea." She poured out water that was still steaming hot, because after all, they were in the Otherworld. "You shall have to tell Us more about this intriguing Human, Alexei. She sounds as though she might almost be a match for you."

As Alexei muttered into his cup, the queen turned to Chewie. "My dear Chudo-Yudo, you have quite made your point. Do please have some of the Water of Life and Death now. You are dripping blood on my good china."

21

Bethany glanced at the clock on the kitchen wall as it ticked noisily past midnight. Her father had gone to bed hours ago, exhausted by his unusually stressful day, although gleeful about his part in their adventures. Or misadventures.

She had been stalling, doing little things around the house, and pretending she wasn't waiting for Alexei to return. But she'd taken Lulu out for one last pee and checked on the puppies an hour ago. It was time to admit to herself what she'd feared all along—he wasn't coming back.

With a sigh, she got up from the table, poured out her cold tea, and was reaching for the light switch when she heard a knock at the door. Her heart might have skipped a beat or two as she walked over to open it.

"Hi," Alexei said, as if he'd just strolled over from the guest house after a normal day. "I saw your light on and hoped you might still be up. Can I come in?"

Bethany looked over his shoulder to see if he was alone. "Are Beka and Chewie with you?"

He shook his head. "They've been back at the bus for a while. I had a few extra things to deal with in the Otherworld before I came back through, so it took me a little longer." He rolled his eyes. "Besides, high tea with the queen went on *forever*. You know, they don't serve beer at those things. What's the point?"

He brushed past her and sat down at the table, staring at the refrigerator until she took the hint and grabbed him a cold brew. Bethany didn't bother to get one for herself. She had no idea how this conversation was going to go, and she felt as though she needed to have her wits about her. What was left of them, anyway.

"Are you okay?" he asked, once he'd drained half the bottle.

Bethany gave him a lopsided smile, the best she could manage under the circumstances. "I'm fine. Some nasty bumps and bruises, my wrists are pretty torn up, and I'll probably have some strange nightmares for a while, but considering that I was kidnapped by pirates, not bad really."

Alexei grinned at her. "That's my girl. And where is your father? Do you need me to help you put him to bed?"

She shook her head wryly. "He put himself to bed an hour ago. Apparently all your nagging and trickery paid off, and he is in much better shape than he was when you got here. Once this crisis forced him to push himself, he discovered that he is capable of doing almost everything for himself now. It looks like we won't be needing a home health aide after all."

"Oh," Alexei said. His face bore a curious expression, and she couldn't tell if he was relieved or disappointed. "That's good, I guess."

"Yeah," Bethany said, her stomach feeling as though it

were filled with lead. "So you don't need to stay here and take care of him anymore. And you fixed all the stuff you broke at the bar, so you're free to travel on to whatever adventure waits for you down the road."

He finished his beer and set the empty bottle down decisively on the table. "Ah, right. I've actually had a few thoughts about that, if you'd be interested in hearing them. If it's not too late, that is."

Bethany got the sinking feeling it was too late for a lot of things, but she figured she might as well get the bad news now instead of later. It wasn't as though she was going to sleep anyway, once he went back to the guest house to pack so he could leave in the morning.

"Not at all," she said in what was supposed to be a perky tone, although it ended up making her sound like a slightly demented cheerleader. "I can't wait to hear where you're going on that ridiculous Harley next. A riding tour of all the dive bars in Alaska, maybe? It's a big state. Might take you a while."

Alexei fiddled with the ends of his beard. "Well, there's kind of a problem with that plan. For one thing, I've figured out recently that I don't seem to find drinking and brawling as entertaining as I used to. It was a disappointment at first, but I guess after all these years, it's only to be expected."

Bethany blinked. "Really? It's kind of hard to imagine you without the drinking and the fighting. Are you sure?"

He shrugged. "I know. Kind of shocking, isn't it? The other problem is that I'm not sure the motorcycle is going to work for extensive traveling anymore. You see, I've gotten kind of attached to one of Lulu's puppies, and she said I could keep him. But it is going to be hard to fit a Great Dane puppy on the back of a motorcycle, even one as big as the Harley. Not to mention that he'll probably keep growing. They do that, you know."

"Huh," Bethany said, feeling a spark of something that felt suspiciously like hope. She stomped on it with a mental boot. "How were you planning to deal with that, exactly? Trade the bike in on a nice practical SUV?"

Alexei looked appalled. "Hell, no. What kind of barbarian do you think I am?" He held up one hand. "Never mind, don't answer that." He gave her that grin again, the one that made her knees weak and her fingertips tingle. "Actually, I was thinking I might try staying in one place for a while. This place, specifically, if you don't have any objections."

"This place," Bethany repeated. "You mean the guest house?" It wasn't what she'd hoped for, in her heart of hearts, but at least he'd still be here. "I guess you could stay there until tourist season starts. Then we'd have to rent it out, I'm afraid. We need the money."

"Ah," Alexei said. "About that. You don't actually."

Bethany felt like she was missing something in this conversation. Maybe a number of somethings. "What are you talking about? Of course we do. Even if my father doesn't need a home health aide, he has lots of medical expenses. The income from the bar barely covers them, even without me taking a salary. We need all the extra money we can get."

"I think this will probably help with that," Alexei said, reaching into an inside pocket of his leather jacket. He pulled out a small pouch and upended it onto the table, spilling out a small handful of old, slightly battered-looking gold coins.

"Are those?" Bethany put one hand over her mouth.

"Yep. I grabbed them up off the deck when I went back to

fetch the amulet. The damned ship was on fire; it seemed a pity to waste them." Alexei grinned at her, looking more than a little piratical himself. "Besides, I thought they might come in handy. Now that your dad is doing so much better, I figured he might want to get one of those cool vans designed for folks in wheelchairs, and maybe one of those fancy electric wheelchairs to go with it."

Bethany blinked back tears. "That's a great idea. But don't you want the coins for yourself?"

He laughed. "I don't have much need for money. Besides, this is just the tip of the iceberg. There will be plenty more."

"What the heck are you talking about?" Bethany gave up and went to pour herself a shot or two of her father's whiskey. This conversation was making her head spin anyway.

"Two things, really," Alexei said, casually reaching out and taking a sip from her glass. "First of all, the queen punished Hayreddin by taking away his hoard, and Beka convinced her majesty to allow us to bring a chunk of it back here to help out the fishermen who were hurt by his actions. So Beka is going to stick around for a while and set up a fund for that, which you'll then administer, if that's okay with you. There would be a small salary attached and Beka thought your legal background would help."

"Wow," Bethany said. "That's great. The damaged boats and loss of fishing put a lot of families into serious trouble. This will completely save the day." She thought for a minute of everything Hayreddin had put them—and her—through. "But just taking away his treasure doesn't really sound like enough of a penalty, all things considered. He was going to kill us all!"

"Oh, that wasn't the only punishment, although losing his

hoard is actually pretty traumatic for a dragon," Alexei said. "She turned him into a newt."

"A newt!"

"He'll get better," Alexei said. "Eventually. The queen usually only stays mad for a century or two."

"Oh," Bethany said weakly. "I guess that's okay, then." She shook her head, trying to rid herself of the feeling that she had walked through a looking glass into a completely upside down world. "You said there were two things?"

"Right. Well, more than two, but two that had to do with money," Alexei said. "You see, it occurred to me that when the kraken brought up those coins, they were probably from Hayreddin's lost treasure, since he'd said they were close to getting it back when we stopped him. We have the coordinates of where Len's boat was when Beka and I caught up with you, so we figured that between Beka's diving skills and your father's boat, we could probably find Hayreddin's old ship and claim the rest of it."

"Holy shit," Bethany said. She was pretty sure her jaw had dropped open in an unbecoming way. "You'd be rich."

"We'd be rich," Alexei said in a firm tone. "Or at least, you and your father would be well enough off to make whatever improvements to the house you wanted, and you wouldn't have to worry about the bar or renting the guesthouse. You could even go back to law school if you wanted. Since I'm going to be sticking around, I could keep an eye on your father." He poured another slug of whiskey into her glass. For a guy who said he wasn't interested in drinking much anymore, he could certainly put it away.

"What would you do with your share?" she asked.

"Would you go back, if you could?" Alexei asked, ignoring her question.

"I don't know. Ever since I realized earlier tonight that my dad might not need me the way he had, I've been thinking about finishing up my law degree. All I have left to do is sit the bar. I'd actually completed the coursework before my dad's accident derailed my plans, but I was having doubts about whether or not a legal career was really what I wanted."

"So you said. And now?" he asked.

"Being back here made me realize that I'd been looking at a conventional path, and I'm not a conventional person. But that doesn't mean I couldn't use my legal degree to do some good. I was thinking I might be able to help the locals when they had issues, and maybe get into environmental law so I could fight for your friends the dolphins and the sharks." She gave him a crooked grin. "I might be the first lawyer in town to hang up a shingle in a bar. My dad wants to get back to running the place part time, but he's not up to handling it on his own."

"That sounds great," Alexei said, a twinkle in his eyes. "I think it would be fabulous to work out of a bar. In fact, I was thinking of taking my part of the money from the treasure and buying into one. That way if I got carried away and broke things, it wouldn't be so bad, since I'd be a part owner."

Bethany stared at him. "Did you have any particular bar in mind, by chance?"

"I am kind of partial to *The Hook and Anchor*," he said. "Having spent so much time rebuilding the damned place. Besides the barmaid is hotter than hell. I could think of a lot worse places to spend my days. You know, when I wasn't out hunting treasure or chatting with dolphins."

"Of course," Bethany said, feeling slightly hysterical. This conversation was not going at all the way she expected it to. "And what would you chat with the dolphins about, just out of curiosity?"

The twinkle got even stronger. "I thought maybe I could work out a kind of treaty between the ocean dwellers and the fishermen. You know, like the dolphins could tell me where certain fish were running, and the fishermen would go out at prearranged times to get them. That way the locals would have better catches and they wouldn't be accidentally netting turtles or sharks or dolphins. Mind you, we'd have to figure out a way to do it without the fishermen realizing I speak dolphin, but I'm sure we could come up with something."

"That could be amazing," Bethany said. She wasn't sure why she was surprised that Alexei had put so much thought into doing something practical and useful. She'd seen his patience and consideration with her father, after all, and how hard he'd worked to make the bar look nice again—well, even nicer—after he'd wrecked it.

"You know, for a guy who puts so much effort into trying to act like he's a jerk who doesn't care about anything, you're a pretty decent fellow."

"Stop it," Alexei said with a grimace. "If you're going to be insulting, I'm not going to tell you the rest of the plan."

"There's more?" Bethany had no idea what to expect. Hell, she hadn't expected any of what he'd told her already. She'd been braced to watch him drive away in the morning, and now he was going to be staying. At least for a while. Maybe longer, if he was serious about buying into the bar. It was always hard to tell with Alexei. "What now? A bridge club with mermaids? A pirate-themed fishing tour?"

Alexei perked up. "That last one kind of sounds like fun. But no, that's not it." Suddenly he looked almost…nervous. She didn't think she'd ever seen that expression on his face.

"What?" she asked. Maybe he was going to buy his own place to live once he'd found the treasure. Why wouldn't he?

"It's about the guesthouse," he said.

Damn. She knew it.

"I thought maybe it would be nice to fix that up to be wheelchair accessible. Your father mostly only uses the living room and his bedroom here, and the kitchen to eat whatever you've cooked for him. The guesthouse would be a lot easier to redo than the house, which has narrower doorways, and then he'd have more privacy."

"Uh, yeah, that's true. But then where would you live?" Bethany suspected her father would actually prefer the smaller, more manageable space of the guesthouse, especially if they could fix it up so it was more accessible. But she'd miss Alexei being right outside her back door.

He flashed her a smile that wobbled around the edges, and cleared his throat. "I, um, I was hoping I'd live here. With you. And Lulu and the puppy. At least one puppy. They're all really cute." Bethany couldn't believe it. He was babbling. But wait, had he just suggested that they live together?

As she watched in disbelief, he slid out of his chair and onto one knee in front of her, then pulled a small leather bag out of his back pocket. He emptied it into his palm, revealing a gold ring in the shape of a dolphin, holding a brilliant and astonishingly large diamond in its mouth.

"This is why I was late," he said. "I took one of the gold coins to an artisan at court—a dwarf known for his metal work—and had him make it into this ring. The diamond is a gift from the queen, by the way. She was very impressed with everything you'd done, and said you sounded delightfully fierce. She's looking forward to meeting you some day."

Bethany opened and closed her mouth, but no words came out.

Alexei grinned up at her. "Want to raise puppies together? I promise to try not to break anything. Much."

She blinked. "You know that is the least romantic proposal in the history of proposals, right?"

"Oh," he said, face falling. "Yeah, well, my brother Mikhail is the smooth one. I'm just the muscle."

"You're a lot more than that," she said softly, gazing into his eyes. The truth was, she couldn't imagine her life without this surprisingly gentle giant, even if that likely meant a future of repairing furniture and cooking meals that should feed an entire pirate crew.

"You're the man I love. I don't need smooth. I need someone who loves dogs and can put up with my crabby father and treats me like an equal." She leaned down and kissed him. "Now, are you going to put that ring on my finger or not?"

His face lit up as he slid the ring onto the finger it had been made for, where it fit perfectly. Magic, no doubt. Then he stood up and pulled her into his strong arms.

"You know, I might occasionally go help Beka or one of the other Baba Yagas out with a problem. It could be dangerous. Would that be okay with you?" He looked into her eyes. "I would like to have an adventure now and again, but I won't go if you don't want me to."

"Life should probably have a little danger and adventure in it," she said, feeling her lips curve up into a wicked grin. "In fact, if you want to live dangerously, I have an idea."

"What's that?" her future husband asked, smiling back down at her.

She reached behind her and shoved the paperwork she'd been fiddling with onto the floor. "How about we see if this old table is sturdy enough to take the weight of an insanely large former Rider and a barmaid-soon-to-be-lawyer?"

"I like the way you think," Alexei said with a roar of laughter, and they proceeded to find out.

What the heck. It was just one more piece of furniture to mend after all.

ABOUT THE AUTHOR

Deborah Blake is the award-winning author of the Baba Yaga and Broken Rider paranormal romance series and the Veiled Magic urban fantasies from Berkley.

Deborah has also written The Goddess is in the Details, Everyday Witchcraft and numerous other books from Llewellyn, along with a popular tarot deck. She has published articles in Llewellyn annuals, and her ongoing column, "Everyday Witchcraft" is featured in Witches & Pagans Magazine. Deborah can be found online at Facebook, Twitter, her popular blog (Writing the Witchy Way), and www.deborah-blakeauthor.com

When not writing, Deborah runs The Artisans' Guild, a cooperative shop she founded with a friend in 1999, and also works as a jewelry maker, tarot reader, and energy healer. She lives in a 130 year old farmhouse in rural upstate New York with various cats who supervise all her activities, both magickal and mundane.

SUBSCRIBE TO MY NEWSLETTER!

Want to stay up-to-date on my newest books, get the latest cat pictures, or have a change to win prizes? Then subscribe to my newsletter! You won't be spammed, I promise, but it *is* a great way to keep in touch!

Just visit my author page at Deborah Blake and subscribe there!

OTHER BOOKS BY DEBORAH BLAKE:

Baba Yaga and Broken Rider Series

Wickedly Magical (Baba Yaga novella – prequel)

Wickedly Dangerous (Baba Yaga book 1)

Wickedly Wonderful (Baba Yaga book 2)

Wickedly Ever After (Baba Yaga novella 2.5)

Wickedly Powerful (Baba Yaga book 3)

Dangerously Charming (Broken Riders book 1)

Wickedly Spirited (Baba Yaga novella 3.5)

Dangerously Divine (Broken Riders book 2)

Dangerously Fierce (Broken Riders book 3)

Dangerously Driven (Broken Riders novella 3.5)

Wickedly Unraveled (Baba Yaga book 4)

Tiny Treasures: A Short Collection of Short Stories

Veiled Magic series

Veiled Magic

Veiled Menace

Veiled Enchantments

Standalone Books

Witch Ever Way You Can

Reinventing Ruby

King Me

Llewellyn Nonfiction books and decks

Made in the USA
Columbia, SC
04 January 2023